OHIO

10

A. V. SMITH

Book Cover: SEVIINTH DEGREE PRODUCTIONS LLC

Editor: TRICIA BARNES

Editing Consultant and Interior Formatting: Kristin Reeg, Ascribe Communications

Warped Writing and Publishing LLC, Columbus, Ohio

ISBN: 978-7351069-0-8

DEDICATION

To my children, Devan, Naiya and Christian:

My prayer to The Universe for you has been sent. You are my life source; greatness awaits you.

I Love You.

Acknowledgements

"To God -The Universe, I hear the words you send. I submit."

To the Jefferson, White, and Burton ancestors: Because of you, I am.

My parents, Diane and Irvin: a child grows best in a stable foundation. Thank you for pushing us to be better every day. I love you.

Fred Jefferson "Pops": Your support and love spreads through me and your grandchildren.

To the memory of departed father Roger Smith, life lessons are learned sometimes in the strangest circumstance.

My siblings: Portia White; Rod Smith; Irvin White III; Troy Smith; (Donald, Cameron and Marcette): I can't imagine a day of my life without seeing the greatness in you.

Michael Armstrong, Jasmine Desiree, Veronica Halko, Dakota Brown, Rebecca Fisher, Tara Kennedy; for inspiring characters.

Carlitha Martez-Allen, Elaine Shady Carter, Graciela Patino for your eyes and voice.

Lori Cooper for exposing glimpses of your life, allowing bits to be shared.

Kary Oberbrunner and Author Academy Awards, for finding merit in my work.

Mary Hoffett; Richard Higgins; Cynthia Stocksdale; Brandon McNeal; Erin and Tony Myers; Valerie Jenkins; Pam Wentz; Lee Krumlauf: Thank you for shining a light in my darkest hours –

Retired Officer Henry Jackson
Cleveland Division of Police
#1384

Late Retired Officer Nick Cooper
Columbus Division of Police
#340

Thank you for your service.

82879

TABLE OF CONTENTS

Chapter One

HerOin

"Pathological constriction, or strangulation, in layman's terms is the cause of death." The Coroner had performed the autopsy but was still waiting on the toxicology reports. The brown tile floor, contrasting against the dull gray walls, was just as bland as the silver carts holding the corpses waiting to be attended. The cuffs of his white lab coat were rolled at the sleeve.

Cole had never gotten comfortable being in cold chambers filled with dead bodies, so, as Sheldon stepped aside, he focused on the ligature marks on the woman's neck. They appeared to be made from some form of thin wire.

Everett let out a sigh, before pointing to the stab wounds and stating the obvious.

"Her blood has pooled together…"

"Yes, there is sign of lividity." The coroner didn't intend to sound condescending, but his matter of fact communication often rubbed people the wrong way.

"That's what I fuckin' said, Shelly." His broad shoulders lifted slightly as he inhaled slowly.

Everett found it easy to match Shelly's gruff tone. He was constantly on edge since separating from his wife, and balancing his family and work was an ongoing struggle. Helping other families find closure by solving homicides tilted the scale lightly back in his favor. He understood she loved him still, but his reluctance to put the family first had been the straw that broke the camel's back.

"This was personal...this seem personal to you partner?" Everett pointed at the facial bruising of the victim.

"Intimate partner, this was intimate. A crime of passion to be exact. This was rage in its purest form. The bruises before the asphyxiation, the postmortem cuts to the body. She upset someone, and I bet whoever it was left something behind for us." Cole thought about the victim's last moments before pulling the sheet back across the body.

"When you get the reports on Ms. Brittany call us." In trying to be respectful, Cole always referred to the victims by name. Upset, Everett stormed out of the morgue.

"Don't mind him, he's not as good at compartmentalizing as he thinks. Call me when the reports get in." Cole finished before following behind.

"Hey E hold up. I'm not jamming all up in your business, but what's up?"

They stepped aside as the door to the elevator opened. An attractive blonde lab technician was exiting, and her face lit up as she smiled at Cole. She hurried past, as if her smile betrayed their secret.

"Are you serious, her too Cole? I wish my life was as simple as yours. Robbi told me she's dating someone. I can't blame her, well I can, but it wouldn't be fair." Everett paused as he received a text message.

"Maybe it wasn't ideal to accept more responsibility by remaining in the military and doing this job full time, but we, we make a difference to so many people by giving them closure. I think we were losing each other before I even came back from overseas."

Everett was conflicted and Cole could hear it in his voice. He knew his partner carried his emotions close to the vest, and that work was what helped him maintain a semblance of normalcy.

"We've got a lead; I'll grab my keys and we can follow up on it right now." Everett didn't wait for a response.

3

The clouds covered the sky, eliminating any remnants of midday sunlight. The car ride had been silent until Cole received a text from the lab technician asking if he wanted to play doctor later.

"Why yes, yes I do." Cole responded verbally.

Everett had grown accustomed to Cole's carefree attitude. Initially there were some reservations, but as their partnership grew, he had learned to accept it.

"Get your mind in the game. Brittany's mother said her daughter had recently broke up with someone. We are going to interview him and see where it takes us." Everett gave Cole a description of the suspect as they pulled into the condo development.

As they exited their black Dodge Charger, the officers observed two male teens dribbling a basketball. Everett moved straight forward to complete their task. Cole took a moment and attempted to take the ball from one of the boys who dribbled around him. A tall, athletically built man adjusting his backpack moved across the pavement to avoid the kids. He flipped his hat forward before slipping into a Mercedes Benz to drive away.

"Good moves...Good moves." Cole called out to the boys as he headed off the court.

Everett had already knocked on the orange door as Cole caught up with him.

"Greg Faulkner, open the door. It's the Columbus Police Department." Cole knocked a second time with no luck.

Everett walked around to the front of the unit. The grounds needed attention. He had to squeeze between the uncut shrubs to access the front window. He could make out overturned furniture along with massive clutter. Looking deeper into the home, Everett saw the body sprawled out on the floor a few feet away from the door.

He backed away from the window, drew his .40 caliber Smith & Wesson, and returned to Cole's side.

"Victim is three feet from the door."

Cole understood as he unholstered his weapon. They would enter and clear the space, still unsure if the assailant was on site.

Everett kicked the door in and checked his left, as Cole followed clearing the opposite side.

"Greg Faulkner." Everett verified upon checking the body for a pulse.

Cole took pictures on his phone and then called for the Medical Examiner and forensic team. Two lovers killed within days of each other was no coincidence. Cole left the apartment to return with gloves and shoe coverings from their vehicle.

"Bludgeoned with the baseball bat, and also strangled it looks like." Everett moved away from the body

"There was no forced entry, the place has been ransacked, and again it feels like a crime of passion. Their relationship is severed and then they both end up murdered." Cole was making observations.

"If these murders are connected, it means there is a high likelihood that the perpetrator is a mutual acquaintance of both victims."

"We need to canvas and speak with their friends and coworkers." Everett said, as the first uniformed officer arrived followed by the Medical Examiner.

"Gentlemen." Malcolm walked in as the last bit of caution tape had secured the crime scene. His khaki pants were a staple, and his colorful shirts under his M.E. jacket were a very strong indicator of his personality.

"This young man has had a terrible morning I see." He pulled both AirPods from his ears.

His unorthodox approach pushed Everett's patience, but he was a valuable part of the team, and for this reason Everett tolerated his behavior.

"He won't be seeing too much of anything anymore." Cole added before greeting Malcolm with a fist bump.

"Malcolm." Everett greeted the Medical Examiner with a handshake.

Malcolm checked the body and wounds inflicted. The forensic team took swabs and skin samples. Cole and Everett rummaged through the victim's belongings before being called back into the front room.

"Strangulation seems to be the method of choice recently, but not necessarily for Greg. Each of these..." he paused as he pointed to several fractures on the head.

"Each of these cracked the skull open, my guess is that the Louisville slugger they tagged and bagged is the culprit." Malcolm finished as the body was secured to be removed.

"The female victim from two days ago, they were lovers." Cole spoke up.

"No, they were ex-lovers." Everett interjected. Specifics mattered and this misnomer, as slight as it was, needed corrected. There were moments when speculation was necessary and he left that up to his partner, but this wasn't the time.

"So, at some point recently they were violating each other before they got violated. That's pretty much the jest of that right." Malcolm hesitated as Cole grinned.

"I can't be certain until more tests are done but these marks are very similar to the female found earlier. We should have access to her electronic devices by end of day." Malcolm bid farewell as a younger detective new to the team entered with a file in his hand.

"I got here as soon as I could. Sheldon had the toxicology report, so I grabbed a copy first. Seems like our female victim had opioids in her system. Sheldon found needle marks between her toes after rechecking the body." He handed Everett the manila folder before sliding his keys into his blue jean pockets.

"I wonder what he did for a living, that art is a month's salary." Travis walked forward to stand in front of a painting on the living room wall. His silver badge hung from his neck and was a stark contrast to the black hoodie he wore.

"That, what the hell is that anyways?" Cole asked as he approached the young detective.

"It's a Fernan Delago, immigrant from South America. Each color represents an emotion, so the paintings feel different to every person."

"This painting is worth six damn grand?" Cole was in disbelief. He took a closer look without touching it.

"Twenty-thousand." Travis corrected Cole, as his intent was adding all their salaries together.

Everett disappeared into the home, wondering why a valuable piece of art was left behind if this was a robbery homicide. Something more valuable had been the catalyst for the deaths of two ex-lovers.

A uniformed officer emerged from a second bedroom with a small, dark, green bag in his possession.

"Sir."

Everett took the bag and placed it onto the kitchen counter before pouring its contents out and revealing a white substance.

"You have a field test?" He asked the uniformed officer who affirmed.

Once the test was complete, Everett had another fact. The white powdery substance was pure heroin.

"So, someone knew that there was something worth more than twenty- thousand dollars, and clearly didn't find this." Travis was speaking out loud to no one in particular. The street value of the narcotics had to have been nearly $200k.

"Good observation on both accounts Travis." Everett gave the young detective positive reinforcement. Travis had promise but was green around the horns. His discernment about documentation being accurate, was commendable, but the over redundancy could be too much.

"Put that away and lock it up. Shit, that's two compliments in one day..." Cole paused as he tapped Travis on the shoulder

"... good job brother."

The heroin was placed in evidence bags and hauled away by the forensic team.

"I think we need to revisit Brittany's mother and ask some questions pertaining to her daughter's lifestyle. Travis, get whatever permissions you need to check both the financials of Brittany and Greg. Everett was issuing direction when his phone rang.

"Hey what's up big Mason? Yeah, yeah, of course I remembered, I will be there soon." Everett had forgotten and was grateful to be receiving this call.

"We can grab some ice cream after. Ok, I'll see you soon. Love you too." He finished the call.

"Change of plans. I'll check their financials when I get done with Mason's yellow belt promotion. You two touch base with Mrs. McKinley and be heavy this time." Everett made sure they both understood.

The mother of the first victim knew more than she let on.

"Call me with anything new." He finished before excusing himself.

"Ok rookie let me show you how it's done." Cole slapped Travis on his back before asking him for the keys to his vehicle.

"Keys?" Travis was unsure of his meaning.

"Give me your keys, just because Everett gets to drive me around, doesn't mean you can. Keys." Cole waited until Travis handed them over.

As they pulled away, Cole could still see the two young boys shooting hoops as the day faded.

"Mrs. McKinley how long have you known about your daughters drug use?" Cole asked straightforwardly. He watched her reaction closely to see what her unspoken body language would reveal. The furniture they sat on was new, as were many of the appliances in the home.

"Huh...what? Drug use?" She asked in return.

Cole knew a rehearsed response when he heard one, but would not let on that he knew she was being misleading. He placed the file in his hand onto the couch and adjusted his gray cargo pants.

"Brittany and drug use? No way, all she did was work. She'd go out occasionally, but when she wasn't at work or home, she would visit here." She was interrupted as a knock was heard at her screen door.

"Barbara, hey hey. How are you holding up?" A middle-aged man entered as she approached the door.

"Oh, I'm sorry, I didn't know you had company. I can come back." His plaid shorts nearly matched his work boots covered in various material. He wiped sweat from his forehead, before replacing the blue bandanna in his waist next to his utility belt. He had a plastic bag in his hand, with a few grocery items, and a book bag across his shoulders. He clinched a smaller green bag in his opposite hand.

"No, it's ok Larry, these are the detectives trying to find Brit's murderer." She ushered Larry into the living room with both detectives.

"Detectives, are you close to finding out what happened to her, anything new at all?" He waited but it was Brittany's mother who responded without emotion.

"They think Brittany was using drugs."

"All she did was work or visit here." His words slipped out easily before handing her the bag of bought items. He opened his book bag to lower the smaller dark green bag into it.

"Can I grab something out the fridge?" He asked.

Cole noticed Travis about to speak up but interrupted him before he was able.

"Mrs. McKinley do you have another bottled water to spare." He pointed in the direction of a half empty one sitting on the kitchen table next to a case of bottled water.

"Oh, of course, Larry grab two bottles please." She called out.

"I don't have any cold ones."

"That's fine. We are going to do everything we can to bring the person responsible for Brittany's death to justice. We will call on you if necessary, again our condolences." He accepted both waters from Larry and walked back to the car.

"Evidence bags." Cole was directing Travis.

"Do I have any, is that what you are asking?" He rebutted.

"Yes rookie, two evidence bags."

Travis retrieved them from his trunk and watched as Cole marked them.

"Larry has bruising on his arms and scratches on his hands. That utility knife on his belt carried a blade about the same length of the stab wounds. The dark green bag was identical to the one we found with the heroin. I hope you didn't have anything planned tonight or tomorrow morning. We need to see who this Larry really is. Call Everett and give him a heads up."

Cole kept his eyes on Barbara McKinley's residence, while listening to Travis leave a voice message for Everett.

"Now we wait."

Everett let his phone go to voicemail. Mason was in the process of sharing his excitement that he passed to the next belt level in karate. Watching his son's accomplishment was rewarding and watching him scoop whipped topping into his spoon of ice cream just as satisfying.

"Do you have to go back to work tonight again?" Mason swung his feet back and forth, as his legs were too short to reach the floor. His white gi was wrinkled, but he made sure not to get it dirty.

Everett would have loved to be able to say no, but he couldn't. He would never lie to his children, or to his ex-wife. They deserved that from him, at the least, for all the time he had spent away overseas.

"Yeah Mason, I do, but you guys are coming over this weekend. I actually have beds for you both now."

Everett was slowly getting ahead with his finances. It was important to be on time sending Robbi money to help with the children. It was his duty, just like it was his duty to seek justice for others.

"Your mom and Becca are home from her band performance. I'll drop you off and then go catch some bad guys." Everett read a message as he wiped Mason's chocolate covered face.

As Everett approached the house, he let Mason turn on his siren. Becca came running out as they pulled into the driveway. She almost tripped over her feet.

"Dad next time you have to come see me play," his daughter ran into his arms and hugged him deeply. She stuck her tongue out at her younger brother.

"Your daughter has incredible talent Mr. Clark." Robbi walked out with an oven towel in her hands. Her cherry brown skin was as smooth as it had been when they met in high school. Her light hazel eyes always seem to be able to see into his soul.

Mason pulled on his new yellow belt, showing it off to both his sister and mom.

"Ok...ok, before you know it, you'll actually be able to fight." Becca began wrestling her brother playfully before saying goodbye to their father.

"We have great kids Robbi; you've done an amazing job." Everett moved closer to stand by her side. He ran his hand over his beard and exhaled.

"A true compliment…hmph." Surprised that he had paid her a nicety, she pushed him playfully in his shoulder.

"I stopped and bought a bucket if you're hungry. I know you ruined Mason's appetite, but if you want to eat dinner with them." Robbi's voice trailed off as his phone rang from a number that she was familiar with.

"It's ok Everett, Cole needs you." She turned and walked away. She pulled her apron off and tossed it over her shoulder.

Everett watched her. She had never lost a trace of beauty, the strength in her shoulders and copper skinned toned legs bore the weight of his family for years. He wanted to say something in response, but he understood the facts, he wasn't going to stay when the job called.

"Yeah." He answered.

Everett listened to Cole explain that Travis and he were following a lead that returned them back to Greg Faulkner's neighborhood.

Everett was making his way to the station; he had received the required approvals to check the financials of both victims.

"Update me along the way." He finished the call as he pulled up to the station. Dusk had transformed into night, and the hustle and bustle that frequented the day had died down. There were multiple emails waiting for him as he opened his computer. There was one that stood out. It was from the forensic department; they had gained access to Brittany's cell phone messages.

He decided to check the financials and noticed large sums of money being deposited into Greg Faulkner's account each week. Brittany received similar deposits every other week. Brittany had recently paid off the mortgage on her mother's home. Her wages from employment were substantial, but the other sums of money deposited made five thousand dollars a month trite in comparison. Greg had several accounts at various institutions. His deposits always fell short of the amount banks had to notify the IRS, but with the small percent earned on his money he was a rich man. One who should have another address than a mid-level condo. Everett looked deeper and saw two separate addresses listed under business names, owned by Greg and another person, T.J. Crowder. After googling both addresses, he picked one to check out first. A second email came through as a reminder the forensic team had information from the female victim's cell phone.

Everett decided to walk two flight of steps down to the forensic lab. Malcolm, holding multiple doctorate degrees, oversaw both the coroner's office and the forensic lab.

"It's about damn time. I could have gone to the casino, played some high stakes poker, and been back before you even showed up. Instead, I used a program that I am developing to gain access to her phone, it's all legal. Case law has set precedent already..." Malcolm paused and tossed Everett the phone.

"Seems little Ms. Brittany wasn't so squeaky clean. Whoever "he" is, has got to be a person of interest." Malcolm finished, as Everett read the final few text messages which were between Brittany and Greg.

"Also, Greg Faulkner was assaulted with more than the baseball bat. A standard twelve-ounce bottle with a distinctive base was used initially, followed by the baseball bat. The strangulation was overkill, get it...over kill." Malcolm laughed and answered his phone before walking away.

Everett took his leave. He had two addresses to check out and hoped Cole and Travis were making progress on their end.

"Is he trying to get into the condo?" Travis asked as he watched Larry struggle with the lock on Greg Faulkner's door.

"Accurate rookie. Head north, I'll cross over by the blacktop. In case he runs we will have both exits covered. Stay sharp." Cole commanded his younger counterpart.

Travis moved slowly, staying in the shadows, while Larry kept struggling with the door.

Cole had already crossed the basketball court and had rounded the opposite side of this condo grouping.

"Hey! That yellow police tape is up for a reason." Cole said loudly, startling Larry, who recognized the detective from the earlier visit at Barbara McKinley's residence.

Larry dropped the keys and began opening his book bag as he turned to run, but Travis had already blocked the exit with his gun drawn.

"Let's have a talk down at the station." Cole patted him down before pulling up his red wind breaker to check the waist band area. He pulled his utility knife from his belt before placing him in cuffs.

"Do you have any thing you shouldn't have in this backpack? Weapons? Or just your prescription medicines?" Cole asked as he tossed the bag to Travis to check.

Travis pulled out two smaller bags from inside. The dark green bag is what drew their attention. Inside was a smaller amount of the same heroin, packaged identically to the stash found in Greg Faulkner's home.

"Breaking and entering, tampering with a crime scene, possession of a felonious amount of heroin. Larry, it's Larry, right?"

"Yeah Larry Mitchell." He confirmed.

"Well Larry Mitchell, you have the right to remain silent, anything you say, can and will be used against you..." Cole lowered Larry's head as he stuffed him into the back of the car and headed to the station.

Cole texted Everett when he arrived and saw he wasn't there. After securing Larry's handcuffs to the interview table, Cole emptied all the contents of the bag in front of Larry.

"Those add up to years, no, actually decades behind bars. The tampering with a crime scene, unlawful entry is nothing compared to the example the court is making against this nasty stuff right here." Cole took his ink pen to push one of the packages of heroin across the table, followed by one of the two bundles of money.

Larry set quietly and listened. Travis noticed his skin becoming flush, Larry was nervous.

"We noticed the scratches on your neck, and the casing of your utility knife was discolored. The bottles you retrieved for us earlier have your fingerprints on them. So, Larry if you have something to say, right now would be the time to speak up." Cole finished and dropped his ink pen onto the table, closest to the wads of money rolled in separate rubber bands.

"If you say nothing at all, these small infractions on top of the double homicides will guarantee you'll be spending the rest of your life behind bars."

The knock on the door halted the interview.

"Malcolm's guys found traces of the victim's blood inside the sheath of his knife, but the fingerprints from the beer bottle came back to a T.J. Crowder." Travis stuck his head in and relayed the message to Cole.

"To be honest with you Larry, this week has been a little challenging..." Cole hesitated like he didn't know what route to take before sitting back down opposite of Larry.

"So, the DA's Office is definitely going to charge you for all that and the murder of Brittany McKinley. Her blood, your knife." Cole was abruptly cut off by the suspect

"Her blood on my knife." He started laughing because he knew he had replaced the knife

"Y'all can get me on possession of whatever, but you're not pinning a murder on me and shit, no way- not today Detective." Larry set back in his chair with the silver linked chain, holding his handcuffs still securing him to the table.

"Oh, my apologies, did I say blade. I meant the sheath of your knife. The brown leather covering, you know, the one with that fancy stitching in it. You see most perpetrators forget something as they panic. Maybe they forget to wipe down everything they've touched, or phone calls and messages they may have sent. For you, well for you Larry, you replaced the blades, but the discoloration on the insignia is because you should have replaced the covering."

As the Assistant District Attorney and Travis looked on behind the two-way glass, they appreciated Cole's closing technique with Larry. Just enough push to create doubt and keep the suspect off balance, but enough room to also let Larry think of all the things he may have slipped up on.

"You see wet blood takes different to the leather, and that's what we noticed initially, I'm sure the skin samples will come back to you. So, it's pretty much a done deal, but what I can't understand is why you would be so gutless and still befriend Brittany's mother? But that wasn't just a friendly visit, was it? You didn't find what you were looking for at Brittany's house after you killed her, didn't find what you were looking for at Greg's home, so you killed him, so you wanted to check Brittany's mom's house too. Here's another thing, we know you had an accomplice." Cole sat back and shut up.

"Killed Greg, fuck that; no nope, you got all that wrong." Larry blurted out. Hearing all the charges and the evidence pushed him to speak his second set of words in over twenty minutes. Cole knew the path of a guilty conscience was opening, so he pushed.

22

"Brittany was probably a mistake right, she got caught up with the wrong people and..."

"Brittany wasn't no damn mistake; she was the mastermind behind distributing, and Greg the connection. Everything was fine until Greg got greedy. It's always greed." Larry set back in his chair and his body language said he was defeated.

"I need a deal; get me an attorney and I will tell you what I know. Until then put my ass in an overnighter." Larry finished and refused to answer any follow up questions.

After an hour wait, a public defender arrived and ironed out a tentative deal. Larry was brought back to the interview room and he shared what he knew with ADA Jefferson, Cole and Travis.

Everett did not find anything out of the ordinary at the first property, owned by Greg Faulkner and T.J. Crowder. A ranch style home with a 1.8-acre lot according to the for-sale sign, posted on the grass. He walked the property, and everything seemed in order. He peeked through the patio blinds and saw that it was empty.

"One dead end." He walked back to his black Dodge and programmed the next address into his GPS. The route took him through an affluent neighborhood. Homes in excess of a million dollars. An older couple were walking their Collie as he came to a security post.

"May I help you?" The guard wore an outfit resembling that of law enforcement, but Everett knew he wasn't one of his brothers in blue.

"Detective Clark for T.J.... T.J. Crowder..." Everett hesitated and leaned out of his window.

"Do me a favor, please don't announce me." Everett added making sure that the guard understood.

As Everett moved forward up the winding road, he checked his rear-view mirror to ensure the guard had not phoned ahead to warn the resident.

These homes near Olentangy River Road were extravagant. Each one designed in their own style, they all had one common theme; wealth.

The long oval driveway was bordered with colorful flowers and shrubs, while the sculpted water fountain in the center of the front yard added substance to the property. A black Mercedes Benz sat next to a heavy-duty Ford pick-up truck with all the bells and whistles. The trunk of the Mercedes was open, and as Everett pulled in, a woman was walking out, followed by a tall, muscular man.

The man whispered something to the woman as he retrieved a box from the Mercedes and closed the trunk. She walked toward Everett, who had parked and exited his vehicle.

"Hi, how can I help you?" She asked with hesitation in her voice. Her brunette hair flowed beneath her shoulders and the green Adidas Crossback Mid Sports Bra showed her toned arms.

Everett watched the man disappear into the house. He removed his sunglasses and introduced himself.

"Detective Everett Clark, I'm following up on a lead to a case I've been assigned. You are?" He extended his hand cordially.

"Terri Crowder." She pulled her hair to one side and waited.

"Is there somewhere we can talk? I'm sure the few neighbors you do have are no different than mine...nosey." He finished giving her a nudge with a truthful statement meant to get inside the home.

"Yeah of course, come in." Terri motioned them inside.

"Troy, this is Detective Clark." Terri made the small introduction to her brother as they walked past a large library and into a smaller den.

"So, what's the visit about?" Terri asked.

Everett noticed how Troy stayed within earshot of the conversation but didn't join in.

"Greg Faulkner was listed on the owner's documents for this and another residence with T.J. Crowder. Can you tell me your relationship?" Everett asked.

Terri's energy shifted hearing Greg's name as Troy approached carrying a juice for her. He sat down next to her and spoke. She pulled off her green and white running shoes and placed them by the front door.

"Greg was a business partner until he took on a different life path. The other residence was our first residential home and this our last. Surely, you've seen CF Purchasing in the financials. However, we haven't had business dealings with him in almost a year and a half." Troy added history to their relationship.

"So, when was the last time either one of you had any contact with him?" Everett watched for any indication that they were being untruthful. Terri stood up and left the room, to return with a stack of letters from Greg threatening them with lawsuits, and a few asking Terri for forgiveness for disrupting their business.

"I haven't seen Greg since he came to a business meeting drunk or on whatever. Nearly cost us a five-million-dollar deal. That was a little over a year and a half. Troy's been dealing with the litigation."

Everett hadn't seen the artwork initially; he was overwhelmed with the multi-million-dollar home, but now he saw artwork like what was found in Greg Faulkner's home.

"Fernan Delago." He motioned to the collection of art. The colors were more brilliant in their piece.

"Very good Detective, quite an eye." Terri paused as she walked to stand by Everett.

"The struggle of immigrants has been a perilous story since the beginning of time. Fernan and his struggle brought to life in color and pattern." She finished.

Everett received a text message from Travis about a big break in the case, followed up by a phone call from Cole.

"Give me a moment". He excused himself to listen to what Cole had found.

"Troy and Greg have been running opioids and heroin for the last five years. Brittany was the distribution channel, and everything was going good until Greg decided to rock the boat. He stole the last shipment, along with the money given to him by Troy. Brittany was an accident. Troy had Larry go see Brittany believing she was in on it and things got out of hand. Troy's sister wasn't mentioned, but she is family." Cole finished before Everett advised him the next steps to make before ending the call.

Everett saw the box removed from the Mercedes sitting adjacent to the picture, when he returned to the den, he took a second route to gain access to the box.

He noticed green bags matching the same found in both victim's homes.

"Troy, with all the litigation you haven't had any contact with Greg. What about Lawrence Mitchell or Brittany McKinley?" Everett saw the concern in Troy's eyes.

"I haven't seen Brittany since our fallout with Greg. We were only cordial acquaintances at best."

"What about Larry." Everett pressed.

"Ok I thought this was about Greg and property. Detective either tell us what your real purpose is, or I have to ask you to leave." Terri had frustration in her voice and was ready for the ruse to end.

"We have a double homicide in which your brother has been implicated, we can get a formal statement at the station."

"So, you came into my house, seeking to entrap him. Get out!" Terri was upset and Everett heard the tone change.

"Troy you are a person of interest, I can have multiple police cruisers appear, in front of your property. I'm sure your neighbors would have a field day, or you can come answer a few questions to help us get to the bottom of this." Everett upped the stakes but with a partial confession from Larry, one way or another, Troy would be sitting down for an interview.

"I will call Matthew and have him meet us at the station." Terri informed her brother.

"I won't handcuff you unless you give me a reason to." Everett received a text from Travis letting him know that he had arrived with members of the forensic team.

"Another Detective is here to secure the box you brought in and search your vehicle."

Everett was explaining before Terri interjected.

"Not without a warrant..." her voice trailed off as Travis approached with warrant in hand.

"Please, don't interfere and they will be out of your hair before you know, I did you the courtesy of having the van unmarked." Everett walked Troy out to his vehicle before returning to the station with his person of interest.

Everett placed Troy in an interview room and left him there unattended until his attorney arrived.

"From what I gather, some ex-convict has fed you a story and you bought it. You found a box containing bags..." Matthew Renault paused as he straightened his tie.

"... that were similar to others found at murder scenes. God rest their souls, but my client has nothing to do with any of that."

Everett and Cole listened to the attorney make a case for his client to be released and not harassed again. When he finished Cole was first to speak.

"I remember you. I saw you at the basketball court the day we found Greg's body. You had a backpack and a black Mercedes Benz."

"Detective, my client has not seen Greg Faulkner outside of depositions from the business lawsuits. Did you speak with my client on said date you recall seeing him? Did you make eye contact?" Matthew countered.

"So, counselor what we do have, since you're asking questions; is a property listed in your client's name, being searched for additional narcotics." Everett was interrupted by Matthew.

"Release my client or the city will receive a counter suit."

"The city will receive another son of a bitch murderer and drug dealer." Cole slid his chair back and stood up.

Two knocks were heard on the interview room before it opens.

"Hey hey hey gentlemen, and that's not my impression of the iconic Fat Albert." Malcolm entered with another evidence bag containing a partially cracked Bud Light bottle.

"I guess you could do worse, dying by Natty Light or Milwaukee's Best. If you gotta go, then go domestic." He placed the evidence bag on the table.

"What, are we going to have a party? What's this?" Matthew asked.

Troy's disposition changed. He asked for a private word with his attorney.

"Just so you know, we have already confirmed through the distributor when this shipment was trucked out for end users. Within the past five days. Fresh is fresh." Malcolm said, leading the detectives into the observation room.

"Nice job, your team is doing a lot better than the last "so-called task force" the city assembled." The ADA commented as the door closed behind. Her micro-braids were neatly pulled into a ponytail.

"Counselor." Malcolm greeted her with a wink.

"Larry has already confessed, depending on the rest of what's secured at the house for sale location, both of them will be going away for a long time." She shook her head affirmatively.

"I thought Larry was getting a deal for ratting on Troy." Cole wasn't sure what had changed since his initial interview with Larry.

"That deal was based on being completely forthcoming with everything he knew, he failed to reveal the house for sale was their staging area. It wasn't going to be sold." The ADA finished as Troy's attorney knocked on the two-way glass.

"I'm up, I only need one of you."

"I'm game let's go." Malcolm spoke out before anyone.

Her initial hesitancy passed before she followed Malcolm out of the door. Her voice was heard giving Malcolm instructions.

"Don't say a word unless you have my permission, is that understood?"

Everett and Cole returned to their desks and exhaled. After a long five days of tracking down leads, they had solved another case.

"That was solid work, by both of you." Everett complimented his team.

"Listen, I don't know what's gotten into you this week, but you're being soooo nice." Cole laughed loudly throughout their open office space.

Travis looked up from the stack of paperwork he was filling out for the team. His obsession with accuracy would pass eventually. Everett was grateful that he was ambitious, but he still had a lot to learn about the streets, about people.

"Thank you, sir." Travis said.

"Thank you, Sir, thank you, Sir... don't be such a kiss ass." Cole continued laughing and even Everett cracked a smile.

"Ok, ok Bill Burr we aren't paying you." Everett watched the ADA speaking with Kellen, as Troy hugged his sister before being booked.

"I can buy a round of drinks." Everett offered.

"I want to finish this tonight, raincheck." Travis answered as he continued inputting information. However, he looked up as the elevator door opened and the blonde lab technician stepped out, twirling a stethoscope in her hand and wearing an oversized lab coat.

"Yeah raincheck for me too partner, the duties of a doctor calls." Cole spun his chair around and greeted her with a slight rub on her back.

Everett opened his email and noticed a message from his military reserve group. Their training had been postponed and he would be updated later. Logging off his computer he received a text message from his children. A video of them saying goodnight.

Everett felt a warmth in his chest and decided he finally earned the right to have a good night sleep.

Chapter Two

HuMAN BeING

The area opened up once you reached the top of the steps. A redheaded woman pushed a mop back and forth across the wooden floor, cleaning the final remains of last night's event. Her arched brows highlighted her eyes, a vibrant color of jade. Cole had been caught off guard; by any measure she was stunning. He stuttered as she placed the mop into the yellow bucket and approached him.

"We are not open for another hour or so." She wiped her hands on the bar towel stuffed in her waistline.

"Oh no...no, no I'm not drinking. I mean I do drink but..." he paused to refocus

"I'm Detective Cole Kennedy, I'm following up on a lead actually." He flashed his badge, holding it longer for her to look.

"Rachel Jenkins." She turned and walked across the dance floor and into the bar area to stack clean rocks glasses. Cole turned and followed attempting to focus on his task.

"So, what's happened that has you here?" She asked pouring herself a shot of whiskey.

Cole pulled one of the photos from the folder he carried, as she drank the whole pour in one take.

"The receipts show that he was in here a few nights ago, for what appears to have been a lively event." Cole slid the photo across the wooden bar. He was enamored with Rachel, he found her breathtaking as she commanded the space around her.

"I wouldn't recognize him dressed like this, no one dressed like that." Rachel laughed and pointed toward a poster for the event held for the transgender community.

"So, you probably know him dressed like... this?" Cole asked as he pulled a second photograph from his manila folder.

"Oh yes, of course I know her. Bianca D. the D is for delicious." Rachel laughed out loud.

"That's how she introduced herself. It's amazing how people can be authentic when they feel safe... anyway..." she paused as a delivery driver needed her signature on the beer order being hauled in.

"What did she get into now, did she try to break into her own car again? Last week she locked her keys in her car and your brothers in blue were complete assholes." Rachel returned to stand opposite Cole across the bar counter.

"There are asshole cops." Cole affirmed. ,

"Was there anything that was different with him, her, that night?" Cole corrected himself. He was an advocate for the LGBTQ community because his sister was in a same sex marriage and he had seen her struggle firsthand. He had even come to her defense against his very parents.

"Nothing out of the ordinary, everyone had a good time, no disagreements. The band played an extra set. Detective Kennedy, is it?" One of her eyebrows raised as she continued. Her lipstick matched her hair color and stood in contrast to the all-black pants and top she wore.

"What is this about for the third time? I usually don't ask more than once." The tone in her voice was firm, not aggressive, and it threw Cole off again. He should've been the one asking the questions, but he found himself answering her.

"She, she was found dead this morning. Fatal gunshot wound. Are you sure nothing was off, not even slightly that night?" He asked a second time.

"Nothing, honestly, Detective but if you have a card, I will contact you if I remember anything. That's really sad about

Bianca, but the word is there are many 'cops' who don't take the reports against our community with seriousness. Hopefully you will give her the same attention as you would a "so-called" normal human being." She moved away from the counter as one of her workers filled the ice bin and another changed out kegs.

"Was Bianca involved with anyone, to the best of your knowledge?"

"Not to my knowledge, she came alone most of the time. Speak with her old roommate, Sara Knight. No, I do not have her contact information. Your card Detective Kennedy." Rachel extended her hand to receive his information.

"Now, I have to speak with these sound check guys for the band tonight." The air of confidence that surrounded Rachel moved with her every step.

Cole watched her walk away toward the raised stage before retracing his steps to exit the small concert venue.

The plastic on the furniture crinkled every time Travis moved. For the first seven years of his life he wasn't allowed to enter this living room. It was reserved for guests of the family.

His mother sat in a chair across from him. Her pink sweatpants and matching top were faded but her words were focused.

"You think you betta then everybody, got your lil college degree and you become a police officer. Ain't one damn cop dun anything for this family, except lock us up. The popo locked up your daddy, and your brother. Stressed so bad had my hair falling out and now you wanna show up and ask if the kids need help with anything."

Travis stared directly into his mother's eyes as she vented about all the negative things law enforcement had done to the family. A homeowner had caught his father and brother breaking and entering and they had been linked to several other break-ins. They had both spent the last decade behind bars. His mother's hair had thinned from a combination of genetics, stress and a past filled with drug abuse. Now she was raising his nephews, and Travis made sure to check on them weekly and provide help to his mother; even when she was being belligerent toward his chosen profession.

"Not all police are bad ma, do you think I'm one of the bad ones?" He asked but he already knew the answer. She did not, she was proud of the life he worked hard for, but her daily struggle had been the same since he had been a pre-teen.

"Boy hush, nobody said you were bad but you the only po-lease officer allowed in my house without a warrant." She leaned forward from her rocking chair to stand slowly. She bent down and kissed Travis on the forehead.

"You hungry?" She asked as she pivoted toward the kitchen.

The split-level home had been new when they bought it, the neighborhood had been a blossoming community until the crack epidemic moved through it. Coupled with factories closing as Columbus became a "service" city, the neighborhood faded into a small shadow of what it could have become.

"7-up cake?" Travis saw the dessert in the plastic container and thought back to moments when his family unit had been healthy and united.

His mother cut him a big slice and poured him a cup of coffee.

"Do you think you can get the boys on the days you do your karate stuff?"

"It's called Jiu Jitsu, and sure, it will teach them discipline and how to protect themselves." A text message came through from work.

"Mom I have to go; I'll pick them up Saturday morning, and here's some cash to hold you guys over. I took care of the electric and the gas bill." Travis cut a second slice of cake, placing it on a paper towel before kissing his mother on the cheek.

"I love you mom."

"I love you too and don't let my screen door slam!" She yelled, but it was too late as the front door closed behind him.

Travis noticed two older teenagers riding their bikes in the street, before he saw an old friend he grew up with. A friend who had taken the opposite path he had.

"What's good pig?" The man approached nodding at Travis.

"What's up criminal?" Travis responded.

The man extended his arms to the side like he was offended.

"That was cold, criminal, why couldn't I be kingpin or lord of the streets or some boss shit like that?" He dapped up Travis.

"Why couldn't I be Officer or Detective?"

They both laughed and caught up with each other. Travis had once considered Rafi his closest friend, now he hoped he would never have to arrest his acquaintance for any wrongdoing.

A second text message came through for Travis, who said his goodbye and hurried to meet Cole at the morgue.

"Traumatic Brain Injury is definitely the cause of death, but from a gunshot wound. More specifically Sheldon, from a full metal jacket which had a velocity of 900 feet per second coming from a four-inch barrel length .38 revolver." Malcolm was expanding on Sheldon's cause of death.

"Furthermore, it wasn't the actual shot that killed him, it was the loss of blood. You're a great coroner but go the extra mile so I don't have to go over your findings." Malcolm wanted to make sure Sheldon understood that missing track marks from one of their recent cases in his initial report wasn't the quality of work he had come to expect from him.

"Understood." Sheldon agreed and walked away.

"He can be stuffy sometimes but was that necessary, in front of me?" Cole asked. He had not seen Malcolm speak with his subordinate in that manner before.

"Sheldon doesn't care about what other people think, only that his work reflects his mental capacity. Have you ever really seen him take anything personal before?" Malcolm paused as he put medical gloves on.

"One shot from the right frontal lobe tip to the forehead would not have killed him, he would've been left with some mental challenges, but it was loss of blood from the gunshot wound that was his cause of death." The small glass containing the bullet fragment was a match to a .38 caliber Bon FMJ. If the murder weapon is secured subsequent tests would match bullet to handgun.

"She... died from loss of blood due to a gunshot from a .38 caliber." Cole put an emphasis on 'she'.

Malcolm was responding when Travis entered.

"About time rookie, be glad Everett wasn't waiting on you..." he paused until Travis could look at the victim and review the preliminary autopsy report being updated.

This is Brian Deetz, better known as Bianca D.... gunshot wound to the head from a .38. The body was found in the garage by her house cleaner this morning. I've already canvassed her steps from two evenings ago. I need you to follow up with her old roommate." Cole pulled the notes he jotted down after leaving the bar.

"Sara Knight. Do background before you question her. Remember don't reveal what happened until it's absolutely necessary, everyone is a suspect until they are not Travis." Cole removed his white Dallas Cowboys hat and rubbed his head.

"Sheldon's writing the preliminary report." Malcolm had taken leave only to return with his keys in hand.

"If you need me, text Sheldon. I'm flying out to a conference I'm speaking at in Miami. With any luck I'll get to Key West before my return. Next week if you get some time off, we can take the boat out to Put- In- Bay, maybe sneak into Canadian waters." Malcolm and Cole exchanged a fancy handshake they created before Malcolm walked out the morgue.

"I heard about his boat." Travis spoke out while holding the clear glass container with the .38 slug.

"A 45-foot Black Diamond Edition is a yacht Travis, and when I say what happens on the yacht, stays ON the yacht I mean it." Cole interjected as he ushered Travis out of the morgue and back up the elevator to their office space.

"Background first." Cole reminded the rookie detective to check to see if Sara Knight had any trouble with the law, before locating her for an interview.

"Our victim was transgender, use both name and gender she identified as."

Cole wasn't looking forward to the next part of his late morning, a deposition on activity he didn't have any firsthand knowledge of, but somehow his name had been brought up, and now he had to sit and answer questions. He debated on being adversarial with the inspector questioning him, just like those he interviewed often had with him. He practiced a few things he heard from suspects.

"I have no recollection of that, I couldn't answer that."

Cole wrote a note on a post it, placed it on a folder of the information on their findings thus far and left it on Everett's desk. He hoped his partner was ready to jump back into the fight upon his return from weeklong drills with his reserve unit.

Everett, for the first time since he could recall, thought about ending his relationship with the military. He had served his country faithfully and with honor for years, but now he felt like he was burning the candle on both ends and something else besides his marriage would suffer. Robbi had been steadfast each time he deployed, but each time he returned he was aware of the subtle changes in her.

"Maybe it's me who changed." He said out loud staring into the mirror as he brushed his teeth. He wanted to get into the office and catch up on the case his team was working, but the long hot shower he had just taken was a must. He pulled his khaki pants up and buttoned them, grabbed a new military sweatshirt before lacing up his boots.

The military had given him a sense of purpose, serving his country. He had only been on the front lines once but found an equivalent amount of danger as a MP. Responsible for investigating multitudes of crimes, even killing in the line of duty.

Everett unplugged his phone from the charger, grabbed a soda from his refrigerator, and left his apartment to head into the station.

The office had a strange vibe to it, that was the first thing he noticed. The second was an apple sitting on an empty desk, opposite of Travis' area.

"What's up Clark?" An older gray-haired man moved past Everett and headed into an interview room.

"Hey Jack." Everett sat down at his desk, turned his computer on and read Cole's post it.

Cole had sent him the information he had gathered over the course of the last few days but being present and back put skin in the game. His next stop would be the scene of the homicide.

Everett looked over pictures of the crime scene as he sat at his desk.

Loud voices could be heard from the room Jack had entered, with someone suspected of another homicide. The man in question kept yelling loudly that he wanted an attorney.

"LAWYER...LAW YER!" There was a pause and then he began spelling out the letters

"L A W Y E R".

Everett could see the strain and exacerbation on Jack's face as he slammed the door of the interview room behind him.

"Fucking piece of shit is caught with my vic's wallet and cell phone and thinks a lawyer can help him. He is going to spend the rest of his life behind bars before spending eternity in hell!" The older detective had not shown this much animation throughout his career, but when the unit was recognized by the Mayor, he intensified his focus on closing cases. With a city clearance rate of less than fifty percent, this unit cleared nearly sixty-five percent of theirs, but Captain Montgomery would never be satisfied with any open cases.

"Jack, where are we with the Reynolds case, you said there was a break in it before I left?" The Captain didn't slow down as he asked the question. He was being followed by a woman, clearly uncomfortable in her new navy-blue pant suit and wedged shoes.

"Clark, my office." His voice trailed off.

His desk was piled with paperwork, and the only modern device in this space besides his computer, was a Keurig coffee maker. He had grown tired of leaving his daily pleasure up to someone else. His salt and pepper hair was the only noticeable indication of his age. He tucked in his shirt before sitting down.

"Vania Aguilar, Lieutenant Everett Clark. This is your supervisor; you report directly to him." Everett felt blindsided because he had not approved of anyone being added to his team.

Everett was familiar with Vania, she was the granddaughter of a former Chief of Police from Cleveland, Ohio. He forbade her from joining the force, believing that women were only responsible for domesticity as was custom in his family. She left the city by the Lake, and joined the central Ohio Police Academy, making sure she kept her family legacy secret until she graduated. Everett had kept tabs on a few promising candidates over the years, and she had made the short list, however; she took a position in Vice. Her personality, fierce; Vania never settled for "no" as an answer." She thought of that word as being synonymous with "I haven't said yes yet".

She had worked a small number of cases, but those cases had major impact against criminal activity in the city, and now that her grandfather gave his approval, he pushed to get her assigned to this unit. Something she didn't fight against, after nearly killing a suspect after her anger had taken over. Video showed that her use of force was warranted. She broke multiple bones, several ribs, and in the end apprehended a fugitive on the run for kidnapping teens and abusing them.

"Vania, can you excuse us for a moment?" Everett politely asked.

Vania went to leave the office, but the Captain overruled his authority.

"Clark, she is on the team, under a probationary term. She made the short list two years ago and her resume has only gotten better. You're short two detectives as is, and what I have in the budget is enough for one of those positions. So, do me a favor, remember when you're in this office I bark the damn orders. Now, the two of you, get out and make it work."

Vania was first to excuse herself.

Everett hesitated. Contemplating if this was a battle he should take on, he relinquished the urge to respond, and closed the door behind him as he exited.

Vania had already been assigned a desk and was sitting on the corner of it cleaning an apple off.

"I'm qualified and you need someone. Teach me what I don't know, and I won't disappoint you." She bit into the apple and appreciated the deliciousness of the red fruit.

Everett, for the second time in less than twenty minutes, was left speechless. He knew she was right, and her straight-forward approach didn't give him enough room to respond negatively.

"I will teach you for six months, my team pushes hard, and I expect you to keep up. I won't hold your hand, but I will assist you. We have a murder scene to visit." Everett picked up the folder containing the information that Cole had left earlier. He handed it to Vania, grabbed his keys before logging his computer off.

"Let's go."

Travis stood at one end of the kitchen island as Sara Knight prepared a concoction in her freshly opened juicer. The modern design of the kitchen provided more space for movement, and as she walked to the refrigerator for additional carrots, her eccentricity was made more apparent.

"You know carrots have always been a favorite..." she hesitated. Her short haircut highlighted her cheekbones, the black muscle shirt under her white robe with Snoopy on it contrasted against her purple hair.

"Bianca gave me this recipe. She was an amazing human being, misunderstood by the sheep of society." Sara did a three-hundred-and-sixty-degree spin after adding the carrots to her juicer.

"Who would kill Bianca?"

Before Travis could answer. She turned her juicer on. Travis waited until she was done before addressing her again.

"Mrs. Knight..."

"It's Ms. Knight detective." Sara corrected him with a wink.

"Was she seeing anyone? Someone from her past even? Any little thing could help us in our investigation." Travis was interrupted as she extended him a glass of juice.

"It would be very rude not to drink this healthy beverage filled with an abundance of nutrients, and to answer your question, Bianca got harassed because she was different. She never expressed emotion about what others chose for their life but being "different", people said the most heinous things to and about her." She pulled up a stool for Travis to sit, before adding butter to English muffins she had pulled from the oven. She sat down on a second stool by the extended island. Her purple slippers rested on the base of Travis' stool as she leaned forward to offer him a portion of the English muffin.

"This place is quite nice, but compared to Bianca's house, you could fit almost two of these in hers. Why did you decide to move out?" Travis asked, declining the English muffin offered. He had consumed the juice faster than intended.

"I loved that house and we were great roommates, we barely saw each other, but we made it a point on Wednesday nights to do something together." She took a bite, leaving a small amount of butter in the crease of her lips.

"And why did you move out?" Travis asked again, she hadn't answered that for him.

After wiping her lips, she took a sip of juice.

"She said she had met someone and wanted to make him comfortable. She said her "interest" was just learning how to accept that his "different" was actually his normal. I guess in a nutshell, Bianca wanted to make him comfortable and me being there, knowing his identity made him…. well afraid."

Travis only had one question left to ask.

"What's this love interest's name?" He stood from the stool to place his glass in the sink but kept his eye on Sara to check for any indication she wasn't being forthcoming.

"I actually don't know. Bianca told me generic information about him, and I would never pry. People have a right to their privacy. I do know that Bianca said she would get to see him in action Thursday night at some event for our community."

Travis received a text from Cole asking him for a status update.

"Thank you for your time, and the juice. If you can think of anything at all, please call and I will follow up with you if there are any more questions." He waited for a response.

"They're having a memorial for Bianca at Club Ekans on Thursday. A special open mic event since that's what she loved most. I drink Cap Rock Organic Vodka." Sara grabbed a napkin and placed her muffin in it and walked Travis to the door.

"Cole was right, it's the badge." He thought handing her a business card as he departed.

He received another text but this time it was from Everett advising him to meet him at the scene of the homicide.

Everett had not said much since their arrival at the crime scene, and even less on the ride to the victim's home. His attempt to focus on the small details of this homicide kept getting interrupted by thoughts of how the dynamics of the team would be shifting. It was great to have another detective, but his patience wasn't as thick as it had once been.

And although Vania had experience on the force, being a good detective required patience and time. Everett knew it would be a challenge, but he understood it would be no more difficult than instructing those in his reserve unit. Clear instruction, room to fail and to grow.

As they canvassed the lower portion of the home, it was apparent that the victim had everything neatly kept. Each object seemed to have its' own place. The simplistic art objects were all black and white, but the paintings on brilliant white walls displayed colors intertwined with others creating mesmerizing schemes.

"Accountants make bank like this huh?" Vania walked up the two small steps from the living room. The room was illuminated from the sun shining through the front glass pane. A twenty foot by fifteen-foot window that overlooked a small ravine at the front of the property.

Everett didn't acknowledge her question; he checked each entrance into the home before he and Vania stepped into the four-car garage.

"Seems excessive for one person to have all of this." Vania crossed over the yellow tape before Everett pressed each switch to open and close the garage doors.

"Check the space upstairs, more specifically the windows." Everett directed Vania, who crossed under the tape as she moved back inside.

Everett was working a thought about the case as he imagined how the murder went down.

Bianca had been slouched over into the passenger seat from the driver's side. A bullet hole through her hand indicated she tried to shield herself. From any angle, she would have seen the perpetrator when she opened the garage door to pull in.

"Why wouldn't she just drive back out or blow the horn?" The ideas wouldn't form a complete picture, but he knew that ideas would eventually lead to action.

Everett reentered the house, checked each window on the first floor. Two bedrooms and an office set on the first floor, along with a full bath and a half one for guests. The upstairs held another three bedrooms. Two of them facing the front of the home, and the third overlooked a man-made pond hidden behind trees on the backside of the property.

"Everything is locked tight and no sign of forced entry." Vania walked down the winding staircase staring upward at the glass chandelier hanging from the ceiling.

"I am pretty good in math, maybe I should think of a career change." She finished as she approached Everett. She noticed that his facial expression soured.

"Too soon?" She joked trying to create a lighter moment.

Movement from the front window caught their attention. Vania distanced herself from Everett, giving them a better vantage point, for whoever was about to enter the crime scene.

"Relax." Everett advised as the front door opened.

"Sir."

"Travis."

"Good to have you back." Travis paused as he noticed Vania standing off closer to the kitchen area. He nodded at her before updating Everett on the interview with Sara Knight.

"So, Bianca was seeing someone that wanted to remain hidden. Hopefully forensics will have more once they get the computer or her other electronic devices open."

"There are no pictures of anyone, not even himself from what I've seen so far. For such a beautiful home, besides the stuff hanging on the wall this place feels cold." Vania's observation drew Travis' attention to her again.

"Travis White. Vania Aguilar. Meet your new partner." Everett said before he walked out the front door.

"Partners?" Travis asked out loud.

"Partners, wow, ok I guess." Vania properly greeted Travis.

"Vania Aguilar, formerly of Vice." She extended her hand.

"Travis White." He responded hesitantly as he returned the gesture.

"There were a few family photos we secured, but none of them are current. And you're correct, this place does seem cold especially after hearing how lively of a person she was." Travis walked closer to one piece of art standing alone. It was positioned directly in the middle of the front window. A figurine of a snake with two heads. Each head painted; one white and the other black. The title "Why fight for food."

"I don't know what it means but I kinda dig it." Vania approached Travis and the artwork.

"I see one body with two mouths. The willingness of each head to realize that there is only one stomach being fed." Travis paused as he watched Everett speaking on the phone through the window.

"So maybe, Bianca understood that there was no separation, and that life would nourish her fully by accepting herself as one complete person, and not two separate entities fighting over food." Travis finished before excusing himself to speak with Everett who waved them both outside.

"I want you two to speak with his colleagues, find out about his workload and if his work had any noticeable changes. Use her birth name, because that's what they knew her by. Check the work calendar over the past thirty days and follow up with Sheldon for any new info. I will check in with you both later at the office..." he paused to check the time on his watch. Vania returned to the home to make sure it was secured. Travis walked toward the ravine and then back to the long-rounded driveway.

"Any chance I can drive." Vania asked out of curiosity.

"Not one." Travis replied as he used the keyless remote to unlock the car doors.

Cole had returned from his deposition, and was sitting at his desk, when Vania and Travis returned. Everett had forgotten to update him on the acquisition of the newest member. Just after 9pm the office was barely a skeleton crew of officers and detectives.

Travis, believing Cole had already been brought into the loop, sat down and began sharing what they had found out at the victim's office, he wasn't sure why Cole was looking confused.

"Bianca was appreciated by the other partners in her firm. Recent audits of her work showed accuracy. The only picture at her desk was from ten years ago from a trip taken to the UK. How was your deposition?" Travis finished.

Cole hesitated and then asked the million-dollar question not seeing Everett approach from the stairwell.

"Who are you?" He said slowly not to be offensive.

"Vania is our new team member; she came over from Vice. So, what did you find out? Everett answered his partner's question before asking one on return.

"Brian Deetz, was an outstanding revenue stream for the CPA firm, his work was exemplary. His relationships were minimal, and although he cracked the whip his employees believed him to be fair. We didn't get any indication that his other lifestyle was known." Vania interjected before standing up to formally introduce herself to Cole.

"Today has been a long day. Travis tomorrow check with the forensic team on what they've found from the vehicle, fingerprints, anything left behind that can help us. Vania coordinate with his schedule. You two can take off. Cole, I need to speak with you." Everett finished as Travis and Vania wrapped up and left.

"There's been another murder with similar traits from three of our unsolved cases. The latest victim was found in Cincinnati, killed three days ago. I don't like how this has been escalating on our watch." Everett stared at his partner recognizing that they both had the same thoughts.

"We have a serial killer in Ohio, and The Captain can't deny it this time." Everett finished.

"Did you get an autopsy report emailed?" Cole was attempting to ask.

"Emailed?" Everett looked at him with his eyes squinting,

"I just got back off the road from speaking with their coroner's office. Can you get a hold of Malcolm? We need him to look this over." Everett acknowledged the file he was still holding onto.

"Malcolm is in Miami until Monday, Sheldon can take..." Cole paused. He knew Malcolm had invested time and energy into these unsolved cases and it was best to send the results directly to Malcolm.

"I'll scan it and send him a copy via email, hopefully in between the sunshine and Mojito's, he checks his email accounts." Cole took the folder from Everett and sat down at his desk to review the findings of the Cincinnati case before sending it to Malcolm.

Like the other bodies found, they had similar traits. Women under the age of thirty-five, wealthy and very active. Two of the three victims in Columbus attended the same gym, but the third murdered woman owned her own dance studio. Each one of the women were found completely dressed, with their shoes off. Their pinkie toe had been severed on their right foot, and their left ring finger also dismembered. Roses were spread on the floor, outlining the bodies in a heart shaped configuration. The bodies were laid in such a position in between the flowers, that they created the separation of a broken heart. They had not made any progress in any of them and Everett had lost sleep over these cases.

"I'm going to review our findings for a little longer." Everett sat down and leaned back in his chair resting his head in his hands after stretching.

Cole stayed until midnight before leaving Everett, who was intently looking at each of the three related cases. He knew his partner would end up staying overnight, it was in his nature. Everett had to catch up on those things he had missed being away with the reserve unit.

Cole found Everett sleeping on the couch in one of the break rooms when he returned the next morning. Arriving at 5:00 am was a bit early for him, but the thought of a serial killer traveling up and down 171 kept his mind racing, and he had barely slept.

Cole didn't disturb his partner until after a strong pot of coffee had been made.

"Everett... E." His tapped him on his shoulder and stepped back in case he reacted strangely being woken up.

Everett focused and took the cup of coffee Cole had extended to him.

He checked his watch and sat up.

The couch had seen better days, but for overnight sleeping quarters it fulfilled its purpose.

"I looked over the info from the Bianca case, you wrote that the General Manager of the bar said that Bianca had been harassed, but you only wrote the number three down, what's that about?" Everett took a sip from his mug before following Cole back to their desks.

"The GM of the bar said Bianca had been harassed by three uniforms after locking her keys in her car."

"So, who were the officers?" Everett asked.

Cole didn't have an answer, he didn't think that uniformed officers assisting someone with locked keys was important to the investigation.

"Let's find out who responded to the call and follow up with them to see if they noticed anything from the norm. Double back around and see if there is footage of this so-called harassment." Everett sat down.

"I promised Becca that I would take her and her brother to breakfast before school. I'm going to take off shortly, but I'll be back by nine. Make sure that Travis and Vania are ready to roll from the moment they step off the elevator." Everett searched for his keys under a stack of papers, and that's when Cole spoke up.

"Give me a heads up when shifts occur to this team. I was like a deer stuck in the fuckin' headlights yesterday."

"Copy brother." Everett decided to walk the stairwell down to the parking garage.

Cole turned his computer on and saw a response from Malcolm. He had reviewed the findings and had already booked a flight from Miami to Columbus. He was foregoing his three days in Key West; he had an investment in finding the killer. The second victim had been a participant in a recent seminar he had been involved in, and her challenging a few of his statements made her memorable.

Cole then called the precinct responsible for the area the night club resided in. After speaking with the dispatcher, he had two names to follow up with later. He put the current case off until 8am when the officers in question would start their daily tour, and he dove back into the file Everett had returned with yesterday from Cincinnati.

"Good morning Cole." Vania approached her desk with a to go mug from Starbucks. Unlike her suit outfit from yesterday, today she dressed more comfortably, with blue jeans and a white cardigan shirt covered by a dark blue blazer. Her feet donned ankle high boots and she seemed more relaxed.

"Good morning Vania." He looked up and smiled.

Travis was a few minutes behind her, and the look on his face seeing Vania had arrived earlier than he had was disappointing.

"Malcolm said the gunshot wound to the head wasn't fatal, that Bianca bled out. The first gunshot wound looked defensive as it passed through her hand, and the second one led to the fatality. See if they found any foreign fingerprints." Cole then challenged them to make a difference today before they left. He spent the next four hours glued to his chair, staring between the folders spread across the surface of his desk and the information on the computer screen. A text from Everett reminded and prompted him to pay the event venue another visit.

The parking lot was full, more than the first time when he pulled into it. Music was playing through the outside speakers for those sitting on the patio. Five tables were full of people being served food. The catering truck sitting closest to the building had caught Cole's attention initially, while a police officer was providing security for an early afternoon event. He made his way inside and back up the stairs to the main room. He expected to see Rachel mopping, but the room had been filled with long tables with more people congregating to eat. Cole saw Rachel speaking with two men in business suits. After making eye contact with Cole, she excused herself and approached him.

"Cole, have you come back to tell me you've found Bianca D's killer?" She was direct, but strangely again not offensive. He was just as stunned the second time seeing her. Her red hair was fixed in pig tails and she wore black French terry Short Overalls with a cuffed hem and designer metal clasps.

"Rachel..." he paused to shake her hand. He kept his eyes trained on hers to not follow the curves of her body.

"We are still working on it and that's one of the reasons I'm here. You mentioned that there were some officers..."

"I said asshole cops." She corrected him.

"Right...right asshole cops that harassed her, do you have surveillance of the parking lot? We'd like to identify them so we can interview them. They may have some valuable information. Any little thing can help." Cole's attention was drawn to the stage as a man and woman approached the mic and the music died down.

"Detective follow me." Rachel walked into a small studio where the D.J. was stationed.

She knocked on the glass pane to gain his attention.

"Hey what's up boss lady?"

"Give this gentleman the footage from two weeks ago on the date he requests. Detective I have to get back." Rachel excused herself.

Cole watched her walk away, he had been with countless women over the course of his life from a variety of backgrounds. Her red hair flowed over her left shoulder, and as the door closed, Cole knew he had been bitten.

Everett had taken the kids to breakfast and was waiting on Cole to return with the footage from the event venue. His kids helped him with clarity that even if he lacked as a husband, he excelled at parenting. After dropping them off at school, he went home to shower and change before returning to the office, where he had his head deep into multiple investigations, trying to balance them all.

"Media Room one, I've got the footage from the night the Vic was harassed. Before we bring them in let's look this over. Maybe there's something, maybe not." Cole said startling Everett, who was highlighting something on one of the reports.

"Yeah ok." He replied checking his Fitbit watch.

"The kids haven't checked in yet." he knew Travis had adequate training under his tutelage, although he hadn't handled many cases hands on. Everett hoped that Vania was following his lead.

Cole heard his partner and thought it wise to text Travis to not come back empty handed.

Travis received the message but would wait to respond. The vehicle hadn't left many results to take back, but Vania wanted to take another look at the murder scene.

Travis walked in first and opened the garage, but Vania walked the perimeter as if figuring out a puzzle.

"Vania." Travis called out for her. When she didn't answer he walked to the front of the house and found her staring up at an ornament extending under the gutter. She then retraced her steps to end up staring upward toward each corner of the garage entrance and noticed two smaller ornaments similar to the first.

Travis wasn't sure what she was doing but decided to wait until she completed her task.

"Something bothered me yesterday when we were here." Vania asked him to follow her to each location an ornament was situated.

"Do you see what I see?" She asked

Travis walked closer to the front of the home and stared upward. Once he saw the device his eyes lit up.

"Oh shit... shit ...shit... shit. Good job." He said as he walked towards the garage.

"All of them?" He asked rhetorically.

"But they took the computer and didn't find anything on them besides work related and investments. The information has to be transmitted to something." Travis finished as he watched Vania enter the house again.

She walked upstairs before coming back down to investigate the bedroom closets.

"So where is all of her clothing? I see Brian's suits and man items but where are her shoes, dresses... where the hell are her wigs?" Vania's curiosity grew.

Travis was intrigued with her questions because they were very valid, and he was amazed that neither Everett nor Cole had asked this same question. He then noticed something odd with the bookcase in the office. From the outside of the house the room should have extended further. He walked out of the room to check the dimensions of the other bedrooms on the first floor.

"The rooms aren't proportioned. There should be at least another eight feet between these walls." Travis then noticed the slight discoloration around the wood floor nearest the bookcase.

"I think there's another space behind this." He said flatly.

Vania approached the opposite side of his position and saw minor scuff marks near the edge of the bookcase.

"Secret Room." The excitement in her voice could not be contained, and immediately she started pulling books from the shelf.

"What are you doing?" Travis asked.

"There has to be a latch, a book to open it up and if we ..." she jumped backwards as the bookcase slid open.

She entered first and the answers to their previous questions came forth.

The room had one long continual shoe rack with all styles of footwear. A small loveseat with paisley print was situated across from a double rack holding Bianca's dresses and gowns. A single chair was stationed in front of a mirror where an assortment of makeup and accessories were fixed.

"Laptop." Travis said as he powered it up. A password was not required, and as they scanned through it, they had another lead from photos of Bianca with what appeared her love interest.

"Let's take this back, but first forensics needs to come do their thing." Travis made a call and when two members of Malcolm's team showed, he and Vania left. Cole told him don't come back empty handed.

"Mission accomplished." He thought pulling out of the oval driveway.

Everett knew the officers weren't giving a true account about harassing Bianca, blaming any misinterpretation on her being drunk. When asked why they let her drive away after getting her door open, neither one had an answer.

"Was there anything strange, anything at all that either of you can think of?" Cole asked without offense.

"No nothing strange on a night people dressed up like..." the officer caught himself seeing the disgust on Cole's face.

"We appreciate you guys stopping down, be careful on the streets. Thank you, officers." Everett excused them.

"That was a waste of time, they clearly razzed Bianca. From their actions on the recording and their demeanor just now." Cole tried to say before Travis and Vania asked them into the media room.

"Bianca had cameras all over the outside of his home, and we found a secret room where she kept all of her belongings, and in that room, there was this." Travis opened the laptop which was already queued up.

"We have a clear picture of the killer." Vania pulled her chair closer.

As the footage moved forward, it showed Bianca pulling into her garage when a man entered holding something in his hand. It turned out to be a flashlight, which was used to blind Bianca's visibility. The first gunshot fired went through her hand, and the second one was the head shot. The perpetrator walked out of the garage after removing the garage door opener from the vehicle. His face was shown as he stared back into the garage at what he had just done.

"Ok, lets print out a copy of the photo and get the laptop to forensics. We have a prime suspect and with any luck we can..." Everett had energy in his voice. This breakthrough was huge. Cole moved Travis to the side and replayed the shooting, and then paused the footage once the killers face came into view.

"I've seen him already, today." Cole spoke up. All three people gave him their attention.

"Officer on site at the event venue, he was the third officer in the video the night Bianca was harassed." The screensaver on the laptop popped up, and it was a photo of the victim with the cop.

Everett left the room and returned with Captain Montgomery. An officer involved in a cold-blooded murder would bring such negative publicity to an already badgered police force. Both Federal and State investigations had left a black mark against the department.

After Captain Montgomery reviewed the recording, he ordered them to be ready to interview him, and within the hour the officer arrived with his commanding officer.

"Stan Frankowich we won't fuck around with you, we know you killed Brian Deetz also known as Bianca D. It seemed like your personal relationship made her happy, why would you murder your lover?" Everett asked

"Who, my lover? I've dated the same woman for the past three years."

Everett thought it peculiar that he was more focused on refuting that they were lovers than he was in defending himself against the actual shooting.

"So why did you do it?" Everett followed up.

"Do what, shoot someone? It wasn't me." Stan answered. The sweat could be seen forming around his hairline. The snug collar of his shirt seemed to tighten as he listened to the detectives.

"So, about a week or so ago, a transgender woman was harassed in the parking lot of Club Ekans. We've interviewed these other officers." Cole chimed in showing him the recording of Bianca being harassed.

"Why wouldn't you stop them from badgering your lover?"

"She wasn't my lover; she locked her damn keys in the car and the guys busted her chops, but we got the door unlocked."

"Sooooo, what you're telling us is that this isn't you?" Cole turned the computer back towards him, showing him standing outside Bianca's home with flashlight in hand after firing two rounds into the car.

Stan sat motionless, silently staring at the screen. The weight he carried could be seen as his shoulders slouched and the blood drained from his face.

Cole and Everett sat quietly waiting to hear what he would say after knowing he was caught.

"She was going to out me after that night because I didn't stand up to the other two, and I let them say demeaning things. I wanted to protect her but … but…" his voice trailed off as both Captain Montgomery and his commanding officer entered the room, followed by two additional uniform officers.

"Stan Frankowich you are a shitty disgrace to this badge." Stan's commanding officer removed the badge from his uniform. He had already relieved him of his weapon before he escorted him to the interview.

Captain Montgomery pulled Stan from his seat and placed him in handcuffs.

"Stan Frankowich you are under arrest, do you understand your right's, or should I read them to you?" Captain Montgomery ordered the two uniforms to take him to be processed and booked.

ADA Jefferson walked out of the room after listening to Stan from behind the double-mirrored glass. Everett exited behind the captain and could hear him speak two words that carried weight.

"No deals." The captain said.

"Agreed no fucking deals!" She adjusted the strap of her attaché hanging across her shoulder.

"Good job Detective Clark. Being in this line of work puts us in contact with the absolute worst."

"Human beings." Vania sat cross-legged in her chair, dipping celery into a jar of peanut butter.

Everett pulled the ADA off to the side.

"There will be cops who won't like how your office will proceed, until all the evidence comes out at least. If you have any problems with anything reach out."

"He is a piece of shit and anyone defending him, also a piece of shit. I will flush them down the toilet too if they want to fuck with me."

Malcolm approached pulling a suitcase behind him.

"All this talk of shit; strangely has made me hungry. Anybody else hungry?" He spotted Vania eating at her desk.

"Darling, do you mind sharing any of that?" he turned and walked to her desk.

"I don't mind at all, but never, ever, ever, call me darling again."

"Fair enough Detective V.A." Malcolm dipped a celery stick into the peanut butter, as Cole sat down at his desk.

"Detective V.A., that's catchy." Cole also grabbed a celery stick.

"Detective V.A.?" Vania asked rhetorically. As she thought about the name, she liked it.

"Detective V.A. that's acceptable." She pulled the peanut butter jar closer to her.

Everett made eye contact with Cole as they understood that this new addition to the team was proving her worth.

"Hey, I'm going to take off, I have a stop to make." Cole said leaving his team behind for the night.

As he walked into the main floor of Club Ekans, he was taken aback by the number of people who had come to pay their respect for Bianca. Her picture was spread throughout, he saw some people crying while celebrating memories. A person was on stage speaking poetry. The piece he could understand was about being authentic, ultimately the goal of human beings.

Cole saw Rachel behind the bar filling drink orders.

He made his way towards one end of the long, curved bar and waited until she had a moment.

"I don't have time to answer or help right now. This celebration is important." She paused to tell the bar back to get more ice.

"I have no more questions, I wanted you to know that we have someone in custody, and that your asshole cop statement was more accurate than I'd like." Cole asked for a double tequila neat.

"Thank you, Detective Cole for closure and giving me hope that justice isn't evasive for my community." She walked away to pour his drink.

Cole had heard her each time she spoke about her community and understood that as much as he was attracted to her, he didn't stand a chance outside of this interaction to learn more about her.

"This is on the house Cole." She said sliding his drink to him on a coaster. She handed him a napkin with her contact number.

"I am free Sunday afternoon, don't make me ask twice." She winked at him and walked away.

Cole couldn't figure out what had just happened until he took his first sip.

"LGBTQ, he put emphasis on the B".

He mingled and celebrated the life of Bianca D with those congregated.

Chapter Three

TRAFFIC STOP

"Yeah ok Robbi, yes...yes I will be at Becca's performance. Yes, on time." Everett kept trying to get a word in, but his ex-wife was drilling him to be on time to their daughter's recital. He had missed her last school concert because he was with his son, but he understood how important it would be to have him in attendance this time.

"Yes, Robbi... ok I have to go. I'll speak with you later." Everett ended the call and stared at his dashboard. Being divorced wasn't that different from being married except the roofs were no longer the same. He was coming to grips that it was mainly his fault, his lack of or inability to change had driven the wedge between them. Love was not an issue, priorities were.

"I will remind you." Cole spoke up. He had been texting on his cellphone the whole time, but being in proximity as they rode together, he heard everything, even Robbi's voice coming through the cell phone.

"Yeah thanks." Everett turned the car off and pulled the keys from the ignition.

"I'll go with you in fact, I don't have plans until later that night." Cole added.

"Has Malcolm got into the Cincy file?" Everett asked as they exited the vehicle.

"Yeah, he has, and he's spoken with the coroner in both 513 and 216. There are some minor differences from what he thinks, the perpetrator is honing his skills. He will hit us up when he makes progress. Should we tell the captain yet??" Cole asked as they walked into the elevator.

A uniformed officer was speaking with the Captain when they exited onto their floor; unusual because it was Sunday afternoon, and neither expected to see him sitting at his desk, with the office door cracked open as a union representative listened on.

Everett and Cole ignored the conversation, but the Captain's voice carried.

"We depend on each other; our brothers depend on you to do your job. You had no reason to pull the gentleman over, and then on top of that you escalate when you were clearly in the wrong. You called for additional back up, a canine unit because his rear brake light was out? Do you understand the liability we may be in? Commendable that you left your cameras on, but just completely dumbass on everything else. Do you have anything to say... either one of you?" He finished by addressing both the officer and union representative.

"Good I didn't think so, you're on desk duty until this shit is over." The captain said before dismissing them both.

"Clark and Kennedy, my office." The Captain called out before they were able to sit down at their desks.

Cole entered first and remained standing, while Everett sat down in one of the three unoccupied chairs.

"Fucking rookies always want their credentials to be recognized." The Captain said as a side bar in reference to the officer just reprimanded.

"Not just rookies Captain." Everett interjected with a quick glance at Cole. His partner's cell phone chimed indicating a text message.

"Aguilar and Travis are working out?" The captain took a sip from his coffee mug.

"Yeah they're like yin and yang." Everett was saying as Cole interrupted.

"More like Cheech and Chong or Abbot and Costello."

"If that's a reference to my age Detective, I take offense."

"Not at all Sir." Cole responded with a sly smirk.

"Good, good, your team is under a watchful eye, especially with as many cases being cleared now. We need this win, for this department, for your careers and for my advancement." The captain hesitated as Cole's phone went off, followed by Everett receiving a voice call.

"Is that all Sir, we've caught a new case." Everett relayed as he stood up to exit.

"That's all, dismissed detectives and close my door on the way out."

Everett was last to leave.

"That is a hard no." Cole said answering the question posed before seeing the Captain.

"Travis and V.A. are already on site of a double homicide on the north side. Let' s roll." Everett was headed to the elevator as Cole detoured to the restroom.

"I'll be down, three cups of coffee this afternoon." Cole detoured to the restroom.

When Cole exited the building, he was nearly knocked over by a man delivering flowers to someone in the building.

"Excuse me." Cole was in disbelief, but the man, with headphones in his ears kept moving towards the receptionist desk, seemingly ignoring Cole.

Cole didn't pursue the conversation knowing that his partner was waiting on him outside.

"1-800-Flowers damn near knocked me down." Cole strapped on his seatbelt.

The drive up I71 was easy but getting off on the Morse Rd. Exit wasn't, as an accident was being moved to the berm of the road.

"You coulda took Cooke Rd." Cole was frustrated.

"Right and you coulda said no to the third cup of coffee but the new barista kept you longer than intended huh?" Everett matched his tone.

Travis was outside the single-family home canvassing the perimeter when they pulled up. They both exited the Dodge Charger and slipped around the yellow tape already put up.

"What do we have?" Everett asked.

"Double homicide. The bodies were found by a teenager, friend of the victim's daughter, Marilyn. Preliminary testing indicates that the deaths occurred between 48-72 hours ago but will be narrowed down once..." Travis attempted to say but Vania was exiting the front door of the home with a revelation. She was more comfortable, and it showed. She donned the standard gear for the team by wearing jeans and hoodies.

"I've called the aunt and she hasn't seen the daughter, and no one has heard from her in several days. We may have a kidnapped teenager." Vania noticed Cole and Everett who were standing just out of her line of sight as she approached Travis.

"Say that again." Everett needed to make sure he heard her correctly.

"This may also be a kidnapping, family has not seen the daughter or heard from her. She usually speaks with her cousin twice per day, but she hasn't called." Vania answered.

Cole had moved away from them to enter the house.

It had a typical middle-class working feel to it. Some family pictures of past events, an older photo of the couples wedding. Cole noticed some pill bottles left on the living room table. He walked into the dining room where the bodies were found, sitting at the table with needles sticking in their arms."

"So why is this a homicide and not a suicide of sorts, damn junkies." One of the uniformed officers spoke up to no one in particular.

"Because the bodies were staged." Travis frowned at the uniformed officer.

"Because they were both shot first in the other room and relocated into the kitchen." Vania added as she lifted the dead man's shirt to reveal two bullet holes and then did the same for the female victim.

"So, as you can see, they couldn't shoot up after being shot, that's why their arms look like that." She finished.

The uniform officer shook his head in agreement before he was embarrassed any more.

"Have either of you notified the new task force?" Everett asked.

He had bent down to check both bullet holes on each victim.

"Yeah, as soon as we found out from the cousin no one has seen or spoken with Marilyn.

Here is a recent pic." Travis interjected showing the photo.

"So, what were this husband and wife really into that they would be shot and made to look like an OD. The killer would know we'd figure this out but what's the purpose." Vania wasn't able to piece it together.

"V.A, and Travis, I want you two to get that photo out. Then first thing tomorrow morning, I want you to go speak with Marilyn's school principal. Find out what type of student she is and her circle of friends. Cole look into the family's background and I will speak with his boss." Everett said in reference to the male murder victim who still wore his delivery uniform.

A small group of the neighborhood had congregated on the perimeter, some asking questions to the officers keeping them out.

Vania walked to the yellow tape, toward a group of teens. As she approached, one rode his bike away, but the rest simply watched.

"Any of you tell me where Marilyn would hangout?"

"She really didn't, hangout with us, she was always busy with her family. Her uncle would pick her up, she really didn't like going with him but..."

"Man... Mansfield get yo ass over here and away from those cops." An older man approached pulling his son away. His dreadlocks were neatly groomed and the t-shirt he wore bore the peace sign symbol.

"Sir we are just trying to get..." Vania got cut off.

"I don't give a fuck what you trying to get, don't talk to mine. Man take yo ass home and eat dinner and get your homework done." He finished by waving his son home as he followed.

"V.A. that's what we run into all the time, are you ready?" Travis waited for his new partner to reply.

Instead she crossed the tape and ran the father down.

"Excuse me, excuse me sir, sir I've been on the other side like you, not wanting to speak with the law so I get it. Nothing good comes out of speaking with 'pigs or 5-0' but in case there's anything you or your son think would be helpful this is my card." She extended the card and waited until he took it.

She turned, walked back and handed out a few more cards. She walked past Travis and then answered his question.

"Yeah I'm ready." They got in the vehicle, strapped their seat belts on and drove in the opposite direction that Everett and Cole had gone.

"They are overwhelmed to say the least, kidnapping and human trafficking isn't something I'd really want to face every day." Travis said as he and Vania left the information, along with a photo of Marilyn, off to a recently formed human trafficking division before they stopped by their desks.

"So, you'd rather work on homicide cases than..." she started to ask before Travis cut her off as he stood up from his desk.

"Yeah, I would because there's no chance for a homicide victim, it's black and white. Don't get me wrong, I would do my job, but I think it would be a lot to carry... the unknown part, but it would never end, the open cases. Ohio is one of the leading states for human trafficking, it would be too much for me at least." Travis interjected.

"Yeah I guess." Vania replied readjusting her black hoodie to cover her gun on her belt holster.

"I can see your point, but I would hope that if somehow, someway I was taken, that there would be someone searching."

"I'll see you in the morning." Travis sat down at his desk and decided to update the notes on the case. His obsession with paperwork and following his duties could be traced back to him being the opposite of his father and brother. They flew by the seat of their pants. Now they were finishing out consecutive sentences. He would not overlook details. The devil was in the details and he would never be the reason a case was lost.

"Man, what are you doing? Is this all you do? Work, work, work, work, work, work? This ain't a Rihanna song." Vania stood to the side of his desk before placing her hand onto the manila folders on his desk.

"Leave this shit, I'm meeting my friend at some arts event, I wasn't going to go but fuck it, you like art and interpretation, I'm sure she would love to hear your take on the work. There's a big buffet and if I'm going to be trusting you with my life you can't say no. So, come on." Vania rolled his chair back away from his desk.

Travis took a deep inhale and decided to go, he loved art and nearly everything needing to be done could wait a few hours.

"There's no dress code for this event?" He asked as they waited for the elevator.

Vania had just finished texting someone when she replied

"Not for us, we are detectives, but if you wanna swing by your place first we have time." Vania answered as she pressed the down button.

"Yeah I've had this on all day since sunrise service. I'll be less than twenty minutes."

"I'll drive and drop you off afterwards. You never let me get behind the wheel, not once and that's not my choice off duty." Vania was allowing more of her personality to shine through. She knew how to play her position on the team, but this was not work related, and she needed to gauge what type of man Travis was behind the person with his head stuck in paperwork.

Travis texted Vania his address, and they coordinated for her to pick him up in one hour. She chose to make a quick detour and decided to pay a visit to a patient in a coma. She had saved the life of the young woman, and in doing so nearly killed the perpetrator. This was the reason for her transfer, to provide her a new beginning, but the victim, always, was in her thoughts even if deep beneath the surface.

When she arrived at the hospice facility, it was after visiting hours. The nursing staff never prevented her stopping in regardless of the time, she was "Alexa's guardian angel".

"How is she?" She directed her question to one of the nurses.

"As stable as she's been, no changes but there's hope."

Vania entered the room and took a deep breath, she had never spoken to Alexa, the young woman was already unconscious when she found her inside of an abandoned home from a tip. After gaining the identity of the offender through fingerprints, Vania set her mark on him and when she found him, she thought she had killed him, but he survived.

The many vases of flowers spread throughout the room provided energy of life and it was the reason Vania sent separate dozens every two weeks.

"Alexa, I mean to stop by more often, but I've got another position. I know how much your family misses you and if you can hear me, I know you miss them too. I'll keep checking on you. Whatever battles your fighting to get back to this place don't give up." Vania stayed longer and read chapters of Alexa's favorite series of books left by the family. She touched her hand before leaving the room.

The emotions weren't as raw as they had been when she made her first visit, but they still brought flashbacks to seeing her cousin in the same condition after being shot on the job in Cleveland as an officer of the law. Vania said goodbye to a different nurse as she left the facility. She had wanted to give herself enough time to change but wearing slacks and a blouse for less than half a day would have to do.

Travis felt like a different man after shaving and showering. He had heard about this art exhibit, but when he went to purchase tickets for opening week, they had been sold out completely. He pulled the comforter across his bed to loosen any wrinkles before adjusting his pillows to fit symmetrically opposite its' match.

His home was immaculately clean, with a small collection of art pieces from different influences. Travis walked into his kitchen, opened the refrigerator to retrieve a bottled water, and took an assortment of multivitamins. The doorbell ringing caught him off guard momentarily. Although he had lived in this condo for over three years, he seldom had visitors.

"Look at you, looking like a baby Denzel." Vania said laughing boisterously.

"Ha...ha...jokes. Man, I tried getting tickets for opening week, you must have some real connects." Travis said as he let her in.

"Water?" He grabbed an additional bottle from his refrigerator.

"Your fucking neat T, I mean clean neat, like you could eat off these floors. No wonder you're always going over paperwork. When I get around to straightening my place you're invited." Vania laughed again, pausing as she opened her water.

"Yeah, she's one of my ex's sister and even though her sibling is a piece of shit, she is someone I call friend. She can be eccentric and at times in her own world, but... well you'll see."

"I'm ready if you are." He slid his handgun into his belt holster.

"Yeah I'm ready Mr. Clean." Vania opened the front door.

"How many names am I going to have before the end of the night? Baby Denzel, T, Mr. Clean." Travis asked as he approached the passenger side.

"I'm not sure Captain Obvious." Vania smiled as they closed the car doors behind them.

It was still dark when Everett woke early the next morning. He appreciated the quietness. The small respite of peace was the best part of his day. Silence helped him put the bits of his life in order that he struggled with, primarily the relationship with his children and ex-wife.

Everett sat on his couch with his legs extended onto the coffee table. Files scattered across the glass top. He had dozed off with the thought of his daughter's performance. His alarm going off in his bedroom startled him awake. Tripping over his shoes laid out on the floor, reminded him his mind was working faster than his body. He regrouped, turned off the alarm before walking into the bathroom to turn his shower on. He powered on his cell phone and opened a musical playlist with "King of The Road" by Roger Miller next in line to play.

Khakis and a white mock long sleeved shirt were the uniform of the day. He put on his newest pair of timberland boots.

He stared at the family pictures on top of his dresser. The kids were much younger; and Robbi still carried hope in her heart, now she had become just as firm in her resistance to try, as he had been in his inability to change.

Everett pulled a carbon case from his closet, before sliding it back, after realizing what he wanted was elsewhere. He pulled a smaller case from beneath his bed and took his Sig Sauer P226 from it and slid it into the belt holster on his waist.

Looking at the clock on his nightstand, 5:00 am. He set his mind on the task for the day. He needed to spend the first two hours combing over the files retrieved from Cincinnati. He sent a text to Malcolm that he wanted an update with any new findings from his perspective. He hoped his text would stir Malcolm awake after a typical night of partying until the last person left.

"A serial killer." Everett said out loud as he rotated his neck to work out a few kinks.

He walked into the kitchen and poured the coffee already brewed from being preset. He put the large mug on the counter-top and picked up his watch. He strapped it to his wrist, before sliding his wallet into his front pant pocket. The text tone was a response from Malcolm.

"Already waiting on you."

Everett smirked because Malcolm had responded so quickly, but that also meant there was a new lead. He grabbed his keys and hurried out the door and into his car before realizing he left his coffee mug on the counter. He retraced his steps, grabbed the mug and drove with haste to the station.

Although Malcolm had responded quickly earlier, Everett was still surprised to see him sitting at Travis' desk, and even more shocked to see Cole already in two hours early.

"You're late partner." Cole said giving Everett a head nod.

"Everett." Malcolm acknowledged him.

"Malcolm..." Everett paused and approached them.

"So, what do you have?"

"It was staring us right in the face..." Malcolm paused to turn the computer screen towards Everett.

"Each victim is positioned almost the same with minor differences. The information compiled including those from rural areas near I71 shows that there are at least nine homicides related to each other." Malcolm exhaled and shook his head.

Everett looked at each photo.

"Similar in every way except...?" He couldn't understand the intent of Malcolm's revelation.

"Their fingers... each victim appears to indicate what order they were murdered in. Our two victims were one and five, Cincinnati has victim number seven. The two bodies in Cleveland are number two and nine." Malcolm was interrupted by Cole

"Mansfield has victim number six..." Cole paused as the sound of the elevator moving drew his attention.

"We need to get the Captain involved and keep this quiet." Cole finished.

"Fuck, how did we miss this, this is simple." Everett shook his head in disbelief.

"Well, we have a solid lead and we need to see what they all had in common. Sheldon and I are the only two working this in the lab. I may bring one more in, but for now that's it." Malcolm said as the elevator door opened.

"Look at you. Travis nice suit." Malcolm greeted him first.

"V.A., I see their early mornings are rubbing off on you." He redirected his attention towards Vania.

"Long night and story to follow, but first can we pull up the footage from the stop that went wrong." Vania moved towards her desk and turned her computer on.

"The stop that went wrong?" Everett didn't quite understand.

"Yeah partner, that Uni that Captain chewed out yesterday..." Cole stood up and continued.

"Wait, you haven't seen it. The media has dubbed it "the stop that went wrong." Cole finished just as Vania accessed the footage.

"This is the street our double homicide is on..." Vania paused and touched the screen with her index finger.

"There." She was pointing at the house and it was in plain view from the cameras in the police cruisers.

"We were watching T.V. after this art event last night with my friend, and this clip came on the news." Vania's voice trailed off as everyone watched the clip of a group of officers and a canine unit searching a vehicle. Supposedly the driver of the vehicle had pulled off to the side of the ride to input an address into his GPS when the first officer pulled behind him. It escalated to him being handcuffed and thrown to the ground and his vehicle illegally searched, before being released and ordered to put everything they had taken out of his vehicle back in, and then arresting him on a drummed-up charge of resisting an officer.

"Damn, he fucked up big time." Everett stated the obvious about the cop who initiated the interaction.

"Yeah but without his fuck up, we don't have this..." Vania paused as a black SUV was seen in the camera approaching the police stop. She slowed each frame down, and the face of Marilyn, the missing teenager could be seen through the front window.

"Go back, go back, there she is." Malcolm spoke out.

"We will but first." Vania found different footage on a different camera from the altercation which showed the license plate of the vehicle. She paused the recording and enhanced the still.

"Good work, good fucking work." Cole shook his head affirmatively.

"It was Travis' attention to detail, he remembered the time of death was roughly the time of the stop when it flashed across the screen." Vania gave credit to her partner because it was true. Her friend and Travis had spoken at length about the exhibit, which lead them all to breakfast and the luck of looking up at the right time.

"Run the plates." Everett said out loud to no one in particular.

"Done." Cole had already moved to his desk when Vania enhanced the license plate.

"Gary Pokinski. 227 Andreas Ct." Cole wrote the address down knowing that he and his partner would be heading to that address.

"V.A. and Travis go to Marilyn's school; staff should be on site in the next hour. Gives you time to get changed. Find out what you can about her. Her relationship with peers, any home issues that drew concern." Everett gave the newly acquired partners their task

"I'll stay on top of things and update you along the way." Malcolm said before departing, nearly bumping into the Captain who was exiting the elevator.

"Let's go check out Gary." Everett nodded at Cole.

"What about..." Cole paused realizing that Travis and Vania were still paying attention to them.

"When we get back." Everett answered already knowing that his partner knew it was tantamount to let Captain Montgomery know that there was a serial killer traveling the I71 interstate.

"You two, get going." Cole nodded at both the two young partners who walked away.

"I think they may work out; they both still have a lot to learn but they're solid." Everett waited for Cole to refill his coffee mug. They didn't know what to expect to find from this Gary Pokinski, but they would be alert enough to meet any challenge head on.

The SUV was sitting in the driveway as Cole and Everett pulled up. Still early in the morning, they were hoping to catch him off balance, but the figure moving past the front window indicated someone was up.

Everett rang the doorbell as Cole stayed a few feet behind to watch the front window.

Everett rang a second time before the door was answered.

"Good morning, how can I help you?

"Gary Pokinski I'm Detective Everett Clark and this is my partner. We have some questions about Marilyn." Everett intently waited for a reaction or lie.

"Marilyn?" Gary asked hesitantly.

"You don't mind if we come in and talk, do you?" Cole said as Everett took a step forward.

From instinct Gary stepped aside, and Cole followed before Gary could object.

"Marilyn, the daughter of Felicia and Timothy Weisner, has gone missing. We have it under good authority that you may have been the last person to see her." Everett thrust the accusation directly at Gary, keeping him guessing.

Cole walked from the living room to dining room before Gary answered.

"Please come back in here." Gary said loudly. Everett slapped his hands together to get Gary's attention, and then served up another accusation through a question.

"When was the last time you saw Marilyn?"

"Felicia asked me to take her for ice cream a few days back, but after I dropped her off I haven't, I haven't seen her." Gary answered.

"Why would they ask you to take her to get ice cream? Are you family? Who does that?" Cole fired off a round of questions.

"I am her god- father like." Gary answered defiantly. He pulled the draw string on his robe before crossing his arms.

"So, what time did you drop her off?" Everett asked.

Gary looked up as if calculating a time.

"It had to have been around fourish, I'd say. We got ice cream and then I dropped her back off. Now what's going on with Marilyn? Is she ok?" Gary believed his response had satisfied the detectives.

Cole slowly edged himself back towards the dining room. On his first scan through the house he saw a computer on the dining room table. It had taken a moment for him to process the images he had seen on the screen.

Gary's face lit up as he yelled at Cole not to go any further because he didn't have a warrant.

"Get out! Get out of my home!!!" Gary yelled attempting to close the laptop screen, but Cole stopped him.

"Gary, Gary, Gary I'm one million percent sure that these girls are underage, oh wait..." Cole paused as he turned the laptop towards Everett.

"Boys and girls are not even in high school." Cole finished.

"Gary Pokinski you are under arrest for possession of child pornography." Everett grabbed him and had him place his arms behind his back, before cuffing him and sitting him down at the dining room table.

"We have you on tape driving away with Marilyn at six. Felicia and Timothy Weisner were murdered around that time. Why did you kill them?" Everett asked.

Gary tried to speak but his nerves kept choking him up like he was gasping in between words

"I... di...didn't...murder... murdered... any." Gary struggled to say but Cole kept him off balance.

"Gary, where is Marilyn?" Cole slammed his hands down on the dining room table.

"Gary, I don't think you murdered anyone, I think you may have some other deep seeded issues, but you don't seem like a killer. Let us know where Marilyn is, and if her parents were a mistake, I'm sure the D. A. will take it into consideration that you're helping. but if something happened to Marilyn too...." Everett shook his head as he abruptly stopped talking.

Cole walked the home, and came back out from a back bedroom, and yanked Gary by the cuffs and led him towards the bedroom.

"What type of sick shit is this, you're going to be dessert every night for a group of hardened criminals. I swear if you don't tell me where she is, I'm going to..." Cole said angrily. Everett had picked up a leather-bound notebook from a desk sitting behind three cameras set throughout the bedroom film set.

The notebook had dates, along with initials and groups of numbers.

"Where is Marilyn?" Cole's voice was tight.

"Who is K.R?" Everett interjected.

"K.R. was with Marilyn two nights ago..." Everett paused again

"These are dollar amounts, you sick fuck. Who is K.R. or I swear to you...,"

"Kellen Richardson, he hasn't brought her back. I didn't kill anyone. I want an attorney." Gary didn't say another word. His sandy brown hair covered half his face, but Everett made sure to maintain eye contact with him.

"This is Detective Cole Kennedy." Cole had already made the call to the human trafficking task force. He paused as he listened to the voice on the other end.

"Yeah that's right, on the Weisner missing child report, Kellen Richardson is a person of interest. He is the last known person to see Marilyn. We may have stumbled onto a child pornography ring. Can you send an address to me for him?" Cole listened attentively before responding.

"Of course. Thank you, brother." Cole texted the address of Gary Pokinski to the special task force contact.

"A uniformed will be here within five minutes to take this piece of shit." Everett said to Cole.

"I've got an address on Kellen Richardson." Cole walked around the bedroom and opened the closet door. Stacks of DVD's filled the space.

"You're not well, a waste of a human life." Cole shook his head in disgust before dragging Gary back into the dining room area.

"I need to step outside." Cole left Everett inside. He needed fresh air and to be free of the dark taint in the house. Two patrol cars pulled up shortly thereafter.

"He's inside." Cole flashed his badge and then directed the officers. A police van approached with two occupants.

"Special Agent Larson sent us...the task force." A short brunette woman said. She wore slacks a white t-shirt and a bullet proof vest.

"Detective Cole Kennedy." Cole shook her hand.

"Agent Yari and Agent Forney." Her partner followed suite in greeting Cole.

Cole walked back inside and made introductions before pulling Everett away.

"Kellen Richardson is a bad dude: child pornography, human trafficking, racketeering and blackmail along with the usual drug dealing, I guess the Weisner's had a huge debt that their daughter was working off. There's no telling what Marilyn has gone through and when we find this Kellen..." Everett paused because he felt his emotions driving him. Emotions created mistakes.

"When we find him, we find her."

"So, what can you tell us about Marilyn?" Vania asked Principal Hawes. The middle-aged woman was overwhelmed with emotion after hearing that Marilyn was missing. Her dark hair draped over her shoulder; just as dark as the blouse she wore under her gray blazer. The secretary pulled the door closed behind them as she exited the room.

The office had photos of past accomplishments the high school had achieved. Broad academic success along with championships in multiple sports.

A family photo with two children was situated on one corner of her desk and opposite it, another with those same children with a man and woman. The additional photo of the woman and the principal on the coffee table made sense as they were sisters.

"Marilyn is such a bright student and inquisitive. She has a good circle of friends, well a group of three, but they were liked by most. But about six months ago her demeanor changed. She became sullen and withdrawn. She's missed more days over the past four months than she has all of her prior school years."

Travis was writing down bits and pieces of her statement.

"So, what changed?" He asked plainly before looking up from his notes. He wiped sweat from his brow. Although his blazer was lightweight, the white hoodie under it, made him hot.

Principal Hawes sat back in her chair and sighed.

"Her foster parents went through a rough patch. Tim lost his job after seventeen years and had to take a job making a substantial amount less. Felicia, recently had back surgery and without his medical insurance it had been rough." She paused to take a sip from a mug.

"How long has she been missing? I bet her parents are heartbroken. Have you spoken to Yvette, their oldest yet? Maybe she's with her." Principal Hawes finished.

"Yvette, is the oldest child of the Weisner's? Then they don't share the same last name?" Vania spoke out loud in reference to the family history they ran. Yvette wasn't listed.

"Right, Yvette was their first foster child, she was rough around the edges until she knew that she wouldn't be moving from place to place. She excelled at athletics and then academically. She is in her second year at State. Yvette Cummings, although on social media she is listed as a Weisner." The Principal stood up and motioned to her Secretary to give her one moment. A parent and his child had a meeting set to speak with her.

"Thank you for your time, here are our cards, and if you can think of anything helpful please give us a call." Travis shook her hand. He gathered his notes as Vania said her goodbyes and followed her out of the door.

"I bet they thought we wouldn't be getting any fruit this morning, Yvette Cummings. No Yvette Weisner." Vania said as she pulled up one of her social media pages on her cell phone.

"Bam." She said before handing Travis her phone with Yvette's profile picture.

"I'll get her addy, maybe Yvette picked her up after Gary dropped her off and we didn't see it." Travis said handing Vania back her cell phone as the morning school announcements were broadcast over the PA system.

"Gooooood morning Vikings. The annual Viking Booster dinner raffle tickets are on sale for another two days. Don't miss out on…" the secretaries voice ended as they exited the High School.

"Is this what high school is in Columbus? In Cleveland it wasn't no Viking Booster club it was just a booster- club, get it. You get it?" She started laughing. Travis chuckled as they got into the car with Vania still driving.

"Yvette Cummings. Chop -chop, let's look that shit up."

Travis entered the name into the ID system in her car.

"Ok, we got it and you're right, if Marilyn is with her sister that's an important piece of fruit that's still good." Travis said as he sent a text to Cole to update their progress. Vania pulled out into traffic with haste as they both secured their seatbelts.

Everett and Cole didn't have any luck finding Kellen at his home residence, but they had found a business address and were pulling up to the building near a strip mall. The building looked to have several businesses. Mostly modeling and photography companies, but as Cole and Everett read the directory of occupants in the building, one company stood out. B. Daylite "Therapeutic Massage: by appointment only."

They continued to the management group's office. When they entered no one was present, but the satellite music radio station, played lowly. Everett noticed a man leaving the therapists office with a young woman waving goodbye to him. Something was off about the whole scene unfolding before his eyes.

"Why is she wearing a robe?" He said out loud, gaining Cole's attention.

"What?" Cole asked when another young woman, barely legal in appearance walked into the front room. Her outfit was highly sexual. The open toe stiletto shoes made her taller than Everett. Her legs toned, could only be imagined in fullness, as her black skirt stopped short of her butt. The nude bodysuit left no room for the imagination, but it was her librarian glasses that filled the room with curiosity.

"There's two of you, I was only booked for one. I'll be right back gentlemen." She left the room shaking her head."

"What the fuck was that?" Everett was certain what was going on.

"Yeah what just happened?" Cole chimed in as the door opened behind them and a man in a business suit entered.

"This is my time, who are you, you shouldn't be here right now. You know the rules!" he said with agitation in his voice.

"No, we got booked for right now, and she just left because they only included one of us, so yeah something is definitely not right." Everett agreed with the man. This was a business, but a business of one of the oldest professions known to man.

"Fuck this, this is unprofessional. I'm out of here." The man said before walking back out.

"I got him." Everett said. They had walked in on something foul that sat right out in the daylight.

"B. Daylite. Broad Daylight." Everett said as he walked out the door to ask the man questions.

"Excuse me." The tall young girl had returned with Kellen Richardson who wasn't happy in any sense of the word.

"Sir I apologize, she said that there were two of you." Kellen said.

"No, it's just me right now Mr. Richardson. I'm Detective Cole Kennedy and I have some questions about Marilyn Weisner." Cole said.

The facial expression of the woman wasn't recognizable easily. Relief or fear, Cole couldn't determine, but Kellen's sudden motion of throwing the young girl into him to give him a chance to run out of the office was an action of guilt.

Kellen had a head start on Cole as he ran out of the building doors. Everett had the businessman speaking to him and had not comprehended what was going on until Cole yelled his name.

"Everett!"

Everett took off and trailed Kellen who was pressing his getaway. He leaped over a parked car before hopping a fence that surrounded his property next to the strip mall.

Everett and Cole followed the same route as Kellen had. He was still within eyesight as he ran across the parking lot of the mall. He turned down an alley between two of the stores but both Cole and Everett had closed the distance down to half. A fence separating the building and the stores was at the end of the alley.

Kellen had removed something from his pocket when Everett yelled.

"Put it down!"

But what they thought could be a weapon were his car keys and the lights flashing to a vehicle just opposite the fence, told them he had planned this.

Cole accelerated and dove into the fence as Kellen reached the top. The shock created stopped Kellen's momentum and he fell backwards off the fence to land hard on the pavement.

"Where is Marilyn you piece of shit?" Cole was breathing heavily. He watched Everett cuff him and lead him back out the alley and into the building and his office again.

The parking lot was less full, as cars were pulling off quickly in all directions, scrambling to not get identified.

"We have a whole bunch of law enforcement coming down, I've taken pictures of every vehicles license plate. But I really don't care about any of that shit. Where's Marilyn? Gary... Good ol perverted ass Gary said you were the last to see her." Cole had anger in his voice.

"Gary, Gary?" Kellen said repeatedly.

"Good ol Gary brought her to me? Gary gave me up to you over Marilyn. All of this is Gary. I work for Gary. Dumb fuck!" Kellen said with more anger towards Gary than his predicament.

"Where the fuck is Marilyn?" Cole jumped at Kellen who shifted and fell backwards.

He hit the ground solidly from his reaction.

"I don't know where she is, but I know where she is going, but I need a deal of some sort. I'm no Saint but I have valuable information about Marilyn and nearly two dozen other females heading out in the next forty-eight hours. Who knows they could be moving their time frame up? I'm sure all the people you let get away have already sent messages up the chain. As an act of good faith." He motioned for someone to pick him up.

"Password is Albatross. Capital A, money signs for the S's and an exclamation point." Everett unlocked the computer.

"Email received at 6am this morning from Gary." Kellen notified him which one to read.

"Now I can help you take down the whole thing and save twenty or so women from being..." Kellen paused

"... being never seen again. I'll serve supervised probation or something, but I won't see a jail cell." Kellen said before standing up.

"So, are we taking a ride or what?" Kellen asked Cole and Everett who were still reading the email. Everett forwarded a copy to his email address.

"Let's go." Everett said watching the police cruisers pulling up to collect all the evidence on site.

Cole accidentally on purpose, brushed Kellen's head against the top of the door frame when he put him in the back seat.

"We are going to get what we need from you one way or another. Believe that." Everett said.

A familiar white Van was pulling into the lot as they pulled out. Both vehicles slowed to acknowledge each other.

"They're active today." Cole nodded at Agent Yari driving as they passed each other.

"I haven't seen her, she's missing. Tim and Felicia are dead...no, no, wait, they're murdered?" Yvette was distraught as she attempted accepting what Vania and Travis had shared with her.

Yvette's silence was deafening as she stared past the younger detectives. She moved to her dining room table in her small apartment and sat down.

"Min, is missing. Not dead." Yvette said like she was speaking with herself as she answered questions she posed internally.

"So, Min is missing, you've checked her friends and they haven't seen her in days?" She asked out loud.

"No, none of them have seen her, the school spoke with them this morning." Vania answered.

"Does the name Gary Pokinski ring a bell?" Travis asked.

Yvette's body position became very defensive in an instant. She swallowed her breath before answering.

"Gary Pokinski used to be a friend of Tim and Felicia, I never liked him. Does he have her, have you checked with him? You have to check with him- he's not a good person." Yvette said as anger built in her voice.

A knock on her apartment door was followed by someone letting themselves in.

"Baby." A male's voice was heard before his appearance. He had on black sweat- pants and a t-shirt with the University logo. He stopped in his tracks as he walked into the dining room.

"Oh, baby I didn't know you had people over, I can come back."

"Drew, Min is missing, and Tim and Felicia are dead...no murdered." Yvette was getting emotional again.

Drew walked to her side and hugged her.

"What happened?"

"We are still trying to figure that out. Is it ok to continue?" Travis directed his attention back to Yvette.

Yvette nodded positively.

"What can you tell us about Gary.?"

"Gary?" Drew asked as if it was a secret that Yvette had kept.

"Min's missing and if Gary is involved, I will tell them everything." Yvette said before going into some detail of the acts of pedophiles. When she was done Travis felt sick to his stomach, as did each other person present, but it was Yvette's fortitude that kept the focus on Gary.

"We are sorry to know; well we won't repeat it." Vania said as she received a text before Travis received the same message.

"Back to the office now." It read from Cole.

"Yvette...Drew, as we make progress, we will update you. Thank you again for your time.

A second message came through, repeating the first.

"We are on the way." Travis text back.

"Gary, this muthafucka and her foster parents were...were...." Vania tried finding the right words to use but words were insufficient to describe the stealing of innocence.

Chapter Four

TRAFFIC STOP

(continued)

Travis and Vania walked into the room opposite of where Kellen Richardson was sitting with his attorney. ADA Jefferson had offered him a deal for information leading to the apprehension of others involved in the child sex ring and the group of women and girls being found safely. He had three minutes left to accept an offer.

"I don't like it either but with the stakes so high, a minimal security facility was all I was permitted to offer." The ADA checked her watch again.

Captain Montgomery stared through the mirror silently as Cole read a file he carried.

"Perp was apprehended on site, fleeing from establishment offering sex acts including minors. Gary

Pokinski has been arrested on charges of child pornography, possession of child pornography, lewd acts with minors to name a few more we haven't added yet." Everett paused as ADA Jefferson exited to see if the offer was accepted.

"Yvette Cummings is the older foster sister, we interviewed her in hopes that Min..." Vania hesitated, realizing the nickname was new.

"She hasn't seen or heard from Marilyn." Vania finished

"Gary Pokinski has been at it, for a long time. Yvette spoke of the times he forced himself on her and when she told Tim and Felicia, they said it was no big deal. It seems Tim had a gambling problem and was in debt to Gary. The Weisner's used their foster children in essence as sex workers." Travis spoke up.

Cole looked up from his file and was clearly agitated.

"And now we have to give this guy less than what he deserves." Cole pointed at Kellen through the double glass pane.

"Making a deal with a devil to stop a deep evil is necessary at times." Everett said without emotion. He had almost lost his cool earlier in the day and it would have blinded him. Now they were getting the location of "the cargo" as it was termed in the email Gary sent at 6am. The time period was ignored as they understood that was no longer relevant.

Time was of an essence because they could be gone already.

"Truck stop in West Jeff, they'll haul the container headed to the east coast. The trailer number and telephone numbers associated with this trip." ADA Jefferson had returned with a piece of paper handing it to the Captain who in turn gave it to Everett.

"Get the task force involved and I will call for a special ops team. Find them." Captain Montgomery finished before ushering the D.A. out of the room.

"Cole, Agent Yari, send details and coordinate thirty minutes from now on site. You two, vests and extra ammo. We leave in five minutes." Everett gave instruction and without hesitation everyone moved to complete their tasks.

The truck stop was typical as rigs were lined up. Some truckers were resting their minimal hours required while others gassed up. A row of unhitched trailers were lined up toward the rear of the building that offered some hot food items. A pick-up truck caught Cole's eye. The door to it was opened as two men stood off to the side of it having a disagreement. A rig had backed up to it but hadn't hitched it for travel. Undercover vehicles had positioned themselves at each exit while the team, in separate cars slowly drove the rows of trucks.

"What's that about?" Cole motioned to the men now arguing. One man shoved the other, who in turn backed down and returned to hitch the trailer.

Everett flashed his lights to see the reaction. Both men, like deer stuck in headlights moved towards their vehicles. Vania had pulled around to block the truck as Everett drove his car close to the pick-up preventing the man from accessing the inside.

Cole jumped out the car as soon as the man started to run, but Travis had already exited his passenger door and tackled him.

"Why are you running?" Cole asked as Travis hauled the man up.

The sound of police sirens caught their attention as two other vehicles had been stopped trying to flee.

Everett walked the side of the trailer, knocking on it every few feet.

"Anyone in here, it's ok." He made his way to the rear and opened the trailer doors. The darkness was overwhelming until the light of the day made its way inside.

A group of girls and women appearing from teenager to late adulthood were roped together and each one gagged.

"It's ok, I'm an officer." Everett flashed his badge as Vania made her way to stand next to his side. Her badge hung from her shoulder across her chest.

The despair that shown initially was being replaced with murmurs through the gags of help.

Agent Yari and Vania, along with four other female officers specializing in human trafficking cases, were first contact. The trauma that they survived would not easily be forgotten. A group of young girls were gathered, and Vania searched for the young girl that began this initial investigation.

"Marilyn...Marilyn?" Vania approached a girl who was sullen and withdrawn. Vania could see the resemblance from the photos, but more importantly from the face that flashed in her mind each time her eyes had closed since learning of the missing teen.

"Min." Vania used her shortened name and that's when the young girl made eye contact.

"Min. I'm Detective Vania Aguilar. Your sister Yvette is so concerned about you." Vania finished and in that instant Min hugged Vania and began crying uncontrollably.

"I know, it's going to be better now. Come on, come on with me and rest." Vania led her to her car which was blocked off from being seen. The news organizations were running live stories about what they believed happened, but no one had provided them any information.

"Thirty souls saved." Everett and his team had done their job, but this did not feel like a win.

"This group has been in our sights for about six months, we could never get close enough to secure evidence. We are going to take the lead in this investigation." Agent Yari paused.

"The credit will go to your department primarily." She finished before excusing herself to attend to the women who would undoubtedly need therapy for a lengthy term.

"We still have a double homicide to close. We are going to take these two with us and they are yours after." Cole said indicating the two men apprehended would be answering their questions in relation to Tim and Felicia's murders.

"Done." Agent Yari left their sides.

"I'm going to stay with Min until she can be reunited with Yvette." Vania approached Cole and Everett.

"Get back as soon as you can. Travis will have to bring him…" Everett said nodding in the direction of the truck driver, cuffed and sitting in the back of her car.

"Yeah, no worries I'll get back." Vania tossed Travis her keys as he joined their core group. He had been speaking with uniform officers who secured both the pickup truck and trailer. He had taken pictures from the inside of the trailer quickly because the stench was overwhelming.

"Put gas in it." Vania raised her eyebrows before she walked away to sit with Min.

"Let's get them back and tear into them." Cole had been in a foul mood since their early morning apprehension of Gary. With the early evening hours fading away, Everett and Cole led the way with their lights flashing and Travis doing the same on their rear.

"Human trafficking, they're going to make you the poster boy for all of this shit. Ohio ranks as one of the leading states and guess who is going to be showcased on network news and major headlines when we walk you outside to be taken to county. You're scum." Cole said with controlled anger in his voice. He walked around the table in the interrogation room as he talked.

The suspect, identified as Raymond Halfshall, had asked for an attorney, so Cole didn't ask him any questions. Instead he painted a picture of the steps he would take to make sure that everyone in general population knew that he kidnapped, raped and trafficked children and women.

"I've heard that they take turns every night with guys like you." Cole finished as there was a rap from the other side of the two-way mirror.

"You're a pretty boy too." Cole winked at the suspect and walked out the interview room.

Travis was flagging Cole down to listen to the truck driver being interviewed. When he walked into the room Agent Burton was standing next to Vania. Cole heard her voice through the intercom before he saw Agent Yari sitting at the table with Everett.

"Nearly every one of them said that there was twice this number held captive here. You are part of a conspiracy which includes murder. It's murder, right?" Agent Yari nodded at Everett who sat silently until then.

"Double homicide." Everett verified

"Double homicide. That by itself, I think gets you dead." Agent Yari hesitated again and stood up.

"We will keep you behind bars with criminals of all sorts who have a disdain for garbage like you and your partners. Held captive for the rest of your life, but if you can help us... help these other victims and children get home safely we may be able to do something for you." She walked towards the double mirror.

"Paul, you're going to have to face charges of some sort, whether you even knew about the double homicide, because it is a conspiracy, you will face the same consequence as those who stabbed that couple." Everett intentionally used a misleading statement to see if Paul Ogden would correct them about the cause of death.

"I have nothing to say about a damn murder, I didn't kill anyone. This was my first run and when I found out what was in the trailer, I told him I wasn't going to do it. You saw us arguing." Paul said as he crossed his arms in front of him.

"We've already downloaded the GPS on your rig and that's not an honest statement. Lie to us one more time." Everett leaned forward and put both hands on the table as he slowly stood up.

"Paul, let's do this. Who is your contact on the other end? We're running down the numbers in your phone, if we get the information first, we don't need you and if we don't need you..." Agent Yari got interrupted by Everett.

"You will be the lowest bottom feeder in an ocean of sharks and killer whales."

Paul stared down towards the table.

"To hell with this let's go." Everett pulled his cuffs out to reintroduce them to Paul.

"No, no, no, I'll tell you straight up this time. Make sure your D.A. knows I am cooperating. There are two separate warehouses with make-shift living quarters. They each have at least four armed guards on site with cameras on every corner of the building. One is in the bottoms and the other near 5th Avenue." Paul Gave them the address and was beginning to share details on the connection in New York the 'cargo' was originally destined to go.

"Agent." The captain entered and pulled Everett to the side to whisper.

"The Feds are here and are pulling jurisdiction. You have about ten minutes. We have a double homicide which stays with us, find out what you can." Captain Montgomery turned and directed his attention to Agent Yari.

"Come with me." He motioned as he opened the interview room door. Agent Yari wasn't finished with Paul but she was given a directive.

"The Feds are in my office arguing with the D.A. Your commander is gearing up to hit both of those addresses. We will do what we can to slow them up. Good work Agent." He finished as she collected her thoughts.

"The Feds don't have..." She attempted, but the Captain got straight to the point.

"I love a good pissing contest, but your guys are already moving, and I'd bet Los Federales will be close behind."

Agent Yari took his advice and left to join her unit.

The Captain walked back into the watch room still occupied with Travis and Vania. Cole had taken Agent Yari's place with Everett.

"He gave up Gary as the point man on everything, he realized he had no other course of action and is naming names, but he doesn't know anything about our double homicide." Vania brought the Captain up to speed.

"I want you both to go back in with Raymon. Don't ask him anything but repeat what Paul has just shared. The Feds only know about Paul and until they catch wind, we have them both let's get what we can."

Travis and Vania did as they were ordered, and when they entered Raymon was laying with his head on the table.

"Guilty." Travis said.

Raymon looked up.

"Guilty, guilty, guilty. It's over for you." Vania added.

"Baby Drax left a little while ago, he's much more intimidating than you two bozos." He laid his head back onto the table with his hands still locked in handcuffs.

"What did Paul say, oh yeah, the warehouse. That's right, he told us about the warehouses. Your connection with the guys in New York. He gave up Gary, after Gary gave all of you up." Travis paused as Raymon lifted his head again. That had gained his attention.

"Gary did what? That idiot. We are dead, all of us except Gary." Raymon blurred out. He was losing the cool, calm façade he had displayed up until this moment.

"Why not Gary?" Vania asked.

"Gary's one of them." He answered.

"Who is them?" Vania asked quickly hoping to catch him off guard. But Raymon didn't answer that.

"Was it, Gary who killed the couple by himself, or did you have a hand in that too?" Travis went in for his line of questioning. The primary goal for this interview was to lead to a murder case being closed.

"Killed somebody, nah, nope not getting me involved in any of that. I have never killed anyone." Raymon had become more agitated, but Travis talked right over him.

"In the commission of committing another felony, it all becomes a conspiracy. You should understand that with your list of criminal deeds." Travis said. They had already learned the history from pulling up his priors. Armed Robbery, trafficking in narcotics, and hindering an investigation to name a few.

"I do know that, and I don't know anything about any of this. All you saw me doing was arguing with some truck driver and then you detained me for some bull..." Raymon was cut off by Travis again.

"Neither myself nor my partner want to hear your lies, the women have already identified you, Paul's text messages from the phone found in your possession shows multiple contacts. Keep playing with us and you'll regret it, I promise. Now who killed the couple? The young girl you tried trafficking was their daughter. Now imagine a jury first finding out about your past convictions, then learning that you actively trafficked human beings, and that people were killed in the process three days ago. Ohio has the death penalty and I'm pretty sure all of this qualifies." Travis sat down across from Raymon.

Raymon's expression indicated that he had not thought that far in advance.

"I did not kill anyone and don't know what you're talking about. I wasn't even in Columbus three days ago. But if it was anyone on this side, it wasn't me." Raymon finished.

The door opened with force and Cole entered.

"We don't need anything else from him. Paul told us everything. Human trafficking, kidnapping, lying to law enforcement." Cole said as he was followed by a uniformed officer.

"Process him and..." Cole started to say before he was interrupted

"I want an attorney."

"I bet, now take him." Cole directed the officer.

When Raymon had been removed, Cole updated the two younger detectives.

"Paul is being escorted by the Feds, and Raymon is going to follow. Unfortunately, neither one was in Ohio at the time of the homicides. We've got some sick individuals off the street and more importantly, all of the victims are returning to their homes." Cole sat down and shook his head.

"All of this and we are nowhere close to solving our case."

"We did good, and it's a few more stripes in our belts." Vania chimed in but she paused while staring into the double mirror.

"Gary's name always came up with everyone interviewed so far. Was his nervousness earlier, simply an act to buy him more time?"

Cole had not thought about that. Could Gary have played both him and his partner.

The door swung open again and Everett stood there in the door frame.

"Yeah, Gary needs more questioning. All roads lead to Gary. Has he lawyered up yet?" Everett asked.

"Not yet." Cole responded.

"I want you two to have a go with him, so be by the book and everything recorded. Don't bring Yvette's name or accusations up until he feels comfortable, and then hammer him, put him in interview room two." Everett finished before dismissing them.

Everett knocked on the glass mirror and shortly after Captain Montgomery entered the room.

"Is it turned off?" Everett asked in reference to the recording device.

"Yes Detective, what's this all about?" The captain asked.

"We have confirmed that there is a new serial killer in the state. The victims have all been generally found close to cities that run the 71 Interstate. Malcolm has confirmed that there are at least nine victims. Besides those working the cases in Cincinnati, Cleveland and Mansfield we have kept a lid on this thing." Everett answered.

Cole had remained seated, but he shook his head in agreement with what his partner had shared.

"I want the details on my desk, and until we have something tangible, I will wait to move it up the chain of command..." Captain Montgomery paused and placed his back against the door so no one would enter.

"If the media gets a hold of this before we are ready." He silenced himself.

Both Everett and Cole agreed.

"Travis and V.A. haven't been read in yet, but once we make headway with this investigation, we will update them." Cole stood up as Everett added what their next steps would be.

"We need to speak with Yvette, the sister again."

"I will leave you two to get at it." Captain Montgomery exiting.

"Let's not forget about Becca's concert partner." Cole reminded Everett about his promise he made to Robbi.

Everett sighed. His mind wanted to keep pursuing each lead, but he understood that if he didn't make the performance his daughter's heart would be broken.

"Ok let's go see her, if Robbi makes it, we can let her ride home with her mother, and then I'll make it up to her later." Everett moved towards the door, but Cole's response made him hesitate slightly before opening it, realizing it was the same decisions as this that advanced his divorce.

"Later isn't always guaranteed partner."

Yvette had kept Marilyn at her off campus apartment with the house still a bad reminder of the tragedy that happened. Stuck on her sister's couch, she stayed under the protection of a large comforter, nestled in one corner.

Neither Cole nor Everett had spoken to Marilyn before when she was rescued, but their faces were recognizable as being some of the good guys.

"Marilyn how are you, Detective Aguilar said she would check on you. She wanted us to tell you to remember "be like the reed in the wind." Everett was first to greet her.

Marilyn swallowed before responding.

"Detective V.A. Is strong and kind."

"You have no idea Min." Cole interjected light heartedly, he paused before continuing

"Do you mind if we borrow your sister for a moment?"

"She's not leaving though right?" She asked.

"No, no, we can talk in the back room. I'm not going anywhere and when Drew gets back with snacks and ice cream, we can do an early evening movie." Yvette directed Cole and Everett into another portion of her apartment.

"What have you found out?" Yvette asked as soon as there was space between Min and the party of three.

The utility room was large enough for the standard washer and dryer appliances that came with each unit and ample room for all three of them.

"Gary and his associates are facing federal charges, none of those arrested have admitted to murdering your foster parents. We know the family didn't have insurance, but the city has found money to pay for therapist visits to help in her recovery." Cole relayed.

"He is a sick human being, wickedly evil and his charming personality hides a vicious persona." Yvette shook her head and turned her lip up.

"We understand it's difficult to speak on certain things and we don't want you to revisit any trauma. Can you tell us if Felicia and Tim had problems with anyone else? Anyone that you can remember having bad words with either of them?" Everett asked. He backed into a few items on the floor as he shifted his weight from feeling his calf cramping. Laundry detergent and a red bucket holding a mop. An aluminum baseball bat sat evenly in the corner where both walls met.

"You can just put that on the shelf please." Yvette directed Everett about the laundry detergent.

"Drew never puts it back when he's done in here. I don't know where I'd be without him. Meeting him during my first year brought a sense of normalcy into my life." Yvette checked the lint cleaner of the dryer before throwing its content into the trash.

"Honestly the time after Felecia had her back surgery, who wasn't upset with them. Her addiction caused him to become addicted and it escalated. Until I was notified about their deaths it was my belief that they were clean. I don't think anyone else besides Gary would actually do it." Yvette finished.

A small towel fell from the overhead rack where Everett had placed the laundry detergent. He noticed the boxes of ammunition.

"Yeah, I got my CCW after Drew recommended it. He said it's better to have it and not need it, than to need it and not have it."

Cole added to the conversation.

"Gary isn't the killer; he was with an associate. We verified it prior to meeting with you today."

Marilyn laughing loudly caught their attention, it was followed by a man's voice laughing just as loud.

They walked back into the main room and Drew was picking himself off the floor.

"Hey babe, I presented the choices for lil Ms. Sweet Tooth and my pirouette left me on my butt." Drew grasped one bag with Caramel and Sea Salt Vanilla ice cream. In the other hand was a ripped plastic bag and on the floor were sugar cones, snack size Reese Cups and Butterfingers.

Drew kissed Yvette on the lips after placing the items from the floor onto the kitchen counter.

"Yvette thank you for your time once again." Everett waved goodbye to Marilyn after being introduced to Drew.

"Min, I will make sure that Detective V.A. Visits before the week is out." Cole bid goodbye to the sister's and boyfriend.

"They've been through more than most human beings. She's only a few years older than Becca. I can't imagine." Everett was walking, talking and checking his text messages.

"Andino," Cole corrected himself.

"Agent Yari, cashed in on a favor and wants to meet." Cole finished as they opened their car doors.

"I just wouldn't with her Cole, she has a gun and a badge."

"I haven't, this is all work related. The thought hasn't even crossed my mind. I've been busy with other things. Let's grab something to eat before we hit the station." It was true Cole had not looked at Agent Yari in a romantic sense. He had too many irons in the fire already.

"That works since you still owe me lunch from last week." Everett reminded his partner.

"Yeah I got it, but I choose."

"Where to?" Everett scanned a few fast food restaurants they were coming up on.

"I am who I am, and that's all that I am." Cole answered in a strange voice.

Everett shook his head understanding that was Cole's way of imitating an old cartoon character; Popeye's chicken sandwiches would be righteous right now.

After waiting in the drive thru for longer than intended, they ate en route to Timothy Weisner's employment. Although they had been instrumental in exposing a human trafficking and sex ring which included child pedophiles, they were still no closer to solving the homicide case.

The building was identical to those that surrounded it. All with sandy colored exteriors, mainly warehouses for global companies, some buildings housed rows of parts and accessories for a wide range of auto parts to restaurant bulk items.

"Right there." Cole pointed to the address they had circled twice to find.

The cameras outside the entrance looked standard, and as they were buzzed in after showing their badges, the bright sterile environment and signs posted relayed that this was a 24-hour facility.

"How can we help you Officers?" A burly man exited one of the interior secured doors. He wore a plaid shirt with purple as the dominant theme. His camouflage shorts were green and his steel toe boots yellow.

"I'm Detective Kennedy and this is Detective Clark. We had some questions about one of your employees, Tim Weisner." Cole said extending his hand to shake the man's hand.

"Kevin Blackstone." The employee made quick introductions.

"What can you tell us about Tim?" Everett asked as they followed behind Kevin.

"I'll be able to tell you as soon as I look at his file. We have a high rate of turnover, so it's rare that I could tell you about any employee until they've been here at least two years." Kevin finished as he walked into his office. The name plate on his office door indicated his position as manager. White boards with sales goals decorated his office, and loose papers were stacked up on his second desk waiting to be discarded. He had rainbow decorations as accessories to his office and the photo behind his desk indicated he was in a same sex marriage.

"Tim Weisner, you mentioned?" Kevin pulled up Tim's employment history.

"Ahh this Tim, good employee. Keeps to himself mostly. He actually missed four days of work this week. No call-no show. Bummer, he was an ideal employee, although if I can recall he was over-qualified for this line of work." Kevin lightly smacked his lips.

"Does Tim have anyone that he hangs with or confides in that we may be able to speak with?" Everett needed something, anything that was of substance.

"Detectives I'm all for working with law enforcement but we do run a business, what's this about? I assume Tim is in some type of trouble. Something we will look into honestly since you are questioning us about our employee." Kevin answered without offense. He picked up an ink pen to twirl between his fingers and waited.

"Tim and his wife were found murdered Sunday evening." Everett paused,

"When was the last time he reported to work?"

"Hold on... I need to go back." Kevin reopened the employee details.

"Thursday, evening shift. Had the weekend off. That's terrible about him, and his wife?" Kevin wanted to confirm that he had heard what Everett relayed.

"Yes, both." Cole answered.

"There's nothing unordinary or unusual that sticks out to you about his employment?" Everett followed up with the same question a second time.

"His supervisor just arrived, give me a second and I'll let her know to come to the office."

After a few minutes wait, a short, frost-haired woman walked into Kevin's office.

"Erin, these are Columbus Detectives, Tim Weisner was found murdered a few days ago. Can you answer any questions about Tim they have?" He also gave her instruction to cooperate.

"Yeah, yeah sure. That's terrible to hear." Erin looked to be mid-forties and fit. She had been with the company for over fifteen years and was responsible for assignments. After quick introductions she shared what she knew.

"Good worker, over-qualified. When things were slow, he talked about how to maximize efficiency of the building. Smart guy. On a few occasions I smelled traces of marijuana, but like we tell our employees if you have an accident and it's in your system your terminated." Erin finished. She hadn't really been able to add anything to what they had already discovered.

Erin excused herself to start her twelve-hour shift.

"Gentlemen if that's all you have for us; I do have a conference call in ten minutes. We are sorry that we couldn't help you any further." Kevin walked them back through the warehouse towards the exit.

"Gentlemen." Kevin bid them farewell as he buzzed them through the exit.

Cole was discouraged and Everett seemed to be in thought.

"Let's think about it. Maybe we are looking at this from the wrong angle." Everett struggled with seeing how everything was connected.

"What do you mean partner?" Cole asked flatly.

"Maybe we should be looking at this from who they got the heroin from." Everett stared across the top of the car towards Cole. Cole's positive head nod was in agreement to his partner and understood they needed information on who was providing this specific drug.

"Let's check with Malcolm and see if he can tell us more about the H, any significant determinations or traits that can give us a direction." Everett finished.

"Well once we get that, we can roll up on Turtle." Cole said as Everett chuckled.

"Right."

Travis and Vania were only allowed ten minutes with Gary before the Feds took him away. What they learned in those ten minutes was nothing new. He denied killing anyone. The Feds had a timeline building from Gary's movements over the past seven days. His ice cream date with Marilyn had been included, his visit to Kellen Richardson as well. Vania and Travis, however, had been informed that Gary's New York family was being rounded up and that they had been instrumental in thwarting a major human trafficking and sex ring.

"None of this is adding up. If Gary and these pieces of..." Vania paused as a father with two children entered their space.

"If their homicides weren't part of this, then what else were Tim and Felecia into?" Vania concluded her thought out loud.

Travis hadn't thought about the murders landing outside of the criminal activities they had uncovered in less than 24 hours. His phone went off and he read a message.

"Damn, damn, damn, we have to make a quick detour." Travis used the key fob to unlock the doors to his car.

Vania got in before asking where they were headed.

"Family emergency." He replied before turning his blinker on to merge into traffic in haste.

When they arrived at his mother's home, uniformed officers had her placed in handcuffs, along with her two young grandchildren. Travis pulled up as close as he could, and they exited the vehicle.

"Hey what's going on?" Travis asked an officer who had his back towards them as they approached. A crowd had already formed, and many were video recording the interaction.

"Why do you have those boys in cuffs?" Rafi's voice was heard from the crowd.

"Get back and don't interfere in a police investigation." Another uniformed officer yelled out.

"Get back this is a police investigation. I don't know why you people think those cameras will save your ass." A larger officer had made his way towards the group watching the police searching Travis' mother's residence.

"What the hell are they doing T?" Vania realized that having the children in handcuffs was not the precedent law enforcement officers should be making.

"You two get back!" The large officer redirected his tirade towards Travis and Vania.

"Sir, that's my mother and my eleven and twelve-year old nephews. Why are they in handcuffs?"

"Don't ask questions, get your ass back. Why do you people always think you can say or do anything you want. They can film all they want but if you don't get your grimy asses back...." The cop was interrupted by Vania.

"What the... did you just refer to us as, yeah you did. Your badge number?".

"I gave you a lawful order, you're under arrest. Both of you!" He yelled toward a second officer to help him arrest them.

"No, you're out of line. Why are there officers inside the house? Where's the search warrant?" Travis escalated, defying the cop who just threatened to arrest them.

His mother's voice was heard over all the commotion.

"They searching, without a warrant. They just busted in and tackled me and threw the boys around Travis. That's why I can't stand these muthafuckas!" His mother was becoming more agitated as his eyes locked on her.

"Put your hands behind your back." The large officer reached towards Vania aggressively, taking control of her wrists.

Instinctively, she reversed his grip before kicking him in the back of his knee to lower his body to the ground before stepping back.

"That's assault." He yelled reaching for his waistband.

"Detective Aguilar and my partner Detective White, instead of deescalating a crowded situation you chose to do the exact opposite. You will be written up and put on desk duty by the time we leave.

Travis walked towards his mother and nephews. He had removed his badge from beneath his sweatshirt to show his credentials, which gave him and his partner rank.

"Take the cuffs off of all of them, who trained you?" Travis approached his mother and removed her cuffs, as Vania unlocked the nephews.

"They said they had a tip that there was stolen property in the house. They pushed me out of the way when I told them to let me see their search warrant. Extenuating circumstances is what they said gave them a right. They tore through the house and I still haven't seen a warrant!" His mother yelled towards two of the uniformed officers.

Travis had tried to maintain professional courtesy but what he kept realizing was that there were segments of society that did not receive legal, fair and safe treatment from law enforcement. He had always known this, and the fact that he was part of the thin blue line, his family was not.

"Where is the officer in charge?" Travis pointed at the large officer Vania had deflated.

"He's still inside." He answered.

"I should've broken his wrist." She followed her partner inside his mother's home. The house didn't have a bunch of expensive items, but they were still valuable. The television in the main room had been broken, and the couches and loveseat had been overturned. The small dining room table was in shambles. A loud crash of glass breaking caught their attention.

"It was a piece of shit anyways." Followed by laughter.

Travis and Vania walked the small hallway towards his mother's room.

At first glance he couldn't recognize it. The bed had been turned over with slash marks in it, the closet doors had been pulled off their hinges. Glass from a broken mirror was spread on the floor.

"Where's the warrant, or what extenuating factors were present before you violated this family?" Vania asked as her partner was at a loss of words as he stood looking at the mess.

The laughter ceased as the three officers turned.

Vania had her badge out. She outranked them and her question demanded an answer.

147

"We got a tip about stolen property and didn't have time to secure a warrant yet." The officer in charge spoke up with authority.

"Extenuating circumstances?" Vania quickly followed up.

"We uh, we had under good authority that this family deals in stolen goods." He tried to say before Travis spoke slowly.

"So, no judge signed off on a warrant and you can't provide a reason." He paused to wait for an answer and with none coming quickly enough he pulled his phone out to take pictures of the mess, the officers.

"Why do you guys care, this isn't even something you guys need concerned with?" One of the additional officer's present asked, and that's when Travis couldn't contain his anger.

"Because shit like this gives us all a bad name, this community needs the same attitude that law enforcement has for families and people in the suburbs, because people like "our grimy asses" as YOUR officer addressed us have the same rights as everyone else, and most importantly because this is my mother's home!"

The officer in charge eyes lit up.

"Brother, we were just following a lead, don't blame us..."

"Who is to blame for violating her rights, who else is to blame for placing children not even teenagers in handcuffs, who else is to blame for destroying this house?" Vania stared at the officer who made the comment.

"Get out." Travis said lowly.

"Brother had we known." The officer who spoke up to Vania had miscalculated the situation, and that's when Travis grabbed him and forced him out of his mother's bedroom before pushing him outside. Stopping short of Blue on Blue crime.

Vania escorted the rest out and listened to her partner.

"What happens to you from this point is all on you." Travis threw the set of handcuffs onto the ground at the officer in charge's feet.

"Don't go back in there. I'll grab some items and lock up. I'll get you a hotel room while this gets sorted out." Travis was speaking with his mom when the one officer who helped release the cuffs approached.

"If you need my statement contact me. This was wrong from the very get go." He informed Vania.

"V.A. can you stay with them while I round up some shit to take with us." Travis was holding the anger inside, but he knew the best way to fix this situation was filing the necessary paperwork against this group of policemen. He agreed with his partner, she should've broken his wrist.

Travis put clothes and toiletries into separate bags. One for his mother and the other for his nephews, while he thought back to when they moved into he and his brother's old bedroom.

They had already lived a tough life. Their mother had died from an overdose after battling addiction and were without their father because he was locked up. Travis heard footsteps walking down the hall. The officer in charge had returned to speak with him about taking another course of action.

"The tip was solid Detective, and I'm sure with a little good will we can resolve this without getting other agencies involved. How was I supposed to know?" He hoped his plea to a member of his fraternity would be heard.

"By doing your job the right way! By following procedure, the right way! By following the oath, you took for all citizens! That's not hard to follow. I've said what I said now get out before I put my hands on you!" Travis was firmer the second time.

"You people always think you're better than us uni..." the officer in uniform tried to say when Travis erupted. He pushed the officer forcibly into the hallway.

"You people?" Travis eyebrows raised.

"Detectives." The uniformed Officer clarified what he meant.

"Get out." Travis had already geared up for a negative reaction and was prepared as the he tried to push him back.

"You don't have to push me out."

But Travis kept pushing him towards the door until he was shoved and forced to gain his balance. If it would not have created a bigger scene, Travis would have taken matters into his own hands.

After retrieving the bags and locking the home up, Travis saw that most of the cruisers had departed, except the cop offering to provide a statement.

"They were wrong and knew it, I'm out of the academy less than six months. I didn't sign up for this." His voice was akin to disbelief.

"Most of us don't sign up for this." Vania took one of the bags out of Travis' hands.

"We will contact you if necessary." Vania walked to meet her partner who had opened the trunk.

"I'm sorry T. My grandfather used to say that weeds grow everywhere and it's important to get them pulled before they spread." She finished without a response from Travis who walked to the driver side door.

"I'm going to sit back here with you guys ok?" Vania sat in the middle to allow the boys to have windows. She had put his mother in the front seat.

"Mom I'm sorry." Travis said before turning the ignition to start the car.

"It's not your fault. You're not one of them, but it's too many of them patrolling our neighborhoods. Crooked and filled with contempt for poor people and people who look like us. I am tired Travis, so tired." His mother finished before staring out of the window.

"I know you are mom." Travis understood that his mom meant more than being overwhelmed from the police interaction, but from life in general. He stared into his rear-view mirror to look at his nephews who hadn't said much, before meeting Vania's eyes looking at him through the mirror as she motioned with her lips.

"I am sorry partner."

Travis took his eyes and placed them back on the road. In this moment his only concern was getting his family situated in a hotel.

"The forensics team found one round in the bedroom in the closet. It must've jammed the gun and the shooter ejected it without retrieving it. So, we can match up both spent and unspent cartridges if you can find the murder weapon." Malcolm was moving around the lab looking for something. His shirt got snagged on the corner of a table and ripped.

"Oh mon, no worry- no cry." He shook his head as he stared down at the photo of Bob Marley on his shirt.

"Ok, the type of heroin they were dosed with is cut with Fentanyl and baking soda." Malcolm finished.

"Both, huh?" Everett asked.

"These days, they're stretching out what they can and stepping on everything." Cole spoke up.

"What caliber of gun was used in our double homicide?" Everett was straightforward.

".380 and 90 grain Hornady Custom Ammunition." Malcolm retrieved a folder with a few sheets of paper inside it that he was reading from and handed the folder to Everett to look over.

"Anything on that other thing?" Cole asked in reference to the serial killer findings.

The door to the department opened and Veronica, the lab technician Cole was seeing from time to time walked in. She didn't notice Cole until she was fully in the room.

"Boss. Detectives." She greeted them in a short non-offensive manner. She had something on her mind and seemed preoccupied.

"Sheldon is working on something he found. Once he can verify his hunch, I'll have more for you." Malcolm was handed the folder back from Cole after Everett shared it with him.

"The building is buzzing with how your team outshined the Feds. The Chief was in earlier speaking with Captain Montgomery. That woman frightens me." Malcolm finished with a smirk on his face.

"She's old school but fair. She was in my father's graduating class and will hold everybody that swore an oath to fulfill it. But yeah, she can be intimidating." Everett responded to Malcolm's statement.

"Have V.A. and Travis checked back in yet?"

They had not received any updates on the interview with Gary.

"No, nothing." Cole checked his cell phone.

"They tried getting some professional courtesy before the Gary guy was hauled off. I think they had about ten minutes, and I haven't seen them in a few hours." Malcolm had watched their interrogation with Gary.

"Cole." Everett called his partners name who was walking towards Veronica standing in a small office with the door open.

"Yeah, ok. Let me call them." Cole responded after Everett reminded him to minimize contact with "friends" at work.

"He will learn sooner or later. No matter the joy of dating someone you work with, there is always pain eventually." Malcolm reinforced Everett's position.

"Straight to voicemail, both of them." He said staring down at his phone as he fiddled with his keyboard.

"I sent them both a text." Cole stated as Veronica emerged from the office with a tablet in her hand and her eyes glued on it, only occasionally looking up to not run into anything. She didn't say goodbye to anyone as she walked out of the department.

A text message was returned from Vania.

"Ten minutes out."

Everett left the lab, leaving Cole and Malcolm to briefly coordinate their plans for an upcoming concert, they would be double dating. He exited the building to walk a few blocks to Crimson Cup. The manager recognized him and began making his order, although two other patrons were in line.

"Everett grabbed the cup holder containing three cups of hot liquid. Two coffees were for Cole, Everett had a Caramel Macchiato with an extra shot of espresso. Today had already been a long eventful day. With a few more details emerging from Malcolm, they needed to sit down and go over everything learned up until this point. He rode the elevator up with Jack, who was on his cell phone speaking with a car dealership about why his extended warranty didn't cover something that is written in black and white that it shall be covered.

Cole was sitting at his desk, texting someone furiously.

"Mandy is coming into town this weekend and wants to spend time with me. She was supposed to be coming next week, but she got invited to speak at some doctor's event." Cole said out loud.

Everett knew his partner would cancel anything for his sister, but he would complain about it first.

"Is Janine coming with her." Everett asked in reference to Mandy's wife

"No, she has an ongoing racketeering case and it's not close at all to being finished."

Travis and V.A. exited the elevator and walked toward their counterparts.

"We didn't get much from Gary earlier. We just went to see if we could get anyone talking from the neighborhood again, but no one knows anything." Vania dove in with information to help Travis, who she knew was still agitated about the earlier incident.

"Malcolm found an ejected shell, matches a .380 and has fingerprints that are not listed in the system. Once we have a suspect, we can tie them down." Everett spoke up in between sipping on his beverage. Cole had his two cups sitting in front of him, drinking from one.

"The heroin was traced with Fentanyl and baking soda..." Cole paused as he looked over to Travis who was sitting down at his desk listening to the conversation, but his attention was elsewhere.

"Travis you ok?"

"Yeah... yeah I'm good. Probably just a lack of sleep." He answered.

Both Cole and Everett knew it was much more than weariness, but they wouldn't pry, everyone needed space to deal with matters close to them.

"Go over all the evidence until we get back. We have to go catch up with an old acquaintance." Everett paused before redirecting his focus.

"V.A. reach out to your old buddies and find out who the players are in Tim and Felicia's neighborhood. If you get any intel forward it to us." He finished, taking another sip of his beverage.

Travis excused himself to take a phone call from his mother.

"You guys are ok?" Everett asked Vania.

"Yeah for sure." Vania kept her answer short and sweet.

"Well make sure you update us if there's anything new." Everett finished as he and Cole departed.

"Cole you want this?" Vania called out before they walked towards the elevator.

"No but you don't even drink coffee." Cole answered as he and his partner walked into the elevator.

"Well you don't know everything Cole. I prefer tea." She said with a smile on her face taking a drink from the mug as the door closed behind them.

"This could be a nice place if you kept it clean." Cole watched as Turtle cleared a space off the glass dining room table. It was true, the convicted felon had a few nice items, but with shoes and clothes spread across each room and a sink full of dishes it looked like a college frat house.

"Well the cleaning lady don't come until..." Turtle paused like he was thinking about when.

"She don't come until next forever. Now what y'all want, showing up at my house, bangin on the door like y'all ain't got no home training." He lit a half cigarette from in his ash tray situated next to half of a blunt.

"I see you're getting the most out of your medical marijuana card." Everett added.

"What do you know about the shot callers or runners for this area?" Everett showed Turtle a map of Tim and Felicia's neighborhood on his cell phone.

"We are gonna have to work on quid pro quo because y'all keep showing up empty handed. I don't want to be in any CI paperwork, but I need compensation for my troubles." Turtle said with his hand extended palm up for something of value to be placed in it.

"Here's twenty dollars to get you some cleaning supplies." Cole placed the money in his hand.

Turtle held it up to the light as if he was checking the authenticity of it.

"You just never know nowadays. It's a start..." he took a second look at the map.

"For H, that's Slim P's square. Fair dude, as fair as drug dealers come." He answered the Detectives.

"What's his signature?" Everett needed to know if they were getting closer to answers.

"Baby Powder or Fentanyl all day." Turtle answered.

"Is he heavy handed?" Cole wanted to decide if his street reputation included murder and Turtle would have that answer.

"Nah, he ain't no killer. He just cuts his ties with you. He may get you jumped, but he ain't got no bodies on him." Turtle finished before exchanging his cigarette for the marijuana.

"My cataracts." Turtle lit it and winked at Everett before he walked them out of his home.

"Use that money wisely." Cole said as Turtle closed the door behind them.

"Text Travis, give him Slim P's alias and have him looked up. I trust Turtles Information even if I don't trust him, and if Slim P doesn't turnout then we are no further along than when we started our day."

An Amazon delivery truck had blocked them in, but the driver returned by the time Everett was ready to pull into traffic.

"Something doesn't add up still, why shoot Tim and Felicia in the bedroom and then stage the bodies in the kitchen, overkill right?" Everett was talking out loud, repeating what Malcolm had said earlier.

"No pun intended." Cole followed up.

"Yeah no pun intended. What are we missing?" Everett had nothing come to mind.

"If it wasn't Gary and his crew, it still had to be someone comfortable enough to spend time moving the bodies around after shooting them, and why wasn't there a report of gunshots fired on the night in question?" Cole asked

"Good observation. I'm thinkin' some type of silencing device, maybe. So, what we do know is they were shot in the bedroom, staged in the kitchen, and the blood was cleaned from where the bodies were dragged from." Everett added factors to the equation.

"So, the perpetrator had to have been strong enough to haul a 200 lb. man, so that leads the suspect pool to a man most likely." Cole continued with the assessment.

"Someone who had access and opportunity." Everett and Cole took turns building the profile.

"But why kill these two specifically?" Cole asked.

"If it wasn't business, it had to be personal." Everett paused as the light turned red. His eyes squinted as he had a realization.

"Right in front of our faces." He said watching a couple holding hands crossing the street in front of them.

"Call the B squad and tell them that V.A. needs to go see Min before it gets too late." Everett's phone went off, and from the ringtone he knew it was his daughter Becca.

"Hey pumpkin pie." Everett said, as he listened to his daughter double checking that he would be at her performance.

"Yes honey, Uncle Cole is coming with me."

His daughter was quick to get off the phone to get ready for her concert.

"I forgot. Damn." Cole looked over at his partner.

"Not me, that's why I've been wearing this rubber band all day. We should have plenty of time to make it to the concert. I'm pretty sure we have a good suspect." Everett pressed on the gas.

"Who because I'm totally blank." Cole texted someone on his phone.

"I want you to look up someone in the system." Everett said louder than intended to get Cole's attention.

"Huh, yeah ok... who?"

"I told you I'd stop back; to see you, this is my partner Lucky T." Vania made introductions between Min and Travis. Yvette was in the kitchen cooking noodles for the pasta sauce brewing on the stove. Although she and Min shared no DNA, they were sisters in every other sense of the word.

Min had been watching the cartoon version of Teen Titans. Even though she had gone through a harrowing ordeal, the television program showed that she still had some amount of youth within.

"That smells good." Travis said, as he helped Yvette with a group of bowls nearly falling out of the cabinet.

"Thank you. That was close. I probably need to get a small stepping stool like Drew keeps pushing for." Yvette thanked Travis before removing a loaf of garlic bread from the oven.

The front door to the apartment opened and Min smiled.

"Drew!" Min pointed at him.

"Did you get the cupcakes for dessert? She blurted out with concern on her face as he stood empty handed. His T-shirt fit him tightly, and the gray sweatpants slipped down onto the top of his boots. But he held nothing.

He smiled and opened the door to retrieve a bag left just outside.

"My favorite, your favorite and most importantly Vette's favorite." He gave the bag to Min who stood up with her blanket still wrapped around her.

"Hi baby." He kissed Yvette.

"Detective Aguilar." He shook her hand as she introduced Travis.

"I could smell that as soon as I got out of the car. I'm trying to lose weight, but your food is sooooo good." Drew walked into the kitchen and stirred the sauce.

"Don't even." Yvette knew her boyfriend would taste test the food.

"Detective V.A. and Travis, we have more than enough, please stay for dinner and no one gets cupcakes if you don't eat dinner." Yvette laughed while offering.

"No, no thank you. I just wanted to stop by. A lot has happened to you both, losing your..." Vania paused.

"Tim and Felicia and you... you're a fighter." Vania sat down next to Min.

A knock on the door came as a surprise.

"Back already?" Drew said as he opened the door.

"Hey, we're sorry to barge in on you, but we wanted to update you guys on how your foster parent's case is going." Cole was standing in the doorway.

"Come in, please." Yvette welcomed them both.

"I thought you'd guys would be gone by now." Everett acknowledged Travis and Vania.

"Don't you smell that? They are thinking about dinner, right?" Min asked Vania who smiled, but before she could Everett asked if there was some where they could talk.

"V.A. and Travis, we are going to speak with Yvette and Drew out in the hall."

"I want to know." Min spoke up but Yvette told her she would share everything with her that she found out.

Cole exited first followed by Drew, Yvette and Everett.

"Over the last couple of days, as you know we took down a major human trafficking and child pornography organization. Federal authorities have taken the case and more than likely an investigator will want to speak with Marilyn. The unfortunate part is that these criminals don't seem to have played a part in Tim and Felicia's homicide." Cole spoke up first.

"So, some criminals are apprehended and Min's safe with her sister?" Drew asked pausing as he reached out to hold Yvette's hand

"I guess that's a good start." He finished.

"From our timeline, Tim and Felicia were murdered between three and five on the date in question. Just to cover our bases we have to ask some questions." Everett interjected.

"Can you tell us where you were last Thursday between those hours." Everett posed the question to Yvette who took a moment to ponder.

"Thursday starting at noon I have classes to until six o'clock, and then I came home to study before working a late shift." Yvette answered.

"We will have to follow up with your professors just to confirm." Everett finished.

"Drew, what were your whereabouts?" Cole asked.

"Uhm, last Thursday I had class too, and then a meeting for a group project."

"What time did your classes and group study start and end?" Cole asked a secondary question.

"Well, Analytics was at 1:00 and group right after." Drew's cadence had slowed as he answered.

"What time was group over, we need to make sure we can rule everything out. We will need the names of your group members to verify. You understand." Everett spoke up waiting for Drew to answer.

"Why are you all asking me these questions, you don't think I had something to do with Tim and Felicia...do you?" Drew became slightly agitated.

"Just answer the question so we can move on." Yvette spoke up.

"Honey I don't like this; how can they think either one of us had something to do with their murder?" Drew still had not answered the question.

"Yvette, when we first interviewed you, we came across ammunition in your utility room. The same manufacturer and brand of bullet was found at the scene. Although many rounds are sold daily the coincidence is too close. If we can rule out your .380..." Everett began addressing Yvette.

"Drew has it, he took it to the gun range and said he would clean it last week." She blurted out. The expression on her face was indicative of how her mind was spinning.

"Drew." She stared at him, waiting for a response.

"I left it at home." He started to say but Yvette had already seen it in his backpack.

"How can you all think I had something to do with it, this is crazy." Drew stated.

"Drew please just tell them the truth. My .380 is in your book bag. Why are you..." Yvette paused realizing that her boyfriend was trying to hide something.

"Yvette can you grab that from your home. Cole will accompany you just for safety." Everett added.

As the two entered her apartment Everett had another round of questioning.

"I can tell that you care deeply for Yvette and Marilyn. You had one charge of assault in your record against your stepfather who abused your mother and siblings. My guess is that you were included in that abuse." Everett paused to take a step closer.

"Sometimes thing have to be done to prevent more unwanted actions. I'm sure Tim and Felicia have done their fair share of abuse with those who were in their care." Everett paused as Drew made eye contact with understanding.

"We have a bullet, probably ejected from the gun jamming, and we have been able to pull prints, my guess is that they will come back to you. I'd rather save Yvette and Min additional stress on a day like today. I can help, but you have to come clean before the D.A. gets involved. You're a not a bad kid." Everett finished as Cole and Yvette reemerged.

"I've got it." Cole held onto the book bag.

"Drew, honey." Yvette started to reply but he interrupted her.

"Baby, I'm going to go answer some questions. You and Min need to rest up." He said as she stared at him trying to figure out what was really going on.

"It's ok." He kissed her.

"Travis and Vania will take him back to the station. We will hold onto this." Cole held up the book bag.

The mood in the hallway became somber and as Travis walked out, he instantly felt it.

"The sauce is..." Travis paused feeling the tension.

"I need you and V.A. to take Drew to the station. Take this to forensics for testing..." Everett redirected his words back to a young woman with the weight of life on her shoulders.

"Yvette we are doing our job, and this is where the facts brought us." Everett finished before he and Cole took leave.

"It doesn't seem fair." Cole said as they exited the apartment.

"Nothing in life is really fair." Everett replied opening the car door to drive to his daughter's performance.

Chapter Five

FAMILY TREES

It looked like a scene from a television show. A domestic disturbance called in between former husband and wife. The father arrived to pick his nine-year old son up for visitation, however the mother had lost her composure knowing the father was drunk and high.

Some neighbors watched behind their front doors, while others stepped into their front yards with cell phones raised to take video of the altercation.

"Sir, you're intoxicated, and we can't allow you to travel with your son, or let you leave in a motor vehicle. We can call you an Uber." One of the two uniformed officers tried to deescalate the situation, but the father wasn't trying to comprehend, instead he kept directing his comments toward his ex-wife.

"Her ass can't tell me when I can get my son. This is my time with him!" He repeated loudly and aggressively took steps toward his ex-wife.

His son sat on the steps of the house watching with tears rolling down his face. This had been one of the reasons for their divorce; the arguing.

"Sir, we need you to calm down or I'll have to put you in the back of our cruiser." the officer turned to face his partner. He felt a hand pushing him forward and his gun being removed. He turned to face the father, but before he could say a word, he was shot in the chest and then the leg. His partner, slow to react, was shot in the head, before the father aimed the gun on his ex-wife.

"All this shit is your fault D. All I wanted was my son, during scheduled visits, but you just want to bury me, erase me. He's my son." He paused as his son began crying.

"Jr. Get in the car, let's go. Now!" He walked to his son and pulled him off the steps. The mother, although concerned about the gun, did not let that slow her from trying to pull her son back to her.

"D, I swear to god. Let go or I will shoot you."

"Daddy no, no please don't shoot my mom." The son was crying hysterically.

The mother would not relent.

"You!" A voice called out, before two gunshots were fired in the direction of the father.

The officer shot in the chest had not been killed due to his vest. The wound in his leg was critical, but he was able to pull his partners sidearm to return fire. Even though both shots missed, it caused the father's attention to shift.

The father snatched his son and threw him into his car and peeled off.

"Officer down, Officer down!" The policeman left alive had reached his cruiser to call for help and to notify of the fleeing murderer.

The mother couldn't stop screaming as she chased after the car. Onlookers wanted to engage, but most had reentered their homes or fled when the gunshots rang out. The mother ran back to her front yard and fell to her knees releasing a bone curdling scream.

The wounded officer attempted to crawl back to his partner but fell short. His leg injury was pouring blood out. A husband and wife neighbor braved their way across the street to lend assistance. They bandaged his leg before flagging down incoming police and paramedics.

Everett was hesitant to pull the sheet back on the Officer. He had already been identified, but the slain man had been a close friend to his father. Nick Franklin was less than a year from retirement and this would hurt many donning the uniform.

"I'm sorry partner." Cole couldn't read the emotion in Everett's face. If he had to guess it was something between sadness and wanting to seek retribution.

"There's an APB on the vehicle. We should have some info coming back soon." Everett relied on emotional compartments to help maintain focus, but all he felt was loss.

"Let's speak with the mother and get possible places this Markus can hide. We need to get the HT Squad Involved right away. There's a nine-year old boy in danger, and we need all the help we can get. Reach out to Agent Yari and I'll meet you inside." Everett walked towards the house leaving Cole outside to make the call.

Everett noticed the family pictures stationed on the deep red walls when he walked into the home. Candles were on the mantle above the fireplace, and as a tortoiseshell cat brushed up against his leg, Everett walked into the dining room where the mother sat in a chair at the table.

"Mrs. Ward. I'm Detective Everett Clark..." Everett greeted her slowly approaching. He pulled out a chair and sat down with her. Her eyes stared off into space while she rocked back and forth. She then focused on Everett.

"It's Ms. Grinnel, no longer Ward, and why aren't you guys out there searching for my son. I wrote down the addresses and contact info of his family members. You guys need to be out there instead of in here. He killed a policeman, so I know your boys in blue want revenge, but the problem with that is my son's safety. My son better not be a casualty." Ms. Grinnel stared into Everett's eyes.

Everett held no reservations that if Markus Ward was found by those affected with the loss of Officer Franklin's life, they would do their job. There was a slight chance that a minimal number of law enforcement would consider taking the law into their own hands; but Everett kept faith in the system he took an oath to uphold.

"Ms. Grinnel, this is a tough situation, no doubt. Our priority is to return your son..." Everett paused as she interrupted him.

"Jr., his name is Junior." Her emotions ran high and her agitation showed as she intermittently tapped her fingers on the dining room table.

"Junior is our priority. To find him and return him safely. I know you've given addresses and names but what I like to ask is, would he ever hurt your son?" Everett needed to know who he was dealing with besides the obvious.

The mother stared off into space before she answered.

"He would never hurt him. I know he shot those cops, but Junior is his namesake." She finished.

Cole walked into the house and situated himself in the opening between the dining and living rooms.

"Ms. Grinnel is there somewhere you can go; anyone you can stay with?"

No sooner had Everett asked the question, than a small commotion could be heard in the front yard.

"You can't go in; this is a crime scene."

"I swear if you touch me one time, I'll sue your ass! This is my home and that is my sister. Now get out of my way!"

Cole walked back outside to calm the scene. From what he gathered, the woman was family but before he questioned her, she ran into the house.

"D, honey, where are you? D." The sister moved quickly into the dining room and interrupted Everett who was still asking questions.

"Baby girl, are you ok? I saw Markus on the news, and he killed people. He took Junior?" She fired off questions until the mother stood up to hug her. They begin crying.

"Honey it's going to be ok. That bastard will get his! Why are y'all in here instead of out there? My client will cooperate however she can, but right now, I need to speak with her, alone." The sister reached into her pocket and handed Everett and Cole her business card.

'Karie Decker. Attorney-at-Law'

Everett made eye contact with Cole. In that subtle exchange they knew it was more beneficial to hit the streets than to have a legal tug of war.

"Ms. Grinnel, we will do everything we can to bring this all to an end quickly, and without any additional loss of life. Here is my card. I will ensure that you are updated with any pertinent findings. We will see to it that you have security until this ordeal is over." Everett excused himself and followed Cole out the front door.

The blood stained the front yard, the yellow tape already placed around the perimeter kept neighbors and news media at bay.

"Detective, Detective, can you tell us anything about this tragic event? What can you share with us?" A local reporter asked them as they walked towards their vehicle.

"This is an ongoing investigation; we have no comment." Cole said as he passed the camera man.

Everett unlocked the car doors and they both got in.

"I wouldn't have even given them that partner. We need to find Markus Ward quickly. Travis is cutting his day off short and is doing background right now. When is V. A. back in town?" Everett pulled out onto the neighborhood street.

"Day after tomorrow, I think. Her Grandfather being honored in D.C by the largest Law Enforcement group is a big deal." Cole answered as he checked his text message.

"We've been requested."

"I wish Captain would let us get going before asking to be briefed." Everett didn't want to waste time going in to brief him about what was already common information.

"Not the Captain partner…. HT Squad, Agent Yari is requesting us at Markus Ward's residence."

Everett acknowledged while watching Cole input the address into the GPS.

"She is a bloodhound partner. Once Travis works up the background, have him meet us. Maybe Yari and he can work together until V.A. returns." Everett knew a good Agent when he saw one. He respected Yari after seeing her work with them in the field, she was tenacious.

"Agreed partner, there's only a few outside of our team that I trust to get the job done…" Cole replied as Everett's phone rang.

Everett looked at the incoming number. He shook his head and declined the call.

"Captain has to wait for now." Everett made certain that Cole understood to ignore his incoming call from their superior until more progress had been made.

Everett blew his horn for a black and white squad to move his vehicle.

"We will find them both E." Cole understood the emotions facing Everett; his partner was a father himself, and Cole knew it was becoming more personal with each passing moment.

"Yeah, we better. We sure as hell better." Everett had lost patience and slowly moved forward to squeeze between two media vehicles with less than a few inches to spare. He rolled his window down and issued an order.

"Ticket both of them for a parking violation." He rolled his window back up and drove off.

"Bruno just do your job. She's the lead and you follow her." The commander of the HT Squad was yelling at an agent when Everett and Cole walked into Markus Ward's home.

Bruno accepted his position and listened to Agent Yari's instruction before he departed leaving the home.

"So, they have you leading the investigation? What can you tell us?" Cole approached her first, followed by Everett, who declined to answer a call from the Captain. He silenced his phone so he wouldn't be disturbed.

"I can tell you Bruno is a good agent, when a man is leading the charge." Agent Yari motioned them out of the room and down a small hallway to a back bedroom.

"Suspect seems like a loner, works for the city in maintenance for the past twelve years. Recently divorced within the past year, besides working and drinking it doesn't seem like Markus has much going on." Agent Yari gave Everett and Cole a few addresses she had gathered to where the suspect could have taken his son.

"We'll take these, and we have Travis coming to assist you." Everett looked over the addresses on the list for a place to start.

"We keep getting tips called in, but between this and another high-profile case that we've kept silent, my department is running thin. I need to give a statement to the vultures out there, so excuse me for a moment." Agent Yari broke away from Everett and Cole to address the reporters gathered outside.

Travis had arrived on the scene. He flashed his badge and walked into the home passing the interview Yari was conducting.

"This is what I could pull up on Markus Ward." Travis extended the file to Cole.

"Army veteran with two tours overseas, honorable discharge. Married for eleven years, and he has two children. One from a high school sweetheart." Cole read bits of the information out loud.

"We are following up on known associates, you will work with Agent Yari. I can't tell you how important these next forty-eight hours are in finding Mr. Ward and his son. The return of the son; Jr., unharmed, is the number one priority. Some officers may seek retaliation for a fallen officer, so it's imperative that we stay on top of this." Everett concluded as Agent Yari ended her brief on screen update for the public.

"These reporters are aggressive." She stated flatly.

"Travis, I understand we'll be teaming up for now. You and I will speak with his mother..." Agent Yari was interrupted by Bruno.

"We have a credible tip that his vehicle has been spotted. Officers have been deployed and we will be looped in soon." Bruno's tone was much better.

"Once confirmed that it is the suspect's vehicle, I want you to process it." Yari paused without emotion.

Bruno shook his head in agreement before walking away.

"Travis I will ride with you, give me one second." Agent Yari walked away to speak with two members of the HT Squad.

"Travis, there will be Uni's seeking retribution but the only thing that matters; well the first thing that matters for Yari is the son's safe return, backing her up is your job, but Markus Ward is your primary. Any whiff or indication we need to know immediately." Everett ensured that Travis had clear instruction.

"Yari has been assigned lead investigator and she's tenacious, be as tenacious as she is." Cole added.

"Well she can't be any worse than V.A." Travis responded instinctively.

"Travis, Travis, Travis you have a lot to learn." Cole shook his head as they walked away.

"Wait, what?" Travis called out after them. Travis missed his partner and the consistency of having someone at his side that he trusted. He also knew it was highly likely that when Vania returned from the D.C. event celebrating her Great Grandfather and Grandfather, that she might not be in the best mood emotionally as she didn't want to attend.

Ba Ba Brazil by Four80East was playing on the smart tv in the living room. The last bit of sunshine peeked through rear patio of Vania's mother's screen door. Two piles of leaves had been left by her nephews, who forgot to get yard waste bags. Vania's mother turned the sound down to listen to her daughter express her feelings.

"I went mama. I did the family thing and supported both; although abuelo did everything he could to keep me off the force." Vania was being as respectful to her mother as possible as she sat at the kitchen table eating freshly made empanadas and chicken with rice.

Her mother inhaled a deep breath. She knew that there were two sides to every coin, her position was always even. Her black robe hung loosely from her shoulders. Vania bought it as a Mother's Day gift along with matching black and red slippers. Eliana Aguilar was still as attractive as she had been when she gave birth to Vania over three decades ago. Her long salt and pepper hair flowed over the collar of the robe, and her copper-toned skin still as smooth as her daughters.

"Mija, they only wanted to protect you. It almost ripped our family apart when Jamie was killed in the line of duty, and then to honor him you want to join the force. It was a lot to process." Vania's mother tried to walk a fine line between supporting her daughter and respecting her father's wishes.

"I know, I know but it's not my problem anymore. I left home mama; do you understand that? I had to leave home to do what I love after having to choose to leave the people I love most. And what's even more hurtful, is that after being a token for his legacy in D.C., he still won't recognize the hard work and success I've had from two separate elite enforcement teams." Vania was venting to her mom. One thing that always remained was the bond between the two of them. Vania shared everything with her, the most embarrassing moments along with memories of elation. She also understood that calling her mother's father, a male chauvinist with overreaching egotistical behavior, would be a bit much.

"He is proud of you; I've heard him speaking to old colleagues about the closing rate of your team. You know he and Detective Clark's father had a history. I wouldn't say they were friends, but they respected each other. Your bis abuelo thought Edward Clark a brave soul to join the force in Columbus long before it became a modern-day city."

Vania's mother had caught her off guard completely. Her grandfather and Everett's father had a relationship. Why hadn't Everett said anything? Did he even know?

"I didn't know, but it doesn't surprise me. You would have thought grandad was a damn rock star. Grown men waiting in line to have their book signed by him." Vania pulled the plate of empanadas closer to her.

"Ahh, you haven't read it yet?" Vania's mother laughed profusely before she stood up and walked into the living room to retrieve the book. She handed Vania the book and then sat back down.

"Vania read the special dedication." Her mother offered.

Vania looked at her mother with curiosity and opened the book. She flipped the pages until she came to the dedication page. She began to read, and her facial expression began to change. A wave of emotion flooded her, and the tears formed in her eyes as she read the words.

SPECIAL DEDICATION

'The years of service passed in the blink of an eye. For many of us our legacies are carried through our bloodline. Sometimes in the least likely soul. Vivi, you are all the best parts of what I had hoped you would become. Protect and Serve the community as you do our family.'

Vania was left speechless. The entire day in D.C. she had not paid attention to people being extra 'nice' to her. Her grandfather had not said anything to her except asking if she had read his book. She felt bad because she had not. How had she become so callous? Was he actually concerned about her well-being while carrying the shield?

"I, I didn't know mama. He never says anything." Vania read the words silently again.

"At least he's been consistent since the day you were born. Truth be told, if he had a favorite grandchild, I'm sure it's you. Now enough of that. How's Rosey? Medical school isn't easy." Vania's mother decided to change the familial subject and speak about Vania's roommate Rosey.

"She's good, busy. With my schedule and her schedule, we barely see each other. She's got a seminar in Dallas in a few weeks." Vania placed the book onto the table before standing to get a can of soda from the refrigerator.

Vania's mothers cell phone rang. She adjusted her black robe and kissed Vania on the cheek.

"I am proud of you mija, and I love that outfit on you." She walked out of the kitchen to retrieve her cell phone.

Vania's white and ivory 'Everyday Lounge Wear' from Victoria's Secret was a softer look than what she typically had bought. Her mother's suggestion of buying more feminine clothing was rubbing off on her, slowly.

Vania ate a third empanada and checked her text messages.

Travis had called earlier to share that a city-wide search was on for Markus Ward. He left details via email along with photos of the suspect.

Vania appreciated her new partner. His excessiveness toward completing paperwork was one behavior she could do without, but she had learned to trust him to have her back. She thought him a solid human being and good cop.

Vania decided that she would leave a day early. She had two days remaining before having to return to work, but there was a cop killer and child abductor needing to be found. She would get her mother out of the house to shop the following day before hitting the road. For now, she would read some of her grandfather's book.

"I haven't seen Ward in forever, I feel for the officer's, but I can't help you." Lamonte Perry was answering the questions posed by Agent Yari and Travis. Agent Yari's all black baseball cap was pulled down to her eyebrows. Her badge hung loosely from her neck and her gun was visible on her hip. Travis followed her lead.

She had decided to run down his known associates. Those whose contact information had been scribbled on a notepad that rested by the phone at Markus Ward's home. Travis kept his hands free and within an arm's length of the man being questioned in his front yard.

"Mr. Perry you still haven't answered my original question, which I'll assume you understood completely. I didn't ask when the last time you've seen your old army buddy. I asked you when was the last time you spoke with him? We can have your call history within the next thirty minutes. Any judge will sign off on anything we want right now as an officer of the law has been killed. Once we do that your name is included in more than just a "visit" side-note. If your records show that you did speak with him, you can and more than likely will be charged with assistance after the fact, you know an accessory. Your life changes at that point. The lives of those you love also change." Agent Yari paused as a teenage girl walked to the front door to stare out the screen at her father speaking with the police agents.

"Look, he called before I knew what he had done and asked to borrow some money. But I swear I didn't see Jr. with him. He was alone." Lamonte explained as he pulled his cell phone out to show his call log to Travis.

Yari knew Lamonte hadn't come fully clean, so she pressed him.

"Besides money and not seeing Jr. with him, what else did he say to you about his plans?" Yari held her gaze on Lamonte. If she speculated, he wasn't forthcoming she was going to follow through with the subtle threat she had given.

Lamonte looked over his shoulder at his daughter

"Close the door honey, I'll be right there." He hesitated until she did as she was told.

"Listen Agents, I had no idea about any of this. He came by and said he was in a fix and needed my help and I gave it to him." He wanted to be clear he had no knowledge of anything that transpired earlier.

"So, you gave him how much money?" Travis asked directly.

"I only had a little over a grand in the house." Lamonte answered.

"So, you gave a little over a grand to someone you haven't seen in forever?" Travis followed up with a second question.

Lamonte's facial expression changed as if bewildered. He looked at Yari and then back at Travis.

"When someone who protects your back or saves your life, asks for a favor, would you say no? Would you say no to your partner?" Lamonte paused before continuing.

"Listen, I gave a friend some money before I knew about the murder and kidnapping. Jr. is his life and he would never hurt him. I know that much; he will protect him with his life. Markus was the best of us, and I mean the very best. Are we done?".

"For now. If he reaches back out to you, you will be required to contact me." Yari handed him a business card and motioned for Travis to do the same.

"One last question Mr. Perry, did you see the vehicle he was driving?" Travis asked

"A black imported SUV, it could've been an Audi, I think." He waited until they walked out of his yard before returning inside his home.

"So, he's switched vehicles and from what I gather he is highly skilled. Can you shoot your boss the information and I'll call into the unit? If Markus contacted one army buddy, I would reason he'd do it again." Agent Yari opened the passenger door and got into the vehicle.

"Were you really going to charge him as an accomplice?" Travis asked.

"If the shoe fits, you're damn right. There is no gray area with the law except our interpretation. You need to fill up before we hit the rest of the addresses on this list." Yari paused as her cell phone rang.

"Andino here."

Travis couldn't help but to listen to her conversation. He had worked two cases with the HT Squad, but this was the first time he learned her last name.

"Ok, thank you for the update sir." When she ended the call, she exhaled.

"Bad news?" Travis asked.

"The second officer has died in the operating room." Yari pounded the dash in the car.

Travis held his tongue and input the next address into his GPS system. He turned on his police lights as Yari looked through the file of information gathered. They followed each lead, only stopping for coffee and restroom breaks for the next several hours.

The sun had gone down like each lead the senior detectives followed long into the next day. Markus was adept at keeping a low profile, no one had any viable information and neither set well with Everett.

Everett and Cole had gone over twenty-four hours straight in pursuit of the cop killing kidnapper. Within that time frame, Markus Ward's vehicle had been found abandoned near the Jewish Community Center in Bexley.

They returned to the precinct to follow up with any evidence forensics was able to pull from the vehicle. The first thing they noticed as they opened the door to the hallway leading to the lab, was the smell of fresh paint. The second, was the doors to the lab were hitched open.

The department bustled with activity with various personnel performing tests. Sheldon was in charge and due to the heightened interest, he was double checking everyone's findings.

"So, nothing. There's nothing found in his car to help us Sheldon?" Everett asked after listening for a second time that nothing processed would be helpful at this point.

Cole listened to his partner question Sheldon. Everett had become impatient, allowing emotions to surface that he typically held in check.

"Unless three sets of fingerprints, two of which appear to be the suspect and his son. The third set has yet to be identified. I am running them through all the databases, and I do mean all. The vehicle was spotless, it seems." Sheldon paused to walk closer to a desk.

"There are some pamphlets on state parks that seem dated, but besides those and vehicle registration that's all we found." He finished by handing Cole the pamphlets.

"Mohican State Park and Hocking Hills. Army vet fleeing into the woods. Sounds like something in your wheelhouse partner." Cole said flatly

"I need to make a call." Everett announced before excusing himself.

Cole remained behind. He had a few more questions for Sheldon.

"Can you run an analysis on any content found in his tire tread?"

"Yes, that is in process but that will take some time. I did forward all of this to Agent Yari." Sheldon included.

"Is there any indication that the boy was harmed in anyway? Scratch marks in the vehicle, anything at all? All indications point that he would never hurt his son, but with two officers killed, perhaps his sense of right and wrong has been shattered." Cole asked a series of random questions.

"Detective, I'm not Malcolm, I don't speculate or form hypothesis no matter how great and grand they are. I rely on facts, scientific facts. I promise we are doing our jobs. I have donated my concert tickets at The Schott for this evening. We take this seriously Detective." Sheldon said dryly.

"Make it the priority. Two officers died in the line of duty. A child has been kidnapped. I don't care what else is going on, this is the only priority." Cole made sure Sheldon understood before he walked out of the forensics department.

Sheldon was very competent at inspecting dead bodies, but this wasn't in his wheelhouse. Malcolm would be much better with this investigation, but he was in Los Angeles assisting on a case.

Cole texted Travis to make sure they had received the Information from Sheldon. No new leads had been made in day two of the manhunt. Everyone that had a relationship with Markus Ward has been contacted and interviewed.

After a couple of more hours of dead ends, the sun was going down again. Several other teams were still working the case, so Everett gave the members of his team time to rest.

Vania was more confused after reading her grandfather's book than she had been before. His actions didn't match his words.

"Well, he doesn't speak much." Vania wondered if she had misinterpreted everything since her cousin Jaime had died in the line of duty. Was he simply protective of her? Each thought led to a different question.

She pushed back against the negative thoughts as she unlocked the door to her home. She felt relief walking back into her safe space. Her roommate was one of the better ones she had ever had. The fact was, medical school kept Rosey busy and they rarely saw each other.

Vania dropped her suitcase in the living room and walked into the kitchen. On the counter was a handwritten note.

'Can you drive ol Shirley and tell me if it's the struts or shocks. Please." The note read.

Rosey's 1999 Honda Civic had less than one hundred thousand miles on it and was in decent condition. Rosey drove it during the summertime to car shows, and Vania had been the only one to work on it over the past three years.

Vania smiled as she saw the Red Velvet Cake in the cake pan. It was Rosey's way of saying thank you in advance. She opened the refrigerator to get milk to go along with the baked sweetness.

There was no milk.

Vania opened the freezer to check for vanilla ice cream but there was only strawberry.

Her cat walked into the space between the kitchen and dining room and sat down. It licked its front paw and then walked the distance to rub herself up against Vania's leg.

"Well I guess I can drive it to the store, huh?" Vania picked her cat up before changing into some jeans and a red hoodie. She put on an OSU Block O hat with red stitching.

Her cell phone buzzed. It was Travis calling.

"Hey T, what's shaking?" She put her 9mm Ruger LCP into her belt holster.

"This case is shaking nothing, absolutely nothing. I've been working with Agent Yari. I thought you were headstrong. Anyway, how was the thing?" Travis wanted to make sure his partner wasn't holding heaviness and if she did, he was there to support her.

"Whew, where do I begin? I'm still processing. I think I had so much shit wrong about so much stuff. I'll be in the office tomorrow to get my partner back."

"Yeah I am walking into my place right now. Over twenty-four hours straight. It's seven-thirty now, and this is the first time in two days I've been home." Travis paused,

"Damn, we just got a hit. Yari is on her way. Are you sure you don't want to join us right now?" He asked rhetorically.

"I'll see you in the morning T." Vania explained she was tired too.

After ending the call, she grabbed the keys to the 1999 Honda Civic and walked into her garage to look under the car before driving it.

"The things I do for Red Velvet Cake."

Vania drove the car a little further than she intended, she needed to put it up on ramps to make a final determination. She turned the radio up as she sat at a red light. The new artist Gov White's, "Interstate Ridin'", was playing on the local hip-hop radio station and she started bopping her head to the music. She glanced over at a vehicle that pulled up at the red light also. She smiled at the driver who looked at her but quickly looked straight-forward.

Vania had to look a third time into the newer model Oldsmobile pulled up next to her. She opened her previous emails from Travis with the description of the suspect. When she looked at him again, she was certain it was Markus Ward.

His return glare induced panic and he fled through the red light.

Vania reached for her cell phone to call the emergency dispatch number, but lost control of it as it fell out of her hand.

The hard-right turn required two hands to steady the wheel of her roommate's car. The manual transmission held firm after twenty years. How she had run across the cop killer was pure luck.

Dusk had just settled, and traffic was heavy. Concert goers exiting The Schott, had congregated at the red light waiting to enter the various parking garages. Traffic cops were directing those already traveling into lanes to make their departure as safe and easy as possible.

A woman tried steadying herself in the crosswalk but lost her balance and was pulled back just in time from being hit as a car screeched to a halt.

"Are you serious? You want to get arrested for jaywalking?" One of the traffic cops yelled at the woman, while her friend pulled her back onto the curb.

The sound of wheels squealing drew everyone's attention to the pair of headlights traveling quickly toward them from the opposite direction.

A bus proceeded through the green light, unaware that it was in the path of a speeding vehicle.

The nearest police officer directing traffic waved his hands frantically at the car to stop, instead, it sped up ignoring him.

A second vehicle appeared behind the first car as it weaved in between traffic. It blew its' horn and flashed its' lights but never slowed.

The traffic officers yelled for everyone to get back away from the oncoming vehicles. Groups of people ran back towards the building. A few people fell but were pulled up quickly by good Samaritans.

The bus unfortunately could not heed the officers command and proceeded forward and only at the last minute did it slam on its' brakes.

The first vehicle hit the back of the COTA bus and spun out of control rolling over the curb to land on its top. The crowd was silenced momentarily, before they erupted, screaming over each other.

The second vehicle swerved from crashing into the bus and slammed into a fire hydrant, before resting between it and a city building. The water leaked from the hydrant but it had not fully erupted.

Vania's head slammed against the steering wheel and bounced backwards to ricochet off the headrest.

She heard the yelling and people barking orders, but she could only make out blurred shadows.

Bodies seemed to dart in and out of the street, some towards the accidents and others to safety.

"Check the passengers!" An officer ran towards the front of the bus as the bus driver opened the doors; the metal contraption had been dented from the force of the collision, but the car had taken the brunt of the damage.

The other officers jumped into action pushing some people further back, who were on their cell phones video recording.

The man driving the car began to slowly crawl out the window with blood covering his hands from the impact. He wobbled and fell backwards onto the car. Blood ran down his nose towards his chin. An officer helped him stand and yelled for assistance.

Vania regained her focus and began scanning for the suspect sought in the connection of two murdered police officers. Her car, smashed into the hydrant, was roughly thirty yards away from the vehicle she pursued. She tasted the blood in her mouth and wiped it away. She squinted through the cracks of her windshield.

Passengers were being taken from the bus; at least those who were able to walk. Others were being attended to on the city transportation vehicle.

Approaching sirens could be heard as Vania attempted to open her driver side door, but it was pinned against the fire hydrant. She couldn't understand why she hadn't been assisted yet as some onlookers pointed at officers to help her.

"Help... somebody help me get out the car!" Vania's voice escalated as she watched more concern going towards the suspect. Vania crawled over the passenger seat and was finally able to scramble out of the vehicle from the passenger door.

"Lady get back, get back and just stay there, right there!" A uniformed officer kept an arm length away, while speaking to Vania in disdain. His apparent concern was not for her well-being.

Vania stumbled slightly back onto the car frame to steady herself. She leaned on the car, still disoriented.

"What's your problem, are you drunk? Lady just keep your ass right there." He reached for his radio and began to call in that an intoxicated woman crashed and damaged several vehicles and city property.

Vania slowly regained perspective as she watched an ambulance being waved towards the suspect, who was propped up on the side of a cruiser, being spoken with by a second uniform. The suspected cop killer wasn't in cuffs.

"Don't tell me what..." Vania tried to speak but was cut off again by the same officer.

"Don't make this harder than it has to be. I bet your insurance won't cover this. Are you even insured?" His tone became more demeaning, and he has still failed to render aid in his first responder role.

Vania felt the blood oozing down her face again from a cut above her brow. She took her sleeve and wiped it away to clear her vision. She tried to walk toward the suspect to make sure he was placed under arrest, because it seemed no other law enforcement could remember his face on a city-wide BOLO.

The uniformed officer prevented Vania from leaving, first by yelling out in an authoritative tone and then grabbing her by her shoulder. He jerked back after noticing that she had a gun on her waist.

"Gun...Gun!" He took a step away from her, drawing his weapon.

"Put your hands up and don't move! Don't take another fucking step!"

"I'm a Det..." Vania attempted to say but the Officer slammed her up against the car and called for back-up.

Vania attempted a second time to speak to de-escalate the situation and apprehend the cop killer, but another group of officers came to assist the uniformed officer. They surrounded her with guns drawn. Many voices were yelling out conflicting orders, until one voice drowned out the others.

"Keep your hands-on top of the vehicle. Now place your hands behind your back."

"I said put your hands..."

Vania was no longer in the mood to exercise patience to deal with complete incompetence.

"I am Detective Vania Aguilar and while you are profiling me and not following procedure, the man you guys are

CHAPTER FIVE: FAMILY TREES

sucking ass up to is the suspect in the child abduction and killing two of our own!"

Officers on site look confused and allowed Vania to pull her badge.

"I'm sorry Detective, I had no idea." The officer who initially refused helping her spoke up.

Vania seeing the suspect finally go into handcuffs turns her attention back to the officer who profiled her.

"You had no idea because you didn't take time to understand. Instead of rendering aid to both car accident victims, your first thought was to appease the man in a fancy car. Instead of making sure I was ok, as you witnessed that I was bleeding down my face, but you ask about car insurance. Instead of doing your job you are quick to pull your weapon!"

"I was just..."

"You were doing exactly what you weren't trained to do asshole, and that's why we've had both federal and state investigations up our ass over the last two years. You are part of the problem!" Vania tried to walk away towards Travis who had arrived on scene, but the officer kept trying to minimize what she would report. He reached out and grabbed her arm to gain her attention.

"DON'T TOUCH ME!" She screamed as her emotions took over.

Vania pushed him into the side of a building, immobilizing his movement, before securing a standing arm bar.

"DON'T EVER TOUCH ME, YOU'VE ALREADY PROFILED AND ASSAULTED A RANKING OFFICER. YOU'VE ALREADY SHOWN YOUR BIAS AND YOU DON'T BELONG ON THE FORCE. TOUCH ME AGAIN AND I'LL BREAK YOUR DAMN ARM AND WRIST!!!"

Travis approached Vania and upon making eye contact, she released the officer from her grasp.

"You ok partner?" He looks at badge numbers and begins reciting them until the uniformed officers walk away.

"We need to get you looked over, come on." Travis waves down a paramedic to look at Vania's injuries.

"You probably need a few stitches and to be checked out at the ER for concussion like symptoms." The older bald man said, after putting a butterfly band aid across her forehead.

"I'm fine for now, I want to get him in the box and get a confession." Vania moved from the back of the ambulance but was held up by one of the Commanders now on site.

He stood under five feet six inches and had a pot belly but held a firm belief that the thin blue line should be held accountable for protecting and serving the community the right way.

"Detective, my apologies for the lack of assistance you received. Do you want to file a complaint?"

The Commander approached slowly with his subordinate in tow.

"I'll think on the complaint Commander, but an apology, both verbal and written will suffice. No need to get unwanted attention drawn on us right now." Vania replied. If it was only on her, then she would ask for his termination.

It meant more to Vania that she raise awareness and that he was willing to correct the behavior immediately. With that behind her, Vania wanted to sit across from Markus Ward and get him to confess to both shootings. After this car chase, she was invested in closing this.

"Ok now that we have that over, let me get you to the ER for head trauma." Travis stared into his partners eyes hoping to convey that her health was important in this moment.

"After he confesses, we need to get to the hospital and interview him." Vania replied before turning to scan the area.

"My roommate is going to be pissed." Vania saw the old Honda being hauled away by a tow truck.

"I think a lot of people are going to be pissed." Travis interjected.

"Detectives...Detectives." A familiar voice called out; it was Veronica from the lab.

"Veronica, what's up?' Vania asked.

Veronica looked over Vania's bandage and shook her head.

"I'm glad you're ok. We found a child's doll in the wreckage, along with a police force issued Glock 22 that we are pretty sure was taken at the time of the murder. Everything is bagged and, on the way, back to the lab." She paused to look Vania in the eyes.

"You're a badass."

"Indeed, she is, now we need to get going before Everett and Cole beat us to the hospital and try to take this one over, Everett is too close to this investigation, and that's coming from Cole." Travis checked his cell phone for any updates from either.

"Veronica, good work. Get that doll to Agent Yari. They've been tracking the abduction." Travis made the simple request, as Veronica walked back to the overturned Oldsmobile.

"Where did you park?' Vania traced her fingers over the wound on her forehead and could still taste the blood on her lip.

"I'm right over there. First thing we need to do is get you checked for a concussion partner. We've got him in custody, and we will question him. Cole can handle Everett." They approached his car. He unlocked the passenger door and opened it.

"It's my head that hurts, not my hands. I can open my own damn door and put my own seat belt on." Vania was agitated.

Travis walked to his side and got in. He strapped his seatbelt on and pressed the ignition button.

"I'm sorry partner, I've got a headache and I feel like I have to..." Vania couldn't say the words as she opened the passenger door and vomited.

"Where is he?' Those three words carried disgust when Everett walked into the hospital looking for the suspected cop killer.

"Sir, sir you're not allowed in there at this time by the order of The Chief of Police." A uniformed officer tried to impede Everett's progress, but it was Cole grabbing his partner by the shoulder that slowed down the escalation.

It made sense that Everett's emotions ran high. The officer killed in the line of duty was only two months away from retiring from the force. At one time, the officer had been Everett's father's partner and for this reason it was extremely personal.

"E, slow down. He's caught and not going anywhere. Let's not jeopardize anything at this point. I'm usually the one riding my emotions partner, let's try and keep it that way." Cole walked toward the nurse's station to ask questions on the condition of Markus Ward when an older doctor approached.

"I am Detective Cole Kennedy and my partner Detective Clark. What can you tell us?" Cole asked hoping to redirect Everett's attention.

Everett kept staring at the patient's door, but he listened to what the doctor conveyed.

"Patient has multiple broken bones from the impact of the collision. He is stable now and can be released in the morning into your custody. His attorney has been allowed to speak with him, but for now he's under our care." The doctor finished and from Everett's abrupt exit he didn't like what he just heard; the suspected killer had lawyered up.

"The warrants garnered evidence, let's revisit what we have so we can go at him in the am partner. A confession will make it easier on both families." Cole followed behind Everett as they walked the halls of the hospital to exit.

The parking lot had more vehicles in it than when they arrived. A black woman was being pushed into the hospital in a wheelchair. From the words being spoken the couple was married and having their first child.

"Baby we're here, we're here." The husband exclaimed but the wife yelled much louder as the pain moved through her body.

Cole tried to make light of the situation to take the edge off Everett.

"For that reason alone; I will never have children, I am totally satisfied being uncle to your two ragamuffins." Cole used the key fob to unlock the doors.

"We need to speak with Sheldon and confirm the findings. This piece of shit is going to confess to murder and kidnapping. Call whoever needs to be called, so that when he is released, he doesn't skip 'go' and is brought to the station...." Everett paused as if he was contemplating a decision.

"Make sure the prisoner is unharmed, and I mean no additional injuries. He will be a candidate for the death penalty."

Cole understood where his partner's emotions were coming from.

"I'll personally escort him in for questioning, we will do this by the book. We need to speak with V.A. and get her account, but more importantly make sure she is ok." Cole said.

Everett pulled out his cell phone and called Travis, but it went straight to voicemail.

"I need an update on V.A." His message was short and concise.

"Let's check with the trafficking unit to see how we can help until Markus is available to be interrogated." Everett needed to help in some way toward the safe return of the nine-year old boy who was also the son of the suspect.

Cole yawned. He had been up for the past day and a half between tracking down leads and Markus Ward.

"The HT Squad does good work. I need to shower and then we can go at it." Cole could smell the must stemming from his body.

"Yeah, I guess that sounds like a plan. You gotta change of clothes at the station?" Everett asked, knowing his bag was still in his vehicle back at the precinct.

"Bro, I will drop you off and then head home. Give me an hour and we can hop back into it." Cole needed his own shower and wasn't going to buy into anything his partner said about cleaning up at the station.

"There's the B-squad." Everett ignored Cole when he saw Travis driving into the hospital turnabout. He blew the car horn to get their attention.

As the two vehicles approached, they rolled the windows down.

"What's up, how's V.A.?" Cole asked looking past Travis into the passenger seat.

"She's concussed, I need to get her inside." Travis replied anxiously.

"We can head back in with you, we were going to clean up quickly and see how we can help the HT Squad." Cole started to turn this car off.

"No, no I've got it. I'll get her checked out and update you. We had Veronica send some of the evidence to Yari directly since she's the lead on the case." Travis pulled into the ER oval and found a wheelchair.

"We need a doctor; she's been throwing up and has been in a car accident. The paramedics on scene believed her to be concussed." Travis approached the check in desk but was told to have a seat.

"Ma'am, I apologize but she can't wait." Travis didn't want to cause a scene, but he wasn't going to take no for an answer.

"I will be with you shortly." The intake nurse stood up and walked away from her station.

"T, it's cool. We can wait, just get me a bucket." Vania said leaning forward in her chair,

Travis had already made up in his mind that his partner was not going to wait again for assistance.

He reached into the intake window and pressed the release to open the doors and wheeled Vania back to another station just inside the double doors.

"Ma'am, we are Columbus Detectives and we need assistance now. Not tomorrow or five minutes from now." Travis raised his voice and it caught the attention of other medical staff.

"Detective, I'm sorry. We have a room right here for you, I'll take her from here." A second nurse took control of Vania and wheeled her inside.

Travis followed behind and gave the first intake nurse an eye roll.

"I'm sorry Detective." The intake nurse called out after realizing the error she made.

"T, don't be a dicktective." Vania said as she was being helped from the wheelchair to the hospital bed.

The nurse began checking vitals and shortly after a Doctor came in to verify that Vania had been concussed.

"You need a few days of rest; I'd prefer to keep you overnight." The doctor gave her instructions for recovery that didn't sit well with Vania after she refused to remain until the morning.

"I don't have a couple of days to rest."

The doctor laughed.

"You guys make the worst patients, well next to my colleagues that is." She walked out of the room leaving Vania and Travis.

"Let's go." Vania put her shoes on and tried walking out but lost her balance.

"I got you V.A., I'll get you settled in before figuring out where I'm needed next. You apprehended that piece of shit. You deserve the whole week off, to hell with a few days." Travis knew the importance of the slain officer's family finding closure.

"Once the little boy is found I'll take a break, until then my medical history is 'my' medical history." Vania wanted to make sure her meaning was understood.

Travis would always have her back, but if she was unable to perform her duty as expected he would not allow it.

"As long as you can keep up and don't jeopardize anything, it ain't got nothing to do with me. But I'm telling you slack one time, and I mean one time, partner and I'll throw your ass in this car and deliver you home." Travis wasn't giving any wiggle room for her to respond.

"Deal." She agreed.

The door to her room in the emergency department opened and her roommate Rosey was walking in with concern on her face.

"If you didn't want to check the Honda, I would've understood."

Vania mustered a grin and reached up to hug Rosey as she approached the bed.

Travis stepped aside and waited until Vania made quick introductions.

Rosey departed to speak with the attending physician, who in turn spoke with her after learning her medical credentials.

With her door left cracked open, Vania and Travis overheard medical staff speaking about the police presence in another portion of the hospital where Markus was being kept.

Travis received a phone call from Yari letting him know the son had been found.

"I've got some good news, they found Jr. Yari has him and she's taking him to meet the mother after being checked." Travis related to Vania who was bent over again.

"Good, good because I am going to take them up on their offer to stay the night. Hand me that trash can and turn the lights down." Vania said before throwing up again.

Travis laid her back and pressed the nurse's button. He walked out of the room and saw the attending physician speaking with Rosey.

"We're going to need a room for two." Travis was not leaving her side. They were partners.

"I think that's the best idea, she's presented with more than a mild concussion." Rosey interjected.

Travis shook his head back and forth as he listened to the doctor speak about the concussion and bruising to Vania's face. He was issuing additional testing to determine if any other concerns needed to be addressed.

Rosey switched her bag from one shoulder to the next as she pulled out her cell phone. She texted Vania's mother to give her the information and to reinforce that her daughter wasn't injured badly. When she was done, she pulled a nurse to the side.

"We are going to need to make it a room for three. I am staying as well."

Chapter Six

SeRIOusLY

SeRIOusLY?

The team had done everything they could to keep the information about the serial killer quiet, but a leak to the media escalated the concerns throughout the state. Citizens voiced their opinion on social media about the lack of transparency from law enforcement officials. Now with someone in custody, news outlets were stationed outside of the precinct.

"Is this really the guy, seriously?" Captain Montgomery asked out loud. He didn't need an answer from anyone else present.

Everett's entire team, along with ADA Jefferson watched Agent Yari behind the double mirror as she sat across from Dexter Ericsson. His ankles were chained together, and his hands fastened to the table.

"Yari Andino. All of them had your spirit." He smiled.

"Who is all?" Yari asked.

He had requested her specifically after he had been caught.

Why? No one knew, but as Dexter conversed with her, his home was being searched in Cleveland. This had been his error; believing the agencies had not pooled their resources together.

His glasses made him look unassuming, but there was nothing simple about him. They believed he had nine victims under his belt originally, but that number wasn't accurate. Only by pure chance had he been caught as he stalked Veronica, the forensic technician. It started off with a few pictures being liked on her dating page and over the course of four months, she had revealed personal aspects of her life to him. He would send flowers, cards and support her from a distance but they never spoke on the phone.

The kaleidoscope roses sat at the corner of the table were the second set he delivered to the building.

Cole remembered him from weeks ago as they bumped into each other when exiting the building.

"All of the ones who broke my heart and walked away from me. Did you know that the unicorn is the national animal of Scotland?" He paused and moved his face closer to the hand restraints as if figuring out how to get loose. He lowered his head to where his hands were fastened to adjust his glasses.

"You're not going anywhere Mr. Ericsson so just settle in. Why did you go after our colleague Veronica? What did she ever do to break your heart, she doesn't know you?" Yari finished.

"When dinosaurs walked this earth, volcanoes were erupting on the moon. I didn't go after Veronica, well, she intrigued me after our second conversation. That guy she dated before is a whore. I think that's why she's still alive. Her self-punishment is torture enough. That Detective Cole Kennedy isn't a good guy. I bumped into him a while back, but he was oblivious, people with narcissistic traits often are." Dexter finished.

"So, you didn't kill her, but why did you take the lives of the other women, we now have the number of victim's up to thirteen?" Yari sat forward and opened the file of information collected of previous victims. She laid the first few autopsy pictures out in front of him.

"Did she break your heart?" Vania pushed a picture forward. Her long ponytail dangled down toward the picture, almost close enough for Dexter to be able to touch it. She wanted to see his response.

"How about her, she walked away from you too? Is that why you dismember their fingers and other extremities so they can never run from you?" She sat back and stared at him.

Dexter looked up at the overhead lights and then over her shoulder, into the double mirror.

"It's not going to be that simple, to get an indictment against me. You have no concrete proof. I only delivered flowers and had online contact. There's nothing to tie me to," he paused again to look at the photos on the table placed just out of his reach. He raised his shoulders as if making a revelation.

"You said thirteen murders? I don't know that number doesn't sound too lucky. Are you sure thirteen is correct? Did you know that the only letter that doesn't appear in the periodic table is "J" like Everett Clark's middle name? He's actually a good inspector, but terrible at family matters. Is it a wonder that his ex-wife is dating a woman now? She ran away from that mess."

Yari had not known any of the information that she was just told by a serial killer. None of that mattered, she needed to get him to slip up, but the longer the conversation went, Yari felt like he was simply spinning her.

The three taps on the mirror was a sign for her to leave him alone. Yari pulled the photos back into the folder and closed it. She left the folder on the table and exited the interview room.

When she walked into the space on the other side of the mirror with the rest of the group, she felt relief knowing everyone else was just as confused as she was.

"He's been studying us, how the hell does he know about Robbi and Sam when I just found out not long ago?" Everett asked out loud.

"Yeah and why did he call me a whore?" Cole asked.

"Because you are Cole." Malcolm spoke up. He had created a program to trace the contacts of those killed from the social media site and came across Dexter's erased messages from several accounts. He wasn't sure how the program would stand up in a court of law, and if it didn't then everything, they found would be fruit from the poisonous tree.

"Well that's beyond the point, we have him slipping GHB into Veronica's drink." Cole said.

"We have him with items identical to those found on each of the victims." Vania added.

Everett stared through the glass at Dexter. He looked more like a predator than a man.

"He stalked Veronica, even at the risk of being caught. Was it the adrenaline that had him deliver flowers inside of a police station? Did each murder provide him with the rush like an addiction?" Malcolm mumbled to himself.

"Let him sit until we hear back from Cleveland." Captain Montgomery advised but Everett disagreed.

"He can sit after Cole goes in. Clearly, he has a disdain for Cole, let's see how that pans out sir."

ADA Jefferson thought it wise but was also concerned that Cole not become combative.

"Don't let him handle you Detective." She watched him walk out of the door.

"That last bit was not necessary Stephanie." The captain responded in kind.

Everett was concerned about his partner. He knew why Cole broke it off with Veronica; he had started having feelings for her. Something he wasn't accustomed to and he forced her out of his life while spending time with Rachel and her girlfriend. It was all mutual between the three of them, and Everett knew his partner would keep it simply fun.

Now, he was going to be sitting across from a stone-cold murderer. A serial killer who quite possibly knew more about Cole; the entire team for that matter, than they did of him.

"Malcolm, pay close attention and see if there are any clues Dexter let's out, let's see if that brain of yours can help get this guy." Captain Montgomery nodded toward the chief forensic specialist.

Vania walked closer to the mirror and turned the volume up on the intercom system as Cole entered the interview room with Dexter.

The tension was immediately felt as the two of them met eyes. The sound of the chain around Dexter's ankle was the only indication of movement.

"I see you're admiring your handy-work Mr. Ericsson." Cole used a sarcastic tone as he sat down opposite of Dexter.

Dexter made no facial expression, although his eyes impressed upon Cole that he didn't appreciate his words.

"A lesser man would've taken that as an insult. Your team is watching you right now, does that make you nervous? Are you going to say something witty to overcompensate? You think you're charming, but you aren't; at least according to Veronica." Dexter smirked. His hair was more grey than brown, but his eyes were dark as night.

Cole picked up one of the victim's photos and studied it.

"What were you compensating for when you killed Kara Timmons? Did she see through your online persona when you met in real life?" Cole shot back the same level of insult to see how Dexter would take it. If he felt he was being challenged, perhaps there would be space to chip away at him.

Dexter laughed uncontrollably.

"Very good, very good, Cole. You aren't just some behemoth who wanted to grow up to be a cop all your life. But here's the thing, I have no recollection of who that woman is. It's a shame that she died."

Dexter looked at a photo closest to Cole.

"She looks like Veronica, don't you think? Milky white complexion, and skin radiant and bright like the Dog Star, Sirius A. But you weren't serious about Veronica were you Michael, because you didn't treat her like a star but like a dog. You wanted her to come when you called. I think she sees through you now. The red-haired woman, she's not like Veronica, is she? Did you know that a single strand of spaghetti is called a spaghetto Detective Kennedy?"

"You see that's the thing about being an adult. The ability to make decisions and choices. It seems like someone left you and you didn't understand her choice. Removing body parts, was that part of taking a trophy, or just a childish way of thinking they could never leave you? Is it some type of weird fetish you have? You talk about my friendships with women, the openness of it all. To put it plainly; they choose me." Cole saw Dexter clinching his fingers the longer he talked. Cole had struck a nerve.

"So why did these women deserve to die, why did you kill them?" Cole laid a few of the autopsy and forensic pictures out in front of Dexter again.

Dexter's eyes traveled from one picture to the next. He tried to reach out and touch the photos, but Cole purposefully left them just out his range.

"This group of women seemed to be exceptional, but their eyes are lonely. Their wings have been clipped. Did you know that a group of crows are called a murder? Kind of an oxymoron don't you think Detective Cole Kennedy." Dexter sat back in his chair and stared at Cole.

"Why did you kill them?" Cole asked straightforwardly.

The overhead lights flickered in the room before the door swung open.

"That's enough for now." A slender pale-skin man walked in, followed by Captain Montgomery and D.A. Jefferson. He wore a smoked gray blazer with faded blue jeans and black wing tipped shoes. His half-framed glasses were black, with what appeared to be clear extenders to help hold them in place about his ears.

Everett stood in the doorway and nodded for Cole to exit.

"It's about time that the adults get to talking Detective Kennedy. A donkey will sink in quicksand, but a mule won't." Dexter laughed as Captain Montgomery closed the door behind Cole.

"This fucker is getting the needle..." Cole paused as Malcolm approached.

"How does he know so much about us? Have we been hacked?" Cole finished.

"I'm sure Veronica unknowingly shared bits about each of us, but Dexter Ericsson is a genius psychopath, and we need to have every T crossed and each I dotted. He has a contingency plan plus another contingency plan I have no doubt." Malcolm had seldom met an adversary that rattled him, but he recognized the evil monster in Dexter. Although they had his fingerprints on the vases at the victim's homes, he was a delivery man. They had strong circumstantial evidence, but they needed to show he was present at the times of death.

Movement over his shoulder had him shift slightly as Travis and Vania exited the viewing room and approached them.

Agent Yari walked out of the Captain's office with another uniformed officer.

Travis waved her down.

"Yari, thank you. I wish we could tell you how he knows so much about all of us. We are going to make sure he has no accomplices." Travis couldn't determine why the uniformed officer was accompanying Yari.

"How's Veronica doing?" Yari asked. She helped protect Veronica after they were certain the lab assistant was in danger.

"She's holding up." Vania touched Yari on the shoulder as an indication of empathy.

"He is too smug, and I don't like the feeling that he has something else up his sleeve. You two build a timeline of his location since the first victim." Everett nodded toward the younger partners.

"We're on it." Travis replied before walking away with Vania.

"Malcolm, I need you to video conference between all the other forensic departments and learn if there are any anomalies that seemed minimal or were overlooked. Dexter Ericsson is going to be held accountable and pay for each life he's taken." Everett was focused. By the time his team was done, the case would be so airtight, there would be no wiggle room.

"Yari can you reach out to your FBI contact to help us get a geofence warrant for any electronic, Bluetooth, wireless devices in those areas around TOD?" Everett wasn't Yari's supervisor and this was the reason he formed it as a question.

"Most definitely I can. I'll update you shortly." Yari excused herself and walked to Vania and Travis' desk to say goodbye.

"His attorney got down here awfully fast. Let's see who this joker is, and I don't mean what we find in the database." Everett addressed Cole.

Cole was feeling something unfamiliar. He thought about Dexter's words and wondered how much; if any, was true. Veronica did deserve better from him, but he never discarded her.

"Yeah, who is this guy?" Cole agreed as his phone rang.

"Howard in Cleveland, tell me you guys found something." Cole put the call on speaker and waited eagerly to hear any good news.

"We think he has another victim somewhere still alive. There's a feed into one of his computers and it's showing a woman tied down and unable to speak because she's been gagged." The voice relayed.

Everett looked at Cole and shook his head.

"Howard can you repeat what you just said?" Everett asked.

Howard repeated what he said and added that there's no indication of her location, and his cyber unit ran multiple traces on the IP address, but Dexter has made it so that it could not be pinpointed.

Everett left Cole to finish the call with Howard, abruptly returning to the interview room with the suspect, both attorneys and Captain Montgomery.

"Have you advised your legal representative that you have another victim who is still alive? Yes, that's right Dexter we found your second home in Cleveland with the live feed. Who is she and where is she?" Everett slammed his hands into the table causing a loud echo in the room.

"Detective I've advised my client not to talk, and if you persist you violate his rights." The pale-skin attorney was cut off by ADA Jefferson.

"Mr. Monroe let me make this clear; if there is a woman who is alive right now and dies as a consequence of your unwillingness to cooperate in saving her life, I will make sure that disbarment is the least of your worries."

Mr. Monroe wasn't willing to back down.

"Threatening my livelihood or perhaps even my life doesn't suit you prosecutor. I need to converse with my client." He finished. If there was an ongoing criminal act, he knew the District Attorney had leverage.

"That's good, you have an imaginative mind Mr. Monroe. We are going to leave you to speak with your client and confirm or deny the detective's information. You will share all information pertinent the ongoing investigation." ADA Jefferson stood from the table and walked out of the interrogation room followed by Captain Montgomery and Everett.

"I'm not trying to cut any deals with that piece of shit. I'd inject him if I could, but we have a woman out there that needs saving. She is our priority." The Assistant District Attorney bid farewell before making calls to her appropriate constituents. She would need to have a conversation with The Mayor, but more importantly the States Attorney General. The Death Penalty was not coming off the table.

$\mathcal{S}$eRIOusLY?

Vania's attitude was more abrasive than usual, so Travis half-heartedly listened to her vent.

"She could've been killed because Cole couldn't be straight up with her." Vania said as a matter of fact.

Travis was unsure where those words came from, but he knew Dexter Ericsson was the only person responsible for causing any harm.

"I wouldn't say all of that. Veronica and Cole had whatever they had."

"Cole was playing work husband and then more than that outside of work. He reeled her in just like all the others. He had no intent of giving her what she wanted after she expressed 'what' she wanted." Vania didn't mince her words.

"They're adults V.A., and that's how I see it." Travis wasn't going to let Vania's personality silence his opinion when he felt strongly about this subject.

Vania felt strongly about her position but realized Travis didn't need to be the brunt of it.

"The subpoena covers everything, every property and vehicle. Every bank account is subject to discovery. Let's take a road trip. There's nothing we can do without access to his computers and files. Clear it with Everett and I'll drive up and you can drive back. I don't necessarily enjoy driving on the highway at night." Vania excused herself to make a phone call while Travis sought out Everett to get approval to drive to Cleveland, Ohio.

"That's a good idea, I'll make the call." Everett agreed with the younger detective's plan. He paused to gain Travis' undivided attention.

"Everything matters. As much as you are anal about our paperwork, be as diligent with your documentation. Take no shortcuts, we have another woman we need to locate."

Travis shook his head in agreement before retrieving the information they had already compiled with the help of other law enforcement agencies.

"V.A. we got the green light and we have a liaison to meet in the next two hours, so we need to hit the road. I want to nail this bastard to the wall. Not only for Veronica, but for the sanctity of our team."

Vania wasn't sure what he meant 'for the sanctity of our team", but she had her own reasons for wanting to help make the case against, 'The Heartbreak Murderer' as he had been named in the news media.

"Yeah I'm with you, this motherfucker is not getting off."

They decided to walk down the few flights of stairs to the garage. Vania no longer showed any residual signs of her concussion, so as she took two steps down at a time, Travis was not concerned.

Vania had become somewhat of a celebrity as portions of her berating the officer the night of her car crash went viral.

"Next thing you know, you'll be the spokesperson and poster child for Columbus." Travis chuckled. He was proud of her, although at times he worried that her ambition to live up to her family's name put her in harmful circumstances.

"I don't want any limelight, just to catch the worst of the worst. We can pop the cherries and inform the counties, so we don't get stopped." Vania opened the door to exit into the underground garage.

"Keys." Travis called out tossing the car keys to her.

"I thought I left them..." Vania was responding when a voice called out to them. Malcolm was running them down. He wore all black, with a black Oakley BG Game Visor; a very different attire than his usual flamboyant outfits.

"Hey, take this with you. It will help break down any password on his devices." He handed Travis a small plastic container with a USB drive.

"All you have to do is plug it in and we will get anything on the drive that has been erased too. He's a psychopath, a genuine, genius psychopath." Malcolm seemed loss in thought momentarily.

Travis wasn't sure if he was admiring Dexter or showing more concern than usual.

"Dexter won't be able to outsmart all of us. His ass is already cuffed. Lawyer or no lawyer he is done." Vania had certainty in her voice.

Malcolm shook his head in a disapproving manner.

"No V.A., do you think he didn't know we'd find his homes? Do you think leaving the live stream of the woman for us to find was a mistake on his part? He knows things about our team, that even our team doesn't know. He's been toying with us this whole time; from Agent Yari's interview to Cole's pissing match with him, he controlled the whole thing. Those little random facts, each one, were true. Were they also clues for us? Does that feel like he's done?" Malcolm took a heavier tone with the young detective.

"You have a point; we can call once we get up to Cleveland." Travis was heading off Vania's rebuttal fearing her previous animosity about Veronica and Cole was escalating again.

"Be careful." Malcolm said and slowly turned to walk away.

Vania was caught off guard, but she called out to the forensic specialist.

"Malcolm, do you remember those random facts? I mean can you tell us so we can write them down. You do have a point. If he's as calculative as you say, then you're absolutely right, we need to slow down." Vania spoke out to halt him.

Travis had not expected her to respond in that matter.

"The unicorn." Travis began to say.

"The unicorn is the national animal of Scotland." Malcolm answered looking upward as if recalling the previous interview.

"The periodic table does not contain the letter J, and a donkey sinks in quicksand, but a mule won't." Malcolm finished as Vania wrote each random fact into her small notepad.

"Thank you." Vania said with humility before catching up to Travis who was walking towards their vehicle. She pulled her baseball cap down further on her head.

"So, you can bite your tongue huh, VA?" Travis looked across the top of the car towards his partner.

Vania met his eyes.

"Shut up T." She shook her head back and forth and opened her car door. She started the car and turned the volume down on the radio.

"If you must know, my grandfather always says that when the smartest person in the room has a hunch, listen to them." Vania strapped her seatbelt on and put the car in reverse.

"So why don't you listen to me more often?"

"You just answered your own question T." she answered.

"I'd pay to see your standup routine VA."

They both laughed uncontrollably. This was the first moment in over two days that humor had surfaced.

$\mathcal{S}$eRIOusLY?

Malcolm knew this was just an act for Dexter Ericsson. He had something else planned. He felt it in his soul. He walked into the forensic department still thinking about the random facts.

Sheldon was standing in front of a white board with papers in his hand. He was double checking the corresponding location of each victim against the time of their death. His lanky frame had not moved in over ten minutes.

Malcolm saw another two technicians working on something under a microscope in one of the sterile laboratories inside the department.

"Veronica is loved by everyone." A freckle faced intern startled Malcolm from his thoughts. She was a senior at a local college. Her college professor and Malcolm had worked a few high-profile cases when Malcolm was up and coming in the field.

"Yes, Veronica is loved by many Ms. Tolls. What do you have for me?" Malcolm saw the promise in her because she had learned to think outside the box. He was teaching her how to erase the box until the box no longer existed.

"We spent hours trying to figure out how he got access to their computers remotely. We couldn't find any hacks or trace programs until we looked closer at the dating website, they were all on. It looks like he hacked into their system making it look like it was the dating company running routine programs. I'm finishing a test now in the bindings used on our victims." She finished.

"Good job Beverly, update me with any new findings." Malcolm responded as he checked his watch.

"If you will excuse me." He walked to his office and logged into the video conference with two of the other three forensic experts in the case.

"Lady and gentleman, we have Dexter Ericsson in custody. We have dispatched two detectives to assist our Cleveland connections. This suspect is highly intelligent, so we need to be extremely diligent." Malcolm said as he looked at his counterparts.

"I've re-evaluated the timeline of my victims. There is trace evidence of cocaine in their systems that I found after running a new hair follicle test, but it's so minute, my only concern is if it was cut with something to inhibit judgement." Dr. Lei Umbrect shared what she could. Her lab wasn't as extensive as the ones Malcolm worked in, but she was a forensic criminalist and pathologist that he respected.

"We are also running those tests." Brad Conners, who specialized in forensic toxicology interjected.

"I've got the samples you both sent and I'm running them through my program. What I found in the blood surrounding the dismembered appendages seems to have been injected with a local anesthetic to dull the pain. These women were alive when he removed their fingers and toes. Sick bastard, if the conclusion is true by counting their appendages, as I suspect; then the victim list is much higher."

Malcolm stared into his computer screen comprehending what he just heard.

"So, he wanted them to be completely aware of what he was doing to them? Besides the dulling agent, have you determined the length of time between removing their toes and the strangulation?" Lei asked. She stood up and exited the viewing screen to return with a file in her hand.

"There were trace amounts of GHB in my second victim's system. How lucky we were to have her sister find the body less than ten hours from time of death. Unfortunately, the shelf life is so fast, this is the only evidence I have relating to this." Lei scanned the file a second time.

"Has your analysis given us a signature on the GHB, can we use your findings if we get a hit in Cleveland?" Malcolm asked.

"That shouldn't be a problem, I have the levels of toxicology for this sample." Lei finished.

"Good, good, let's reconvene tomorrow morning after my team investigates his home and life in Cleveland." Malcolm said his goodbyes and returned to Sheldon's side for an update.

"The tests and analysis are being done and in progress. I won't let anything go unnoticed. This evil man was going to kill our colleague and for that he must pay." Sheldon showed more emotion than usual.

"How is Ms. Veronica?" He asked.

No one had spoken to Veronica since the ordeal began. Agent Yari had been the closest contact. Veronica was being guarded in an unknown location.

"From what I gather, she's still managing. It has to be unnerving to be on the other side of an investigation..." Malcolm paused looking for more accurate words but Sheldon being his stoic self, added to the conversation.

"To nearly becoming a victim in the investigation. Especially, this one." Sheldon excused himself and Malcolm went back to work; looking at some of the initial testing to determine if his victims in Columbus had indications of what Lei had shared. Malcolm felt good about how the information was coming together, but a small voice in his head kept him aware that Dexter Ericsson was leading them down the rabbit hole.

SeRIOusLY?

Pressure had mounted from multiple directions once the media ran stories of the victims. Special investigative reporting increased with national coverage crews moving into the city. The Captain handled all the questions to leave his detectives insulated to do their job.

Cole looked over a file as he sat opposite of Captain Montgomery, who sat upright in his chair reading an email from city hall.

Everett paced the Captain's office and it was making Captain Montgomery feel uneasy.

"Sit down or stop moving so much, I can't think Clark."

Everett looked at Captain Montgomery and realized he in fact was also feeling uneasy.

"Sorry Cap. There are so many loose ends surrounding this case. Having the same type of rope and candles is at minimal... minimum. We can confirm that he bumped into Cole. Which gives him an alibi for the eighth murder." Everett got interrupted by Cole.

"But that time of death isn't set in stone. The lab is double checking everything, and once VA and Travis update us with the evidence in 216, we can add it to the equation." Cole took his hand to rub his temples with his thumb and middle finger. His headache was a combination of stress and lack of caffeine.

Everett understood where his partner was coming from, but he hated feeling like he was playing from behind, trying to catch up with whatever Dexter had done and planned.

"There has to be a way to determine the video stream, we can't even determine if the woman is North, South or here in our city. I need to speak with The Chief, the Mayor has been riding her ass and she's been up my shit. After this call it's going to run downhill to you. Get me something, anything we can work with." The Captain had protected his team from the higher ups, but he needed his team to step up like they always had. With the public's concern high about a serial killer traveling up and down the Ohio highways, people were on high alert.

Everett and Cole walked out of the captain's office. The buzz in the office had escalated from the moment Agent Yari had called in that she had a suspect who tried to use roofies against Veronica.

Dexter's apprehension went without escalation. He obliged them without resistance and maintained his innocence the entire time.

Cole's cell phone went off.

"I need to take this." Cole walked away to have his phone conversation.

Everett saw Rachel Jenkins photo when the call came through. Everett had no skin in the game when it came to Cole's love life, but if any of what Dexter had said in the interview earlier was true, Cole was the reason Veronica was still alive. Ironically Cole's lack of commitment to a woman he truly cared for is what spared her life.

Everett walked to his desk and sat down. There were messages from Robbi on his work voicemail. He had not taken any of her calls because he was busy, also because he wasn't prepared to discuss her personal life, and how Dexter knew these things about his ex-wife. He leaned back in his desk chair and stared up at the ceiling before calling Robbi back.

"I've been swamped at work Robbi, are you and the kids ok?" Everett asked waiting to see how loudly he was going to be yelled at.

"We are fine, they're both sitting down doing their homework. Why is there a cruiser sitting across the street?" She answered him and asked her own question. She had not yelled at him, and was concerned about his well-being, but he needed to tell her what had transpired earlier in the day.

"The serial killer." Everett began to speak but was interrupted.

"The Broken Heart Killer?" She asked.

"Yeah, the murderer of thirteen women, that we know of so far. Well, he stalked Veronica, and if it wasn't for an agent we work with, she would've been killed. The black and white is for you and the kid's protection." Everett didn't want to go deeper into detail.

"Our protection, what's going on E?" She asked.

Everett decided to reveal what he could

"This guy knew about you and Sam. I thought Sam was a guy. Have you noticed anything strange Robbi? How well do you know this Sam?" Everett paused because he knew he had not asked the question he really wanted.

"When were you going to tell me that Sam is a woman?" He asked flatly.

The ensuing silence on the phone seemed forever.

"Yeah I wanted to tell you. This is all so new to me. I'm not sure how I feel about it all, but I do enjoy her company." Robbi waited for a response from Everett. She knew it took a lot for him to bring it up because it was personal.

"The cruiser will remain until we know for sure he does not have an accomplice. I need you to be very observant of your surroundings. Kiss the kids and tell them I love them." Everett ended the call. He leaned back in his and exhaled.

Cole had returned to his desk while Everett spoke with Robbi to share information.

"Dexter Ericsson doesn't have much of a background. No parking or speeding tickets. No criminal history. If Yari had not caught him stalking Veronica, I wouldn't be sure he was the guy."

"So, him telling you how shitty of a dating man you are isn't accurate? Or how Veronica gave you more than you deserved?" Everett's emotions didn't help him bite his tongue.

"E, I'm not sure what's going on with you, but my love life is my love life and I'm sure you're the last person I should take relationship advice from." Cole rebutted.

They stared at each other intensely before the elevator door opened and ADA Jefferson stepped back into their department.

"Gentlemen, follow me." She said as she walked toward Captain Montgomery's office.

Everett pushed his chair back without looking at Cole. He knew he had made it personal with Cole and it really wasn't what had him upset. The safety of his family was weighing on him but having his business about his ex-wife dating a woman released to his coworkers, boss and DA's office was rubbing him the wrong way. He kept his personal stuff close to his vest.

Cole let what Everett said slide for the time being. It wasn't enough to hear Dexter call him out, but to know his partner agreed with Dexter didn't sit well.

When they walked into the office ADA Jefferson took the lead.

"I've been in a pissing match with both Cincinnati and Cleveland DA's office. They are trying to make a case about trying him in their localities first. I advised them that the first known murder in the string of events happened in Franklin County, and that we have him in custody." The emerald green pant suit she wore was rich. Her diamond studded earrings were visible; not only because of their 2-carat size, but because her micro-braids were pulled back revealing her profile. She paused to address Everett.

"These detectives that you've been working with outside of Columbus, do you trust them?" She asked plainly.

Everett had only met Howard at a convention over two years ago but had kept in touch periodically as they both still served in the reserves with similar designations.

"I trust him to do his job. We have a decent professional relationship." He answered.

"Well let's hope it stays that way. I'm sure he's going to get a call to limit Detective Aguilar and Travis. I have a call with the Attorney General and there's no indication what her thoughts are on the subject. Work fast." She looked at her watch.

"I have to go boys, keep me abreast of where the investigation is leading." She picked up her attaché case from one of the chairs across from the Captains desk and exited.

"Have you heard from the B- squad yet?" The Captain asked.

"Not yet sir, we wanted them to get brought up to speed from the Cleveland findings. One of us will phone them within the hour." Everett concluded. He was just an anxious to get something new.

Cole had been more reserved than normal, and the Captain sensed it.

"The truth can be difficult to accept, but it remains the truth. If you want a new truth, you have to change behavior." He paused to let his words sink into both partners.

"Now get me something I can use to stop this social media ridiculousness."

$\mathcal{S}$eRIOusLY?

The moment was tense. Vania couldn't curtail her emotions and the sharpness in her voice was meant to offend the two officers in the Cleveland office who stood in their way. The eyes of other detectives fell to them from the desks spread out through the space.

"What do you mean we can't have access? We got the computer open and we have the suspect. What the hell is going on?" Vania couldn't understand the shift in working together with the detectives in Cleveland. Searching the home and sharing information went smoothly. Once they returned to the office, that sense of brotherhood had been lost.

Travis was standing by her side as they faced down two detectives that had not been at the suspects house. Personalities notwithstanding, the energy felt like they were simply following orders.

"I don't know how you guys do it in Columbus, but we do follow our command." One of the two Cleveland detectives answered with an attitude.

"How the fuck are you gon talk to us about command? Without us, those electronics would still be locked. This is why I told her we shouldn't trust..."

"Ok, let's take a breath. Everybody just relax for a second. It's not on them, it seems our District Attorney wants to garner the limelight." Howard stepped in to lessen the tension.

The two detectives who had confronted Travis and Vania turned and walked back to their desks.

"What's that got to do with us just taking a look at it? We aren't trying to take it. Shit, you can sit there with us and share the findings. We are the ones who got it open." Travis returned to being rational in his usual manner, but Vania was irritated.

"This is bullshit Howard and you know it. We drove up here under the assumption that we would be fully cooperating with each other. All of these murders span the state and we have to work together." She watched Howard's partner walk away with one of the forensic technicians.

"It's not up to me." Howard wanted to help in any way he could, but there was no way he'd go against the order of his boss.

"Let's go, these asshats aren't budging." Vania walked towards the glass door exit, bumping into Howard on purpose.

"This ain't right and you know it." Travis shook his head and caught up with his partner.

When they returned to their vehicle Vania made a decision.

"My mom's house is like fifteen minutes from here. Let's go regroup, I'm sure she has something cooked up and if not, she'll still feed us."

Travis had never heard much about her mother, he simply listened when she vented about her grandfather not being supportive about her career path.

"There's a woman that needs to be saved and they want to play politics. I only like Cleveland's sports teams." Travis opened his door and sat back. He was frustrated.

The neighborhood Vania's mother's home was in looked like a suburban copy of every other middle-class family.

She pulled into a long, paved driveway that wrapped partially around the back of the home.

A picnic table sat in the backyard, with two men sitting at it. Not too far from it was a custom-made stone BBQ pit.

"Those are my cousins; they check on my mom constantly." Vania pulled the keys from the ignition.

"So, they're cousin-brothers, got it." Travis got out.

One was slender and stood about Vania's height; the other was overweight, bald and a little shorter than Travis.

249

"Yo, this is my partner Travis. That's Marcos and the bald one is Jorge."

Travis threw his hand up in acknowledgment and continued following Vania into the home.

A two-vehicle carport extended from the home where they entered. The home, all-white with blue trim and blue shutters was spacious. Vania's cousins took on the responsibility when her father died from cancer when she was nine years old. They took pride in helping her mother maintain the property.

"Take your shoes off." Vania advised before she was ambushed by her mother. A splitting image of what Vania would look like in twenty years. She was a few inches shorter with the same build.

"Mija, you should have told me you were coming." Her mother greeted her with a huge hug.

"You must be Travis, my Vanilita tells me you are the best partner she's ever had." She greeted Travis with an equivalent embrace.

"Come in, come in. I have something I'm cooking right now. You have to eat before you leave."

"Thank you so much." Travis followed behind the two women. It felt good to be recognized as her best partner.

She had been his only partner, so there was no measuring stick for him.

They had to pass by the kitchen to enter the living room.

"Senora Aguilar, it smells really good." Travis couldn't help complimenting her. His taste buds were watering.

"Thank you so much, I hope it tastes as good as it smells. How long are you staying mija?" She asked as Travis and Vania sat down in separate recliners.

"Not long mama, the detectives aren't playing nice, well the DA's office isn't. We drove up thinking we were sharing everything about this case. They only computer that got opened was the one Travis had a program for." Vania tried not to show how much she was frustrated but her mother knew her child.

"I'm sure it's all going to work out mija," She kissed Vania on the forehead.

"Let me finish this food." She walked into the kitchen. Her black capri pants were freshly ironed and the V-Neck, Women's Cavaliers T-Shirt with logo fit perfectly against her frame.

"Vanilita, ok, ok." Travis smirked.

"I need to call Everett. He's not going to be happy." Travis reaches for his cell phone.

"No, not until after we eat. I don't want to ruin my appetite." Vania made a strong suggestion to her partner.

"Agreed." Travis saw a photo album under the coffee table mixed in with magazines.

He sat at the edge of his recliner and pulled it out.

"It's ok?" He motioned towards it.

"Uh no, don't nobody need to see how much of a tomboy I was." She tried to get it back from him when her mother walked back into the living room.

"Travis, let me show you how beautiful Vania was." She grabbed the album and opened it.

Vania gasped and left the room when her mother sat down next to him.

Her mother shared a few pages before leaving him with the album to make their plates.

"Mija, la comida esta lista."

Vania interrupted her mother acting like she was affected from Travis seeing her as a child.

"Yo se, Yo se Mama."

They sat down and ate as Vania's mother said she needed to make a call.

Travis cleared his plate and was served a second when she returned.

"Pollo con arroz, empanadas and bacalao." Vania shared what each dish was called.

Travis smiled.

"Chicken with rice, pastry with meat and a fish dish. Heaven." He repeated in English.

"Ah, tu hablas espanol." Her mother was impressed.

"Just enough to get by." He answered.

Vania stared at him and wondered why he had never told her.

Travis sensing her question, answered before she asked.

"It never came up VA." He left it at that.

"My Vania speaks four different languages too." She smiled at her daughter with pride.

"Now I have to make a phone call." He took his plates and rinsed them off before walking into the living room.

"Travis, he's a good man. He has a good energy mija." She walked to the sink and placed the dishes into the dishwasher.

"Ok, ok good news. We are back in good graces. I don't know what happened, but their captain called ours to apologize about being uncooperative. I think though, it had more to do with logging back into the computer. It shut them out and they need us again. This time, we set the rules." Travis had positivity in his voice.

"Mama, we have to go. I'm sorry." Vania pushed back from the table and hugged her mother.

Travis repeated the action and followed behind Vania to put his shoes on.

Once outside, he smelled the marijuana in the air.

"Really?" Vania said towards her cousins.

"It's for my glaucoma prima." Jorge said while Marcos laughed loudly.

The drive back on I-90 was slow due to stop and go traffic. Travis concluded that rush hour traffic was not the same everywhere.

Howard was waiting for them when they entered back into the Cleveland department.

"The Captain wanted to see us before we get back to our joint investigation." He led them into his captain's office.

"Now that we have lawyers out of the way, we need you to get back into that computer. Howard and his partner will assist. Everything is shared." Howard's captain directed the last portion to Howard before he dismissed them all.

SeRIOusLY?

Yari showed her credentials to the officers as she exited the elevator. The DA's office decided it best to keep Veronica under police protection; being the only known witness that could testify once the case proceeded in court. The hotel had history. It was built over a half century ago. Over the years it had been refurbished with both minor and major upgrades, but the essence of The Grand would never be erased.

The deep mahogany walls held the memories of countless ages and the energy remained light.

Yari walked the corridor. As she approached the room Veronica occupied, she saw another officer at the far end of the hall guarding the emergency exit.

She knocked three times, and then another three times.

The door finally opened with Veronica in the door frame. Yari could tell she had been crying.

Veronica hugged her and then allowed her to enter. She locked the door and put the latch across the top.

"How are you holding up?" Yari thought it best to ease into dialogue, to let Veronica set the pace of any discussion.

The room was larger than Yari expected. It had a full kitchen with a microwave. A half refrigerator was situated neatly against the wall. A small square table with two chairs was available in the space to eat. A loveseat and couch were pushed back against the wall with a small coffee table as they walked further into the hotel room. A large king-sized bed could be seen in the reflection of a mirror opposite the room they sat.

"I'm, I'm grateful." Veronica finally answered. Her blue-eyes showed she had been crying.

Yari had no doubt, had she been the target of a serial killer, she too would be emotional.

"I'm grateful too. The odds of me being at the same restaurant, at the same time your date pours GHB into your drink." Yari slowed down because she could feel herself become more animated.

"I had no idea, none. He seemed perfect online, witty and he listened. Yari, I...I told him personal stuff, more than I should have." Veronica rocked forward on the couch and began to bite her nails. Her blonde hair was pulled into a ponytail. She wore a white t-shirt and light blue shorts that matched the color of her eyes.

"It's ok, none of that matters. What matters most is that you, you are safe. That we have his ass locked up." Yari didn't want to go into details with her, she had a lot to deal with.

Veronica stood up and walked into the kitchen. She came back with a box of donuts and carafe of coffee.

"When I get nervous." She said offering Yari her choice of pastry.

"When I'm on my cycle." Yari laughed causing Veronica to smile in return.

Veronica poured two cups of coffee and sat back down and crossed her legs on the couch.

"How's Cole?" She stared into her coffee cup.

Yari had thought about a few topics she wanted to steer clear of on her drive to the hotel. This was one of them.

"Everett and Cole are following up on some loose ends. You know Everett won't let this go down any other way than Dexter Ericsson going to jail forever and if we are lucky; the needle."

"I appreciate you; I mean your way of giving me what I needed to hear. I didn't know that I had fallen in love with Cole. I thought accepting his behavior, allowing him to come and go when he wanted was a way to prevent feelings from growing, but I fooled myself. Now I'm stuck in a hotel because I was having a self-pity party and needed attention."

People simply thought that Cole and Veronica were messing around, but the truth of the matter was, they had taken weeklong trips together and he had an item; a toothbrush at her residence. They had never said 'those three words', but Veronica had met his sister once over the past year. More than any other woman had since he was in college.

Yari interrupted her.

"Emotional splits, hate em." She then changed the subject.

"I can run to your place and grab some items if you need. I have no idea how long you have to be quarantined." Yari's fingers gave the signal of quotation when saying quarantined.

"Not that I can think of, I get tired and want to lay down, but then I get nervous because I see the news and social media calling him The Heartbreak Killer. Am I broken?" Veronica asked as she tugged on her ponytail.

The question caught Yari off guard, but she still gave an honest answer.

"Everyone is broken babe. In some small way or some big portion. A lot of us have had time to deal with the truth of ourselves." Yari got a text message for an update. She ignored it.

"I'll stop back later, Pizza or burgers? Don't worry I'll bring another box of donuts." Yari smiled.

Veronica smirked and ate the last bit of her donut.

"Ange's pizza, only Ange's pizza because I'm a pizza snob..." she paused.

"If any of the team wants to stop by and see me let them know it's ok." Veronica finished.

Yari understood who the message was really meant for.

"Ok, yeah I'll tell them."

They stood from the couch, Yari went to pick her coffee cup and napkin up to discard but Veronica said she'd take care of it.

"Ok cool, well I'll see you later. Hit me up if you need anything Ronnie."

Veronica shook her head and hugged Yari before unfastening the locks.

"Stay safe my friend." Veronica watched the door close behind her.

$eRIOusLY?

Sheldon and Malcolm were working with precision. Each sample they had was being run for their respective tests. Sheldon, for the first time in several months, was leading the way Malcolm needed him to.

"Ms. Tolls rerun the CRP and ANA." Sheldon called out.

Malcolm had begun background on Dexter Ericsson as soon as they had him in custody. His standard Google search only shared basic information. He reached out to an organization of information gatherers he used previously to hack into systems he couldn't legally.

"What the hell is a CRP and ANA?" Cole asked. He had walked in for an update after sitting at his desk.

"They're blood tests designed for auto immune deficiencies. Something didn't feel right when he was booked in. In his possession he had pills for people with certain genetic markers, but as we tested the blood from the glass at the restaurant, he has no reason for these pills." Malcolm finished.

"So why would he be in possession?" Cole started to ask but Malcolm cut him off.

"Cole, let us do our job and I will pass along our findings. Is the feed still live?" Malcolm asked in reference to the woman still yet to be found.

"Yeah, and we are no closer to her location...." Cole paused

"Last question and then I'll get out of your hair. Is there a second suspect, in your opinion Malcolm?"

Malcolm looked at Cole, calculating what his response should reveal in this moment.

He pulled Cole into his office and closed the door behind him.

"I've always thought there were more than one person. Why do you ask?" Malcolm walked to his file cabinet and pulled one out.

"There was a second feed that I found in the broadcast stream. The IP address I couldn't pinpoint, but I know what I know. While we were grilling Dexter, another source was found logging in to watch. I have put my hacker guy to try and trace it." Malcolm finished.

"So why are you now just telling us, don't you think we should have known..." Cole was frustrated.

"No, I don't think you should have known until I had more to offer. Listen Cole, I'm going to do my job and so will everyone else that you see." Malcolm hesitated as he nodded in the direction of all those working in his forensic lab.

"But your guilt is not helpful, I know you Cole. Focus and finish this case, if there is anything you can give Veronica right now, it is a case that leaves Dexter without a chance of seeing daylight again." Malcolm put the file back into his cabinet and locked it.

Cole thought about responding but understood he was in his feelings over Veronica. He said goodbye and walked out of the lab.

Malcolm received a message indicator that he received an email. When he opened it, there was an attachment with several videos of the victims being assaulted. Why he received these videos was a big question. Was someone trying to throw them off the trail they were on. Did Dexter Ericsson set this up to be emailed at a certain time? Malcolm had no answer, so he called two members he trusted to search for metadata imbued.

"Look at me, only I get the result of anything you find. Only me." He reiterated.

Malcolm knew this error was a huge mistake by whoever sent it. Not only did this email give a path to trace back to its origin, but the videos were sure to contain location information.

"Dexter, Dexter, Dexter, the walls are closing in and you have no idea." Malcolm thought before he forwarded the video to an outside source he trusted, one of his hacker associates.

Sheldon walked into Malcolm's office. His usual stoic disposition didn't accompany him, he was animated.

"Information from the blood tests, first, Dexter does not have an autoimmune deficiency. Second, the pills found are a new test drug and after speaking with the manufacturer, only a few hospitals have been included in the trial. The medication is being tested on patients exhibiting hearing loss from an Auto Immune Inner Ear Disease. One of the hospitals is in Cleveland." Sheldon finished.

"Good job Sheldon, good fucking job." Malcolm replied

"It was actually Ms. Tolls who went the extra yard. Now we just need to get access to the list of patients under the trial." Sheldon turned and walked out of the office.

Malcolm searched his white lab coat for his cell phone and called Everett to share the information.

"Hey, your partner just left but I have something you guys can tear into. Are you still in the office?" After Malcolm confirmed, he locked his computer and office door behind him before taking the stairs up to the Homicide department.

SeRIOusLY?

Travis pulled Vania away from the computer they still combed with Howard. They had been in touch with Everett, who had remotely been watching through Vania's Facetime capability on her phone, as they scavenged through Dexter's computer and other hard drives they could access.

"We need to go speak with a doctor at Cleveland Clinic, alone. How far are is it?" Travis asked.

Vania looked over her shoulder at Howard and his partner who kept going through the computer files.

Travis walked back into the media room, leaving Vania outside the space.

"We need to run and get some products for my partner, will be back shortly. If you turn the computer off, you're going to lose access until we get back." When Travis concluded he noticed the Cleveland detectives had barely looked up to listen. He walked back out and left the station to seek out answers about the trial drug testing.

Cleveland, Ohio contained two of the best leading medical facilities in the world. Everett was working with ADA Jefferson to build a warrant for the medical records, with only slight pushback from the District Attorney's office in Cleveland.

The specialty department inside the hospital had a minimal amount of people in it. Besides a younger couple sitting together, the only other person visible was the receptionist.

"Good afternoon, how can I help you?" Her short salt and pepper hair was the only indication that she was older than she looked. Her dark skin was smooth, like Travis', and her teeth bright white, she was pleasant to look at.

Travis words were caught in his throat.

Vania squinted at him recognizing he was about to stumble over his words, so she took the lead.

"I am Detective Aguilar, and this is my partner Detective White. We need to speak with Dr. Minsah."

The receptionist made a call to inform the Doctor, who walked out to greet both detectives.

"Detectives, I'm Dr. Minsah, how can I be of assistance?"

"Is there somewhere we can talk in private?" Travis asked.

Dr. Minsah ushered them into his office. He motioned them to sit as he walked around his desk to also sit.

"I've never had Detectives in my office, so this is a novelty. How can I help you?" Dr. Minsah's Eastern accent was strong.

"Dr., we are investigating a case where an experimental or trial drug has been found on the scene of a crime. We've spoken with the manufacturer and your name is associated with using it in your drug trials. The family classification is from something called methotrexate." Travis explained.

"Our office has been sampling new methods and a new antimetabolite antineoplastic agent is more than overdue. I've only used if in a sample size so far, for those who are beginning to transition with their auditory functionality." He pulled up something on his computer before reaching back into a file cabinet.

I will answer what questions I can, but specific patient's names I cannot share; doctor and patient confidentiality of course."

Vania debated on how much of their investigation they should share and if his information could help, she would do what we was necessary to secure it.

"How many patients have you used it on?" Vania asked.

"Only ten so far, but again these clients are fairly new. The second round of testing is still nine months away."

"Of those ten, can you say if any of them stick out. I mean when you think about the candidates, do any of them show signs of any personality disorders or anything like that?" Vania asked a second question.

Travis was unsure where his partner was headed but he let her stay the course.

"No, quite contrary. Most of them are humble as they learn about their autoimmune disease. For many of them learning that they may be losing their hearing. Well ..." he paused.

"There was one that pressed me, I mean initially he wasn't included in the original set for the trial until someone dropped out. It wasn't necessarily the patient, but his guardian so to speak, that wouldn't take no for an answer." Dr Minsah shook his head as if remembering said conversation.

"If I show you a photo, you can tell us if this is someone that you're familiar with. We aren't asking you if he's a patient- just your familiarity." Travis pulled a photo of Dexter Ericsson out and from the look on Dr. Minsah's face they knew he had seen Dexter before.

"I've seen him." He answered.

"Is he a patient?" Vania asked.

"I can confirm that HE, is not my patient." He paused and looked intently at both Detectives.

"Please, I need to know what's going on?"

"We can't fully discuss it, but what we can share is that there has been a substantial awareness on crimes committed up and down I71 and ..." Vania tried to reply before she was interrupted

"Are you saying The Heartbreak Killer, that he's the Heartbreak..." but Travis interjected

"We aren't at liberty, but to confirm, he's not a patient but he has been in your office before?" Travis asked.

"Yes, yes he has." Dr. Minsah replied as a knock on his door took their attention to it.

"Dr. Minsah these Detectives also have some questions for you." The receptionist walked Howard and his partner into Doctor Minsah's office.

"Thank you for everything, you've helped greatly." Travis and Vania stood up to leave.

"Don't go anywhere." Howard said as he handed Dr. Minsah a sheet of paper.

"This is a warrant for any information relating to your study." Howard's relayed leaving his partner in the office with Dr. Minsah.

"You two left us to follow up on this. My captain said to share everything." Howard had disappointment in his voice after they had worked together for most of the day.

"We didn't want to pull you away from breaking open the hard drives, we didn't need you holding our hands." Travis thought diplomacy best.

"Come on brother, that's not right. We both have skin in the game." Howard spoke lowly to not be overheard.

"Howard, I like you but that's about it. So, if you're Captain presses you, just tell him that in Columbus we follow a chain of command too." Vania made sure he understood that the altercation from earlier was still on her mind.

"Touché, I got you. Are we passed the pissing contest yet? Can we get this done together?" He asked.

Vania looked at Travis for direction.

"Yeah, let's finish this so we can get back. Dexter is done."

The three walked back into Dr. Minsah's office.

SeRIOusLY?

There was a constant air of focus in the forensics department. Sheldon was overseeing all the work. He had one small outburst when a technician took too long running samples. Malcom watched the entire space from his office. He opened a second program on his computer to run additional analysis.

"I got the file about an hour ago from the B squad, they should be headed back by now. I am still looking it over so be patient." Malcolm didn't have it in his personality to be micro-managed, but he knew this was different for everyone involved.

Out of respect, he took the third phone call from Everett. He had been looking at all the information on the test subjects from the Cleveland Clinic. The answer was in the details he was sure, but he just couldn't see the connection.

He stared through his glass pane into the lab. Everything his lab could test had been tested. Now analysis needed to be applied. He leaned back in his black leather swivel chair and looked upward towards the ceiling.

A knock on his door drew his attention. He ok'd their entrance.

"Agent Yari," He paused,

"Why don't you go by your last name, Andino, I've always wondered. Not that it matters to me per se, but I've always wondered why?" He greeted her with a handshake.

Yari shook her head and handed him the file in her hand.

"Dare to be different right? I just think the crimes I've dealt with in human trafficking are so personal and I want the families to know I take it personally." She finished.

"Interesting." Malcolm responded and opened the manila folder.

"The data from the geofence warrant for the locations, there are a few anomalies that have my attention. Do you have some type of 'wutchamakalit' to extrapolate it all?"

Malcolm's eyes lit up because anomalies meant the needle in the haystack had another possibility of being found.

"Actually, we do, follow me." Malcolm headed out of his office to approach a group of servers in a remote part of the lab. The equipment in this room seemed more up to date than even the upgrades the department had received.

"My work-space within the department." Malcolm scanned the information into the system.

"I have to get back to Veronica. She's doing ok before you even ask." Yari hesitated as she turned to leave.

"When you see Cole, tell him if he..." She prevented the next set of words from coming out and simply shook her head back and forth. She walked back through the lab and out.

Malcolm stared at the documents, but he couldn't determine anything until the program ran fully. He went back to his office and pulled up the footage of Dexter's earlier interview to watch. He watched repeatedly, but nothing new stood out. He ascertained that the random facts were just used to throw them off.

'Anything sinks in quicksand.' He thought back to what Dexter told Cole when he interviewed him. Malcolm saw the expression on Cole's face each time Dexter had mentioned Veronica. Self-doubt or hate was easily recognizable for Malcolm, because he had once been face-to-face with his own.

Dexter's lawyer's entrance didn't seem organic. He seemed out of sort. Malcolm rewound the footage again and watched Dexter wink when his lawyer walked in. Originally Malcolm believed it was to take one last shot at Cole, but after further review it was directed towards his attorney.

Malcolm watched it again, slowing down each frame and that's when he saw it.

"I got you, I got you both." Malcolm sat down in his leather desk chair and called Everett.

"I need you to come to my office now."

$\mathcal{S}$eRIOusLY?

Dexter Ericsson and his attorney set in the interrogation room full of themselves. The demands they placed on ADA Jefferson seemed reasonable for innocent men to be asking. The fact that the circumstantial evidence was great, did not guarantee a conviction. Dexter would plead to charges pertaining to the GHB and quite possibly 'hacking', but under no circumstances would he be pleading guilty to any murders or mutilation charges. In his words, he wasn't some type of 'sick puppy'.

Travis and Vania had just returned. Their trip back had been delayed as Vania took the opportunity to pick up Cleveland Style BBQ, after hearing Malcolm had solved the case, and Yari and the HT Squad had located the woman left alive. Malcolm's outside investigative source, Avery, had found the IP address hidden in the meta data and from that information, any device ever connected with the IP address had been identified. Yari and her team were onsite securing evidence.

"We waited on you two, without your investigation in Cleveland we wouldn't have gotten the last few pieces of the puzzle. Malcolm is bringing everyone up to date." Detective Jack was first to greet the two younger Detectives.

As Vania opened the door to the viewing room of interrogation ADA Jefferson and Malcolm were exiting.

"Good job you two. Now watch and learn." Malcolm said as he carried a laptop computer into the room with Dexter and his attorney.

"So, what say you?" They asked in unison.

"Funny you should ask, what say you?" Malcolm answered while he opened the computer.

"Your arrogance and believing you're the smartest person in the room was the first mistake you made. A small one, but nevertheless a mistake. Your second mistake was creating too many investigations." Malcolm ran down one more mistake before he started a program that disrupted hearing aids or equipment used to enhance sound.

The lawyer pulled his glasses off in discomfort and Malcolm had the final piece to put them both away.

"What the hell?" Dexter's attorney yelled out.

The look on Dexter's face said it all. The blood was draining out.

"Release my client, we don't have time for this." He said but Malcolm assured him that neither one of them would be leaving.

"Did you know that some cats are allergic to humans?" Malcolm paused as he brought up the feed to where the woman was found alive. He turned the screen towards the two men.

Their eyes flashed despair at the same time.

"You see we've been working the 71 corridors, just like you and your neophyte. None of this made sense until we discovered a trial medication at two of the locations. Your attorney has an autoimmune deficiency which causes hearing loss. But you already knew that, because it's been confirmed that you attended all his doctor visits at the Cleveland Clinic. We've already searched your home and office Mr. Monroe, and of course we've found the missing appendages. We've run Fingerprint analysis and low and behold, only two sets of prints match." Malcolm paused as ADA Jefferson stepped in.

"Neither one of them are ours, do you wanna take a guess who the other two belong to or whose cell phone was traced back to five of the locations?"

Dexter fidgeted in his chair while his attorney stood up to walk out of the door.

"This is ridiculous, more than that... it's outlandish." He opened the door to leave, but Cole was already standing in the frame to bar his exit.

Cole moved forward causing the attorney to back up before returning to his chair.

"Did you know that M&M's stands for Mars and Murrie?" Cole paused as he walked behind Dexter.

"Maybe I'll put an order on your commissary of M&M's to remind you that you almost got away. You and your lawyer are sick puppies."

ADA Jefferson enhanced the charges on both men before updating her counterparts in the other cities involved in the investigation.

Travis and Vania were speaking with Everett about the case. The food they had brought back sat patiently on their desks.

Yari and Cole disappeared to have a talk and had not returned yet.

"Malcolm, that my man, was precise." Everett dapped up Malcolm.

"Go after one of us and you go after all of us. I know y'all brought some back for me. Please tell me you brought some polish boys." Malcolm said as Vania handed him one of the smaller bags.

"This is fantastic". Malcolm found himself sitting at Coles desk while he ate a polish boy and wings with sauce.

"Yeah I can't lie, Cleveland Sports teams and this BBQ might be the only things I like about that city." Travis said.

They continued making small talk as they ate. The feeling of closing this case felt different; it was personal.

SeRIOusLY?

The lobby to the hotel wasn't as full as it had been. The legendary happy hour of top shelf liquors and live music was always a draw. The only requirement was a waitlist, unless you were one of the fifty people who held a lifelong membership. The who's who of the State frequented the bar of the hotel, to make deals, and listen to top notch musicians play in an elegant atmosphere.

The police officers nodded as the elevator doors opened.

"I brought you guys one too. I hope you like pepp."

The officers took the large box and said thank you.

"Your hands are full let me knock on the door. Thanks again." The Officer said.

The door opened slowly.

I coulda sense thee pizza..." Veronica said in an Italian style voice; but the words stuck in her throat when she looked out. Veronica stood in the doorway completely caught off guard.

"I heard you were hungry. Can I come in?" Cole asked.

$\mathcal{S}$eRIOusLY?

Chapter Seven

BLAST FROM THE PAST

Captain Montgomery set in his chair and stared out the window of his office. He arrived early to prepare for his meeting with Internal Affairs who were investigating allegations that officers in his department were violating their oath. It helped that his team of detectives were clearing cases and the department was finally coming together the way he had envisioned. It had taken him over three decades to feel like he was making a real difference.

Captain Montgomery thought back to his beginning on the force and the night his trajectory in law enforcement changed. He recalled the conversation from over thirty years ago, as if was happening in the present.

"Montgomery, you are never going to be more than a beat cop. Most of the men in this unit have stared death in the face in a country that didn't belong to us. Honestly son, you're not cut out for this, and no amount of affirmative action is going to make me change my mind." The Sarge spoke clearly to the younger ambitious officer.

"Sarge I get it, but I can do the job they do."

The sergeant pulled the young officer to the side and was completely frank with him.

"Do you see any colored people on the squad? There is no room for you, even if you were qualified. I can see the potential in you but being honest, I won't stick my neck out on the line when I know the point is futile. You're a smart boy, play the long game. They will need good colored boys like you to put a progressive face to our law enforcement community. Hell, they've already got a Mexican or Puerto Rican Chief of Police in Cleveland." The Sarge finished.

Officer Montgomery was speechless. He appreciated being plainly spoken to, but the same doors that failed to open his whole life, seemed to remain closed, even after graduating at the top of his police training class and having a bachelor's degree.

"It's nothing against you David, but we still have a hill to climb before all this equality stuff makes sense." The sergeant shook his head and walked away.

Members of M-Squad could be seen walking into a briefing room to get their assignments for the night.

This squad, in the early 1980's was the elite force before Swat became a major tactical force to be used. During the silliness of big hair and neon clothing of the 80's, this squad was serious, deadly and did not hold themselves accountable to anyone.

The night progressed, and David sat at his desk listening to dispatch calls while filling out paperwork.

Nothing noteworthy had come through, just an occasional rowdy crowd or domestic violence call.

He thought about his new pregnant wife and how he could make a career out of law enforcement even with the obstacles faced.

Two voices were heard in the distance in the squad room. David listened and remained quiet. He was often overlooked by his fellow officers, until someone wanted to make a joke about race or ethnicity. Often, he smiled to show no offense was taken, but he was offended. He had more education than ninety percent of those wearing blue. He scored one of the highest ever in the academy, and he was relegated to paperwork.

"We have west of Broad St. tonight; it should be an easy enough shift. We can arrest a few people for our numbers but I'm not trying to do much Kuup."

David could make out the voices before he saw them. Officer Kuper had shown David the ropes when he was first hired. He acted as a shield when others weren't so quick to accept David.

"Yeah I don't have any problems with that. I have to take my wife and daughter to Circleville tomorrow for the Pumpkin Show." Officer Kuper's voice was heard.

"Montgomery, what the hell are you doing here so late? Don't become a paper pusher or you'll be stuck behind a desk. What are you doing anyways?" Officer Kuper asked, approaching David as he gave him a handshake.

"These robbery reports have to be updated by the morning and Captain McIntosh was adamant about it." David lifted one report to show him.

"These burglaries lately have been escalating. Breaking and entering when no one is home is one thing, but home invasions leaving families injured is another." Kuper added and handed David back the form.

"I ran across a few similar home invasions that occurred in Dayton. Same MO, and..." David was interrupted by Kuper's partner.

"Rookie, you think reading shit on a piece of paper gives insight. You think a few similarities from crimes an hour and a half away make it the same burglary ring. Jesus, Kuup this boy don't get it yet. There is no way you don't know this. You're a token David and I'm all for more equality and all that shit, but Columbus ain't a city like Cleveland or Chicago. You are the most diversity this precinct has ever seen. My partner likes you for the most part and I don't dislike you, so that's a start...." He paused to redirect his attention back to his partner.

"If this 'bonding' session is over we need to be out."

Kuper's partner walked away, leaving him with David.

"It's true Montgomery, you are the first black to ever work in this precinct and I'd like to say everything will turn out ok; but I can't. You are much braver than I am." Kuper touched him on the shoulder and walked away.

For the next two hours David finished all his paperwork while listening to dispatch calls. A call came through about a home invasion and then the description went dead. Something made him turn to the channel that M-Squad used to communicate, and he listened.

"We need back up, immediately!" A voice came through the walkie talkie.

David heard Kuper's voice next.

"En route, eta ten minutes, passing Town and High Street..." Kuper's voice trailed off as his partner's voice was heard next

"We shouldn't go..." and the communication went dead.

David thought about driving to the scene, but after hearing that he was simply a token and being called boy repeatedly, he locked his desk drawer and clocked out.

When the news hit the office the next day of the officer shot in the line of duty, David still held onto the anger from being treated and spoken to disrespectfully. When he heard that Officer Kuper was shot, his disposition changed.

From that moment thirty years ago, to now, the case always stayed with him because no one was found guilty for shooting an officer.

Captain Montgomery heard the knock on his door, bringing him back to the present.

"Come in."

The waitress refreshed both cups of coffee and placed the bill equally between Everett and Robbi.

Breakfast was Everett's idea; a way to keep open a means of communication.

Robbi wished she could simply say she was no longer in love with him, but nothing was ever that simple with them.

"I heard Sam was over for a few evenings last week." Everett picked up the check and laid his credit card on it.

"Yeah, she was, and she will be over a few nights this week too. You can't police my life E. I love you but you don't hold the rights to my attention anymore." Robbi added creamer to her coffee and stirred it before doing the same for Everett. She added three packets of sugar to his cup.

"I know that, I'm just saying. Forget it." Everett took a sip of his coffee.

"Exactly. The kids are keeping a scrapbook from all the little headlines your team keeps making. It's one of the two things that you're great at. Thank you for breakfast but I gotta run." Robbi slid out from the booth and kissed him on the cheek.

"The red looks good against your skin Robbi."

She looked back at him and smiled as she walked out the door.

"Old dogs can learn new tricks I see."

Everett missed his family but he had failed them so many times and he didn't know how to change. He had yet to decide if he would renew his commitment to the military. He had nothing else to prove, he served his country faithfully.

"Can I get some coffee to go?" He asked the waitress as she picked up his check and card.

"Absolutely, I've got a fresh pot about ready. I'll be right back."

He ate the last bit of French toast on Robbi's plate and took a ten dollar bill out and placed it on the table as a tip.

Everett heard the laughter before noticing an older couple holding hands and sharing food from each other's plates. He could see the light in their eyes. Unaware, he was smiling as the waitress returned with his receipt and copy to sign.

"They've come here twice a week for the past ten years. Still in love. Hopefully you and your wife will be like that in about forty years." She smiled and cleared off the table.

"Ex-wife if we're speaking the truth." He said without realizing it.

"Well it's good you two can still talk. Thank you again and have a gorgeous day."

Everett had not heard that phrase before and thought to himself,

"I am going to have a gorgeous day."

He walked out of the diner, pulled his keys from his pocket and that's when the first drop of rain hit him.

"Damn."

"I'm sorry I could only spend a few hours with you before I fly out, but I'll be back next week." Cole sat in the car with his sister at the terminal listening to her say goodbye. This University Airport had more chartered planes flying out of it, and her firm had sent their company plane for her.

A security guard walked to Cole's window and tapped on it. His navy-blue security uniform fit him loosely.

"Play nice bro." Mandy mumbled as she stroked her deep auburn colored hair with a comb she had pulled from her bag.

Cole rolled his driver side window down.

"This is for unloading only, not sitting and talking..." the guard held the words in his mouth as Cole flashed his shield.

"I'm dropping my sister off. Give us a minute and I'll be out of your way brother."

Mandy waved at the terminal guard with her itinerary in hand.

The guard smiled and nodded at both as he walked to the car behind Cole and ensured they were moving along.

"I promise to visit you guys in Chicago as soon as Everett allows us a real vacation."

"I'll hold you to it, and if you need me to call him and make that happen I can." Mandy checked her purse and made sure she wasn't leaving anything behind.

"No, you leave him to me." Cole hugged his sister and then popped the trunk. He got out and thanked the terminal guard for being patient before pulling his sisters traveling luggage to the curb.

"Coley, you seem happy for the most part. A bit of advice though, when the fun dies down; it's good to have someone around that loves and accepts you – for you. I'll see you in a week or so. I hope Columbus can be interesting for two weeks." She gave him another hug and motioned for a valet to pull her belongs to check in.

"Call me when you touch down." Cole waved one last time before hopping back in his car.

Pulling away from the terminal, he thought about his sister's words. He had been having fun for so long that he barely made time to sit still. When he wasn't working, he was having fun, and when he did neither, he felt lonely.

As the thought faded, a text message came through from a yoga instructor named Bethany, he met two weeks ago at a grocery store. The attraction was intense from the start and grew quickly after the first time they had sex when he visited her studio.

"I have a few minutes to spare before your shift starts if you want to practice downward dog or some other canine position".

The light changed red before he merged into traffic. A rainbow could be seen in the distance and Cole took that as a sign that he should do what makes him happy and replied to her text.

"Of course, I have time, but you'll have to stretch me out first."

While Cole had his fun, Vania was giving back to the community by teaching a self-defense class.

"This is called what?" Vania called out to the eager eyes looking at her as the participant tapped her arm three times.

"An Americana Lock." Half of the class spoke up.

"I didn't hear everyone's voice. You have a voice. Again, what is this called." She asked a second time and each voice was heard loud and clear. Her Black Gi had become undone from the exercise as was expected, she continued to instruct.

"Good, that's good. Remember, the elbow must look like an arrow for this to work. When you have them mounted and they cover up, pick an arm to control the wrist first. Grip the wrist, drop your elbow to the side of the neck of the arm you control to limit your opponent's head movement. When you're done, their arm and elbow should look like a rectangle. Then slip your hand under and grip the hand that still has leverage. From there grip and reverse 'throttle'. Now what's the most important part of this technique?" Vania asked the class in general.

"Don't panic." A man's voice called out.

"That's true, always true in any situation." Vania gave him positive reinforcement.

"But what is the most critical part of the..."

"Your attacker's wrist 'must' be pinned to the ground for leverage." A woman spoke up over the group. She had only been learning for a little under six months, but she was good at remembering the small technical details.

"Exactly, perfect." Vania told them to grab their bottled waters as she gave them their last lesson for the morning.

"The last thing I want you to remember is that you can avoid almost one hundred percent of fights. Now there is that one to two percent chance that it can't be walked away from but remember the other persons' problems are not yours." Vania made eye contact with each student.

Being on the mats felt normal, although she had not been to the Brazilian Jiu Jitsu studio in nearly three months. Learning how to defend herself had been instilled by her grandfather and father alike. She learned how to box before the age of fourteen; and had studied BJJ for the past ten years. Her black belt hung loosely from the waist of her Gi and she could feel the sweat dripping down her back.

"Strong mind. Strong body." She repeated two additional times before dismissing the adult class.

She spoke briefly with a couple of students who wanted to pick her brain as she drank down two bottled waters.

"Thank you, that was a great class." A newlywed couple waved on the way out of the gym.

"How's it feel to be back?' A lanky red-head man said walking across the matted floor.

Vania smirked and met him halfway.

"Ed, what's up? I feel tired and still have a long day at work. You guys are doing great work and the classes are full, I wish I could be more available, but such is life." Vania looked at the clock on the wall as Ed's wife Lynn walked into the gym.

"Vania. What in the world, is it snowing in hell?" She laughed as she kicked off her shoes and gave Vania a hug.

"Next time I'll come a little earlier and teach you two a couple of things." Lynn then gave Ed a kiss. Lynn was the highest ranked belt and had been Vania's mentor since she began training years ago.

"I'll take you up on that offer, but unfortunately my day job is calling. Can I get a hold of you guys about my birthday celebration later?" Vania watched as they both rolled their eyes at her.

"I'm serious I will call before the end of the week." Vania backed off the mat and disappeared to grab her gym bag and shoes. She decided not to change until she was back home and it was still early enough that she could order breakfast takeout from a local diner to get some calories back into her body. Vania felt the soreness in her shoulders but knew it would pass.

Her Satellite Radio station was tuned in to modern hip-hop and she bopped her head to the artist Gov White and tracks from his album 'Dues Paid' as she turned out of the parking lot and onto the street.

She got caught behind a city bus and put her blinker on. She was surprised that traffic allowed her to easily switch lanes. She waved at the car to acknowledge the kindness.

"Today is going to be a good day."

At least that was her thought until a car ran through a changing red light and slammed the vehicle she was traveling behind.

She hit her brakes in time and before she had realized, she was out her car door, running towards the crash in her Gi.

The bullpen was bustling with energy. Detectives had taken Captain Montgomery's words seriously when he made it clear that he expected results from anyone under his directive. The older detective Jack had taken on a partner and had cleared two current investigations and one cold case off the board.

"Clark, you and your team won't be the only ones making the news." Jack's partner said lightheartedly.

Everett looked up from his computer and shook his head to acknowledge Bryan Waterford. Bryan had been at a different division of detectives but with merging departments, he was re-tasked under Captain Montgomery.

"You know if it was up to me, I'd avoid all of the attention. It's really not my thing."

"It might not be yours partner, but did you know that men practicing yoga are called 'yogis' and the women 'yoginis'? Cole was loud when he entered, shaking Bryan's hand in greeting.

"What do they call partners who show up with lipstick on their neck?"

Jack and Bryan looked at each other and replied in Unison.

"Cole." They laughed and went back to finishing paperwork

Cole walked to the restroom to remove the lipstick and returned to his station.

"If you knew what my morning was like, ooh wee!" Cole was excited, but that quickly changed as a woman walked out of Captain Montgomery's office. It appeared she had been crying.

Cole looked at Everett, who shook his head in response. He had no idea who the woman was or why she was meeting with their Captain.

"Clark and Kennedy, my office." The Captain's voice was louder than he intended.

The woman looked into Everett's eyes as she passed and then did the same with Cole.

There was sorrow in her eyes, but Everett also saw the anger. She mustered what appeared to be a grin that was quickly replaced.

"Hey, Captain what's up?" Cole was holding onto the last bit of positive energy for as long as he could. He went to close the door but was advised by their superior to leave it open.

"Take a look at these crime scene photos." He handed Everett and Cole copies.

"What, are these pictures from when I was born, what the hell Captain." Cole laughed as he pulled up the sleeve to his cotton knit shirt.

Everett glanced at him but didn't say a word.

"I said look at the damn photos Kennedy and tell me what you see." The seriousness in Captain Montgomery's voice changed the atmosphere in the space immediately.

"Captain, you wanted to see me?" Malcolm entered the office. He nodded at Cole and Everett to acknowledge their presence.

"Tweedle Dee and Tweedle Dumb have been looking at these crime scene photos. What can you tell me at first glance Malcolm? Don't think, just your first reaction."

Malcolm took the photos out of Cole's hands. He looked at the first two that showed a body lying in a small gated area. A third picture showed a gun about five feet from the body, and two sets of legs of people who had secured the perimeter.

"First thing is that these pictures have been doctored. The scaling is off. What is this, some old Mod Squad crime scene pics." Malcolm laughed and it was short-lived.

"Sorry Capt." he quickly surmised the level of seriousness from the intense stare that Captain Montgomery shot.

The Captain walked back to his desk and sat down.

"Close the door. Sit or stand." He finally directed.

Cole and Malcolm stood behind Everett who had taken a seat opposite of Captain Montgomery.

"This case has been a cancer to me since I came on the force. The body in the photo was a home invasion suspect in the early 80's. I had only been on the job for about a year. Back then, realize everything was different. People of Color didn't have but a minimum number or positions. After earning my bachelor's degree and graduating the top of my class from the academy, I should have been fast tracked, but instead I sat behind a desk, filling out paperwork and verifying everyone else's. I had one, only one person that showed me kindness. That person ended up shot by the person sprawled out in the photos." The Captain stood up and looked out of his office window. The rain was coming down in large drops. After his meeting with Internal Affairs, Officer Kuper was still on his mind.

"Sorry to hear that Captain, thank God times have changed a bit." Cole tried to lighten the mood, but it didn't.

"What I am about to tell you is why I need your help. The woman who just left, was the daughter of that officer. For over three decades she's investigated the scenario the night her father was shot, and why that man in the photo was never tried in a court of law, was given a payout from the city, and had his record cleaned." The Captain looked back at the group.

"Shiiit, the only people with power like that are us and lawyers." Malcolm interjected.

The look Captain Montgomery shot back sent chills through each of them.

"This file has everything that I could find by piecing together things over the years. Many of the names in the file have passed. But..."

"These are names that my dad worked with too." Everett paused as he looked through the file.

"Most of them are from M-Squad."

Everett was beginning to see why they had to tread lightly. These were the elite police specialists. Everett had heard stories from his father, but could never decipher which stories were true, because they all seemed so far-fetched as a child growing up.

"The soon to be retired Commissioner, was his partner. Everything led me back to him, but then I ran into dead ends and the file has been stuck with me ever since. I need you all to handle this discreetly. I simply want answers. The statute of limitations has run out, and to be honest I have no real thoughts that you three can make heads or tails out of something from thirty-years ago. I just know I owe it to that woman to get her answers."

"Of course, Captain, is there any other 'evidence' available to us?' Malcolm's demeanor had taken a more serious turn.

"Here is the onsite forensic report done the night of the shooting..." Captain Montgomery handed Malcolm another folder.

"No one but you three." The Captain made it clear he trusted only them.

"Put White and Aguilar on the Powell case. You think they can handle it?" The Captain asked.

Everett looked at Cole who shook his head positively.

"Yeah they can handle it." Everett answered.

"Good...good, now get out of my office and close the door behind you."

The three men exited and formed a quick group before they went separate ways.

"These guys, from this squad...had problems with authority. We need to tread lightly. Investigating former officers and the current Commissioner, well you both know the risks."

Everett walked away as Cole and Malcolm held a brief secondary conversation.

"Travis, where is your partner?" Everett asked as he approached the younger detective.

"She, uh, there was a major accident. She's running a little behind sir." Travis had been taken off guard. He had not seen his boss approach.

"Is she ok?" Everett asked.

"Oh yeah, yeah she is but..."

The words stuck in Travis' throat as a fire alarm sounded.

"Everybody, you know the drill. Take the steps and don't trample each other." Captain Montgomery stood in his office door and watched his team take both exits, to lead downstairs and out of the building.

"This is some bullshit." A few voices were heard as the Detectives stood close to the building to limit getting drenched.

Travis was one of the few who had been smart enough to grab an umbrella.

"When V.A. finally shows up for work, the Powell case on my desk is yours to work." Everett motioned for Cole. Now was as good a time as any to help Captain Montgomery get answers to question's he had for three decades.

Cole and Malcolm did their special handshake before Cole gave Travis a bit of advice.

"It took me over a year to have a case assigned to me without supervision. This can make or break you rookie. Don't let us down." Cole finished as Vania pulled into the precinct, to exit her vehicle.

"We won't." Travis watched Cole get into Everett's vehicle and slowly back out.

Vania slapped the hood of their car as they pulled out as much out of reflex as it was to acknowledge them.

Travis closed his umbrella while Vania held the door for him.

"You good?' Travis asked as people filed back into the building.

"Yeah, I'm good but this morning has been, very..."

"Strange." Travis finished her sentence as he noticed she was wearing a martial arts Gi still.

Travis and Vania regrouped after she showered and changed into more appropriate work clothes; khaki pants and button-down shirt. She kept a blazer in her car when she needed to look more the part.

"I'm going to get the boys signed up later this month. You should've told me you were an actual instructor, you just said you knew the owners." Travis was still amazed to learn that his partner held a red/black belt in Jiu Jitsu, and he was still working on passing to his brown belt.

"Well, I'm sure you have little things that I don't know about yet."

Travis agreed before taking a sip from the water fountain.

"The video at the dealership is grainy, so I'm thinking we should speak with the family of the victim first. Being shot at a car dealership, is a helluva way to go." Travis caught up with Vania who kept walking to the car.

"You want me to drive after..."

Vania unlocked the doors and got in the driver seat.

"I didn't get in an accident T, why would I want you to drive?"

"Whatever, I'm just trying to help but since you want to insist, let's go Ms. Daisy."

Travis input the address into the GPS and checked his watch.

Vania shook her head in disagreement.

Travis read the file for most of the ride to the home of the recently deceased.

Calvin Powell was fifty-five years old. Married for over two decades, he was survived by his wife and three children.

"Car salesmen, I can't believe more of them don't get shot for some of the shit they pull." Vania turned onto the street the house was located.

A collection of cars lined the street. Model year vehicles with dealer plates on them were parked intermittently between others.

"I think today may be the memorial." Travis could see two tents with people gathered under them. Some with small plates of food, others with drinks.

Vania found a place to park a few houses away.

A large banner with Calvin's photo was stretched across the front patio, and groups of people congregated around the home even though it sprinkled intermittently.

"Katherine, we are so sorry. The one thing we know for sure is that he loved you and the kids. If there is anything at all we can do, don't hesitate to call us. We must get back to the dealership so I can get the checks cut. We will call on you later." A strawberry blonde woman hugged the wife of the deceased. Her blonde hair was full, and the black two-piece skirt suit she wore, showed wealth.

"We picked up the bill for his casket and the services." The woman's husband added before kissing Katherine on the cheek.

Vania smiled at the couple as they passed by. Travis approached the widow and offered his condolences.

"We had no idea that his memorial service was today, so our apologies." Vania added.

Mrs. Powell pulled Vania by the hand and walked her and Travis into the house. She traveled to a den in a portion of the home that no one occupied. She slipped off her black Kate Spade Cecilia Pumps before her feet sunk into her carpet.

"Thank you. I'd rather help you two bring justice for my husband's murderer. Entertaining people has never been my strong suit." She offered them a seat before pouring herself a drink from a heavy glass container. She took a sip and began coughing profusely.

"Mrs. Powell is there anyone you can think of that would want to cause your husband harm?"

Mrs. Powell shook her head.

"Calvin could rub some people the wrong way because he was blunt. Not always a good trait to have as a salesman, let alone a General Manager. He busted his ass for the last ten years at those dealerships and was going to be awarded the rights to his own. That or a piece of Tamara and Bills'." Travis looked at a family portrait that was placed along the dens wall. He saw pictures of the Powell family and the couple who had just departed the memorial.

"So, the couple who left when we arrived owns the dealership?' Travis asked.

"Yeah, they hired Calvin when he first got into the business and groomed him. Other dealerships offered him positions with six figure signing bonuses, but my Calvin was loyal. He was always a loyal man." She stood up as a few people entered the den to say goodbye. Her black Admiral Crepe Sheath Dress draped her silhouette and the grace of a wife and mother encompassed her presence.

"If you want answers I would stop by the dealership, I'm sure his colleagues will have plenty to say about him. He spent more time there, than he did here."

Travis smiled at others who were now filing in from outside as the rain started again.

"Mrs. Powell, one thing before we go. With your husband passed, what happens to the percent owed to him?"

The look on Mrs. Powell's face said that she had not thought about it.

"I'd ask Tamara or Bill; I am sure they have all the details..." She paused and walked to the desk in the den. She scrambled through some papers in the desk drawer and turned on one of the laptop computers. Mrs. Powell printed off a few pages and handed them to Travis.

"Here are copies of all the contracts and drafts. If you'll excuse me, I must get back to the guests who came to honor Calvin. You can show your way out?"

She excused herself and approached a group who wanted to say goodbye.

Vania and Travis eased out and walked down the street to the car.

"We can have Veronica look over these contracts and then you and I can go car shopping." Travis strapped his seat belt across his chest.

"I bet you're really a minivan person." Vania took a jab at her partner.

"With our salary, more like an entry level compact."

Everett wasn't exactly sure where to start a thirty-year old investigation, but he knew the importance of it to Captain Montgomery.

"Malcolm's going to find the original negatives. I think we can agree that we steer clear of the Commissioner's reach for as long as possible."

Cole listened to his partner, but he had thoughts of his own on how to proceed.

"Former Officer Terry Scarborough was first on site of the shooting. He was the one who called in the 10-999. He's in Grey Stone Nursing Home, that's where we should start." Cole was still reading through the report.

"These photos were taken over the course of an hour. No one rendered aid to the victim. Officer Kuper arrived at the hospital at 2:47am. The call was made at 2:20." Cole paused as he shuffled through the papers in the folder.

"This photo was taken over an hour and a half after the officer had been removed for medical assistance. First question; why didn't Officer Kuper's partner, the good ol' Commish not call it in? He should've been first on scene. Secondly, Officer Kuper's statement indicates he only discharged his weapon twice. One of the bullets hit the suspect, but there are five gunshot wounds. The couple who returned home that night to find the intruders said that before Kuper pursued the suspects, he pulled them to safety. They swear that before Kuper engaged in the chase, they heard two gunshots and then one of the suspects emerged from between two garages. Where did those first two shots ring out from, and where was his partner?" Cole finished as Everett pulled into the parking lot of the nursing home.

"So, it wasn't Commissioner Grahl who called it in?" Everett asked.

"No, and his statement taken that night doesn't add up." Cole watched an aide pushing a resident of the facility along a path as Everett parked.

Two other seniors sat on a bench holding hands, as they tossed small morsels to squirrels that had become accustomed to being fed.

"God, I hope this isn't what I have to look forward to." Cole smiled at the couple as they walked toward the entrance.

"I don't think you have to worry about old age if you stay on the path you currently walk." Everett opened the door to allow Cole to walk in first.

Apart from a few residents reading newspapers, the energy in the building was more vibrant than they both expected.

"Good morning, welcome to Grey Stone. How can I assist you?"

The receptionist greeted them with pleasantries. Her name badge read 'Penny'. Her lowly shaven head was tapered, and the clear frame glasses gave her a unique look. The red horseshoe nose ring contrasted against her green eyes. Although she was heavyset, she carried the weight well.

"Detective Clark and Kennedy. We're here to see an old colleague of my father, Terry Scarborough." Everett wanted to keep this as simple as possible. He flashed his badge.

She pushed a clipboard across the receptionist station and had them sign in. She motioned for a nursing aide to inform Mr. Scarborough that he had more guests.

"He will be happy to have a second set of visitors this week. It's tough on people who have outlived or fallen apart from their families over the years."

"I can only imagine, but, Grey Stone seems more active than most." Everett held a conversation with Penny as Cole wrote his name in the sign in book.

Cole scanned the visitors log quickly to locate the name of the other person who had visited Former Officer Scarborough.

"We do a good job and they make sure people who work here, are truly caregivers. People should have peace in the later portions of their lives." Penny motioned them toward the nursing aide pushing Terry into a greeting area for them to speak.

"When you are done, please make sure you sign out." Penny smiled, adjusted her glasses and answered an incoming phone call.

"Grey Stone, a better quality of life. How can I direct your call?"

Terry watched them approach as the nursing aide poured him a cup of coffee from a coffee station in the room. His face recently shaven with a spec of blood dried under his chin. His hair was shoulder length grey, with minuscule traces of black.

"Clark? You're Arthur's boy?" Terry asked as he added sugar to his black coffee.

Everett was surprised that Terry remembered his father, who had been killed in the line of duty over fifteen years ago.

"Yeah, Arthur Clark was my dad."

Everett felt a sense of familiarity and it made him think back to his father.

"He was a good cop. A damn good cop. I remember you from his funeral service. Even back then, a father couldn't have been prouder of his son."

Everett had seldom brought up much about his father. Although the pain had dulled after losing him, the memories could pull scabs off emotional scars that had not fully healed.

"Yeah he was a good cop and better father." Everett sat forward and dove in.

"I remember the stories of M-Squad he would tell. You guys were the cream of the crop. I'm hoping you can answer a few questions about the night..."

"The night Kuper got shot." Terry interjected before Everett could finish his statement.

"Thirty years later and finally people are asking questions." He paused to take a sip from his coffee cup.

"Laura Kuper-Coates was just a child back then, she had questions I couldn't answer thirty years ago." He finished.

"Couldn't answer or wouldn't answer?" Cole could sense that the trip down memory lane had thrown his partner off his game.

"Ha, good question Detective. I couldn't answer them, nor could I answer her questions yesterday.

I've got a decade left, at most, of living a good life. Some things should stay in the past." Terry took a sip of coffee.

"Why did it take so long after Kuper was taken to the hospital, to tender any aid to the victim?" Everett asked straight forward.

Several groups of seniors were congregated in the room. Two women walked in and said hi to Terry.

"Hi ladies." He smiled and blew them a kiss.

"I'm living a good life Clark." Terry stared at Everett, contemplating if he would share anything at all.

"If the first bus arrived to take both suspect and Kuper, why was the suspect left. Why would anyone order no one to touch the body or render aid? Why were the guns firing that night re-positioned before CSI showed up nearly two hours later? Where was the current Commissioner at the time, who should've been also pursuing the same suspect?"

"Why did the suspect, who shot an officer, not spend one day in jail?"

Terry looked up and met Cole's eyes. He was on to something.

"Exactly." Terry answered affirmatively.

Everett pulled out photos of the crime scene and showed it to Terry.

Terry pulled glasses from his front pocket in his robe.

"Wow, this, takes me back." He paused as he looked deeper into two of the pictures.

"Where are the photos before they took Kuper away? When I arrived on scene, he was still slightly pinned under the suspect. This body..." Terry pointed to the suspect.

"He was lying face down. Listen I'd love to help you, but this is bringing up some memories I'm not too fond of. I wish you safety and success, but I can't help you anymore. Thanks for the visit."

The Detectives knew he was done, and no amount of pushing would make him share more than he had already.

They signed out and left the building.

311

"Kuper-Coates was listed in the visitors log." Cole informed Everett as they pulled out of the parking lot.

"Let's check with Malcolm before we pay her a visit. We need to make sure we can distinguish between fact and fiction before that conversation with her." Everett's cell phone indicated he had text messages from Becca, asking if he could take her to a father-daughter dance at her school in two weeks.

"There is no other place I would rather be princess." Everett replied.

An assortment of emojis with smiley faces were sent back with an "I love you dad."

"I love you more, but there is one thing I need to know... can you dance?"

Becca responded with a gif of a stick figure breakdancing.

The car dealership looked like a typical business. Surrounded by other car businesses, 'First Motor Group' was the largest on Auto Lane Blvd. With more than seven dealerships within a two-mile radius, FMG had been the first to break ground over twenty-years ago.

Vania parked near a gate on the same side of the building the body had been found. A tow truck was hauling a vehicle towards the body shop.

A few people walked the lot alone, but others were being escorted by salespeople showing them the features and benefits of the vehicles.

"Hey, hey welcome to FMG. I'm Jess. If you just want to look around or kick tires, please do. I have a delivery but will be right back to you." The brunette saleswoman had an air of confidence about her as she walked away. The customer who had just purchased a car from her was smiling from head to toe.

"Jess, I can't believe I was able to buy my first new car. Thank you." An older black woman hugged her and then got into her vehicle and drove away.

"Anything in mind?" Jess asked as she approached Travis and Vania, who had continued to walk the car lot.

"We didn't think you guys would be open, we heard about the dead body found late last week." Vania spoke up to get a general conversation started.

"It's been a tough couple of days, the services were today so we didn't open up until noon. It's going to be an adjustment for everybody. Calvin was a good boss because he let people know where they stood. So, you two might be getting a good deal today if you find your car." She winked at them.

Jess was called back into the showroom for her second car sale of the day, as her customers were coming out of the finance department.

"I didn't catch your names."

"Travis and Vania." Vania introduced them, leaving out the title of detective.

"I will be able to spend all of my time with you, just give me about ten minutes." Jess walked away with an air of confidence.

"She doesn't seem too bad for a car person." Travis said, as an older man made his way out from a side door of the dealership and approached them.

"Hey guys, what's up. I'm Frank. If you're looking for a great deal, then I'm your man. What kind of car did you want to buy today?" His beige polyester pants fit snuggly around his waist, and the navy-blue, short sleeved short had a coffee stain next to his shirt pocket.

"We're just looking, and Jessica is helping us." Vania spoke up and gave a fake smile.

"Everybody is just looking, until they're not. I have some cars that we've marked down that might be in your price range."

"How do you know what anyone's price range is, that's a big assumption?" Vania did not appreciate the aggression of the salesman.

"When I've been doing this job for over fifteen years, I can prequalify just about anybody."

Vania had enough and walked away.

"Did I strike a nerve with her? Look you're the man and it's going to be your money getting spent right, don't end up driving a minivan off the lot today if that's not what you want."

Travis looked at him in bewilderment and Frank knew he overstepped.

"Look, I know that I am not everyone's cup of tea. Here's my card." He then walked towards a different pair of customers who had just parked and got out of their vehicles.

"Hey folks, welcome to FMG and we have some CRAZY deals going on today and today only. I'm Frank, what are you guys looking for today?'

Travis walked away and caught up with Vania who was looking inside of a brand-new Ford Explorer.

"That's why car people get a bad name, are you ready to get down to business?" Travis asked, as he looked inside the SUV.

"Yeah, the sooner we get answers the better because now I'm getting the itch to buy a car or with our salaries like you said; half a car." She followed Travis inside of the dealership.

As soon as they walked in, they were greeted by a third salesperson. Instead of going through the same meet and greet process, Vania asked for the General Sales Manager.

The salesman pointed towards a desk area which was elevated on a ten-inch platform for better visibility

Two men sat at the sales tower staring into one of the three computers at their disposal as the detective's approach.

"Excuse us, but which one of you gentlemen are in charge." Travis asked.

They both looked up at the same time.

"Who is your salesperson?' The first one asked straightforwardly. He came across as being impatient and had no time to answer questions.

Vania didn't like his first impression.

"Which one of you is in charge, and you, what's your name?' She asked again and flashed her badge at him.

The demeanor of the impatient man changed, and he became apologetic.

"I'm sorry, but trying to run a dealership when..."

"Kevin, I got it. Structure these next two deals, give them the manufacturer's rebate and five-hundred above invoice. We keep the dealer cash and we get a point and a half on the back end." The second man excused himself from the sales tower. He wore a white shirt and tie with tan slacks. Standing nearly six feet six inches, he had a towering presence.

"I'm Donald Lentz and please excuse my associate. Added pressure will often bring out the truest self. I'm sure you have questions about Calvin. To be honest, tension is running high, with all of us fearing the unknown." Don walked them into an office away from the sales floor.

During the interview they ask standard questions, like any problems with employees or noticeable changes in his behavior, but Don can't think of anything out of the norm. He seems honest about the answers he shares.

"We would like to speak with Tamara and her husband. We see the convertible they drove to the memorial is back." Travis pointed at the vehicle which had been washed and now on display in the showroom.

Bill was on his cell phone walking onto the sales floor, with Tamara walking towards the convertible. She pulled the magnetic dealer tag from the rear license plate when Don excuses himself and flags them down.

"Tammy. Bill"

Vania sees the owners of the dealership walking towards the room, in the reflection of a picture hanging on the office wall.

"Tammy, Bill, these are detectives investigating Calvin's murder."

Travis stood and shook hands.

"Can we speak somewhere private?'

"Absolutely, honey, can you take them to our office? I need to speak with Don, and I'll be right up." The wife said, as the husband led the young detectives away and up a back flight of stairs to the upper business offices.

Travis and Vania appeared relaxed a bit and were drinking beverages when Tammy makes it her office.

"I'm sorry to keep you waiting. So many things have changed here since Calvin is no longer with us." She walked to her desk and sat down.

"Don said that nothing seemed out of the ordinary the last few days he worked with Calvin. Is there anything that either of you can recall that could help in our investigation?" Travis asked as he took another sip from his water bottle.

"Calvin was an acquired taste until you got to know him. He was all about business, and that's why my father hired him over fifteen years ago. His business acumen and ability to weigh risks has grown my business by over fifty percent in the past five years.

"We understand that there is a contract to share a percent of ownership in your dealership if certain goals were met and maintained."

The husband's body position tensed slightly, but it was noticeable.

"That is true. We gave him operational control over all three dealerships, and he didn't let us down. The contract stipulates that he gets a percent share of the company, or we would back him with the manufacturers for his own dealership." Tammy swiveled her chair to a filing cabinet and pulled out the contract.

"Everything is on the up and up...." Tammy paused as her husband made a revelation.

"You were at the memorial service this morning for Calvin."

"You're just realizing this." Tammy raised her arms in disbelief.

Vania recognized the disconnect between the two but needed to keep the conversation on task. She noticed pictures in the office of the Powell's with them at various vacation getaways.

"You all seem very close. How was Calvin's marriage in your opinion?'

Bill looked at his wife before answering the question. He walked to stand slightly behind her chair.

"Calvin loved his wife and she loved him. The only complaint either of us ever heard was about the fourteen-hour days he would spend at one of our dealerships. Other than that, they loved and supported each other." Bill finished by placing his hand on his wife's shoulder.

"Calvin's typical day was like, fourteen-hour shifts?" Vania asked.

Both husband and wife agreed with her question.

"So, if he had operational control and it freed a lot of mundane tasks, what roles do you play besides collecting the money...not to sound offensive." Vania was prying.

Travis had his head in his notepad, jotting down statements.

"I'm here first thing in the morning three days out of the week for purchasing options in our parts department and I have other interests."

"Bill, playing 18 holes of golf every day is not an interest, it's an addiction." Tammy spoke up causing a forced chuckle between the married couple.

"Golf can be addicting, that's true..." Travis interjected to keep the conversation on track and directed the next question to the wife.

"What hats do you still wear?"

Tammy let out a genuine laugh and shook her head.

"I usually am the one closing the office or leaving when the last deal is done. I still sign checks and authorize every electronic payment distribution. My father's first car lot had three cars for sale and one of those was our family vehicle. It was his hard work and business savvy that grew that into three more dealerships that offer new and used cars, along with in-house financing for those with marginal credit. We are the number one dealership based on new car deliveries for the past three years, that was an achievement solely made possible by Calvin's dedication."

"Yeah, Calvin was the big savior." Bill walked to a wet bar in the office and poured himself a drink of Vodka. Tammy's expression showed disapproval.

"It's ok honey, Mark is picking me up. I'm not driving to the clubhouse."

Travis thought they had received enough information and motioned to Vania.

"Is there anything at all, that you can think of that…"

"Well, we did hear about a customer who got irate and belligerent on the showroom floor about a week ago. The customer had to bring their vehicle back after the bank declined to purchase their loan. Calvin attempted to put them in a used vehicle and get them signed up with our financing, but the customer wasn't happy." Bill looked at Tammy and then excused himself.

"Detectives if you have more questions, you know where to find me." Tammy accepted their business cards before the Detectives left the business office.

Jessica was speaking with the General Sales Manager at the tower, when she saw Travis and Vania, she approached them again.

"Detectives, Calvin was a good guy and I hope you find out who did it!' She had genuine concern in her voice.

Vania nodded toward the used car salesman who had approached them earlier.

"Frank. Frank is a unique taste." She laughed along with the detectives who agreed with her.

"I take it no one is buying a car today." She asked as she shook both detective's hands and gave them business cards.

"No, not today."

"Whenever you're ready, give me a call. I'm fair and professional." She cut the conversation short as an appointment came in to discuss purchasing a vehicle.

Travis approached the sales tower.

"Tammy and Bill said there was an irate customer who threatened Calvin about a week or so ago. We need their information."

"You still have the reject file?' he asked his counterpart, who still had his eyes glued to the computer screen.

"Yeah it's in the office." He said flatly.

The General Sales Manager looked at the younger man and then turned his computer screen off to gain his undivided attention.

"Go get it!"

With that directive the younger man walked to an office to return with the intake sheet from the customer. He handed it to the GSM.

"Without a subpoena I can't give you more than this, but it has his address, place of employment and contact numbers."

Travis thanked him for his help and caught up to Vania who had already made an exit to the car.

Frank was approaching her again but this time she pulled her badge out and he abruptly turned around.

"We can interview him after lunch." Travis held up the contact sheet.

"You mean dinner T, it's almost five o'clock."

Travis looked at his watch and couldn't believe how fast the time was passing by.

"Well let's handle this first and then eat. We can give Veronica time to look over these contracts and meet with her first thing in the morning." Travis said as his stomach grumbled.

"The contracts are on the up and up. Mrs. Powell is set for life, there is a clause written in it that in case of an untimely death or illness; the principal and interest is passed to his wife. Have you spoken to your boss yet?" Veronica scanned over to where Malcolm and Everett were sitting in

Malcolm's office. Two other people no one recognized were also present.

"Not since yesterday. Why, what's up?' Travis asked.

Veronica put her back to Malcolm's office before she answered.

"I don't know but we keep finding files, doctored. From what I gather, someone has taken in interest in the lab and your team. That's all I know."

Vania started to laugh but the other two couldn't understand why.

"Veronica, I need all the files you are working on that have yet to be placed in the system." Sheldon approached with a man on his heels.

"This is Mr. McCallum, he is doing a brief onsite audit today." Sheldon kept it simple.

Veronica looked at Sheldon and then the auditor who simply stared.

"We will catch up with you later for happy hour." Vania hugged Veronica and gave an evil stare to the auditor.

Travis walked out, taking one final look into Malcolm's office. Neither Everett nor Malcolm seemed pleased with their morning so far.

The parking lot was vastly different early in the morning. The young partners had come to a hitch in their investigation. The customer they had tracked down had an alibi for the time period Calvin Powell had been murdered.

"I'm surprised no one is here yet. Didn't the husband say he was here the first thing in the morning."

Travis stretched after stepping out of the car. He straightened his tie before grabbing his coffee mug.

"Yeah, well he didn't seem like he had the best of character or paid his wife attention." Vania closed her door and opened a folder she held in her hand. It contained crime scene photos of the victim pronounced dead on the scene.

The security gate to the body shop opened slowly and a young technician walked from behind it smoking a cigarette.

"Good morning, won't nobody be in until ten o'clock." He kept walking the lot.

"Excuse me, I'm Detective White and this is my partner. What time does Bill usually get here? We spoke with he and Tammy yesterday. We're trying to find out who killed

Calvin." Travis called out and caught the technician's attention.

He turned to meet them. He took a drag from his cigarette and put it out on the ground. He pulled a small sandwich bag from his front work pants and placed the butt in it.

"Bill will show up early if he wants to change out of his Demo."

"His Demo?" Vania asked.

"Company car basically. They can drive anything they want up to a certain number of miles and still title the vehicle as new." The technician answered.

"Oh ok, that makes sense." Vania shook her head like she understood.

"What's your name?" Travis asked. He needed to document each contact made on the case.

"Tyler. Have you seen or heard anything that might be able to help us solve this murder? I don't care how silly it sounds, because honestly are wheels are spinning." Vania asked in much a nicer way than usual.

Tyler smiled as his eyebrows raised.

"Everybody liked Calvin after getting used to his personality. He was straight forward but fair." Tyler had not taken his eyes of Vania as he replied.

"There's gotta be something, nobody is perfect." She took a small step closer to Tyler.

"I try to stay out of people's business or rumors, but I liked Calvin, he loaned me money when I first started working here eight years ago..." Tyler hesitated.

"I saw Mrs. Tamara and Calvin together late at night a few times."

Vania looked at Travis.

"Together as in?" Vania asked.

"You know what I mean, I need to get back to getting this lot ready for opening..." he paused

"...and I disagree with you about nobody being perfect." He touched her on the hand and went back to work.

"An affair opens up all types of possibilities T." Vania had a bit of excitement in her voice.

"Well we have two new suspects...actually three, if we include Mrs. Powell." Travis took another sip from his mug and opened his car door.

"T, you know what this means don't you?" Vania asked as she stared across the roof of the car.

Travis shook his head because he didn't understand her question at all, so she answered.

"It means I'm perfect."

Vania greeted Tammy and Bill when they stepped off the elevator into the office. Bill, wearing golf pants and an emerald- polo shirt was talking on his cell phone. Tammy wore a beige pinstriped suit with chambray stripes. Her powder blue shoes matched the color of her Coach Duffle Purse.

"Hey guys, thanks so much for coming down."

Tammy looked at Bill who was still on his cell phone.

"Hey, we can double it up tomorrow but I gotta go." Bill ended his call.

"So, you said your guys found some inconsistencies with the contract?" Bill asked.

Vania shook her head to affirm.

Travis walked out of the Captain's office and met the group still congregated.

The couple had no idea that Katherine had been interviewed a second time. In which, she advised them she knew of the affair and provided an alibi for time of death. She also revealed that someone had sent anonymous videos of Tammy and her husband having sex in the office at the dealership via email.

"Wow, that was quick. Bill, if I can speak with you, it will only take a moment." Travis asked in a manner that didn't give him time to say no, and as Travis turned to walk away, Bill followed him instinctively.

"Detective, what's going on?" Tammy asked.

"Oh, it's nothing. Just standard procedure to separate, and honestly, I need to ask some personal questions." Vania then motioned her forward to a separate interview room.

"Do I need a lawyer?" Tammy asked as she sat down and saw the camera placed high in the corner of the room.

"Maybe a divorce lawyer. How long was your affair with Calvin?" Vania went straight to the core of the matter.

Tammy's eyes widened and her response got caught in her throat. She shook her head to deny the allegation and then took a deep breath.

"Six years. We had been together six years, and yes I loved him but things, things were complicated." She sat back in her chair and placed her purse on the table.

"Complicated how, your husband would take half of your business with divorce?" Vania sat forward.

Tammy denied the charge.

"My husband signed a pre-nuptial agreement. In the case of divorce, he leaves with two hundred and fifty thousand dollars, in addition to ten percent for each year we are married. My business is worth over twenty million dollars." Tammy sat forward and slid her purse to the side to leave nothing between her and Vania.

"Katherine is my friend, genuine friend. She doesn't have much time left and we decided to wait. We had been selfish enough with the affair and didn't need to add that log to the fire." She took another deep breath.

"So, Katherine didn't know?" Vania kept pressing.

"Are you being serious detective? I love her, and no she didn't know. No one knew."

Vania looked deeply into Tammy's eyes and she believed her.

"Katherine knows. She's known for two weeks." Vania said it forthright.

"There's no way." Tammy tried to respond but Vania pulled up one of the multiple video clips sent to Katherine showing Calvin and Tammy having sex.

"Oh my God, oh fuck...I have to see her. How did she...Who recorded me....wait, this..." Tammy paused.

"This is my office." She got quiet as the picture unfolded and one name slipped from her lips.

"Bill!"

Travis excused himself, after making sure Bill was comfortable with a bag of pretzels and diet soda from the vending machine. He and Captain Montgomery watched Vania speaking with Tammy. Now that the affair had been confirmed, he could fire away because Bill had motive and opportunity.

"That had to be devastating for Mrs. Powell." Captain Montgomery referenced Travis and Vania asking her a second round of questions to reveal the affair. She told them she already knew about the affair from the videos. They confirmed her alibi that she was receiving treatment the night of the murder.

Travis walked out of the room, leaving Captain Montgomery behind to view him with Bill from the adjacent room.

Travis entered the room with Bill and closed the door behind him. He sat down slowly, giving the captain time to adjust the volume and record the interview from behind the double mirror.

"Why'd you do it?" Travis asked

Bill looked at Travis questionably.

"Sending videos to Katherine was a shitty thing to do. I guess misery does love company." Travis looked at Bill with a frown on his face.

"Videos, what are you talking about?'

"You do realize that we are the police. I mean the real police, where we have departments on departments to check everything. Every bit of evidence that we get is researched and researched again.

How long do you think it would take a state-of-the-art department to trace the IP Address of the email that sent the videos to Katherine? How long do you think that would take Bill?" Travis rubbed his face.

Bill had the look of a deer caught in headlights.

"Yeah, that was distasteful but not a crime, I don't think. I may have to have our cyber unit check on that though." Travis stood up and looked at his reflection in the mirror.

"I bet that pissed you off. Seeing your wife having sex with another man, in your office, on your desk and floor. Why would you keep tormenting yourself?"

Bill stood up.

"Sit down, I'm not done!" Travis commanded.

Bill sat back down.

"You were friends with Katherine, and you know she doesn't have long to live. You could've walked away with a little over a half-million dollars. That's enough money that you would never have to work again. Why destroy another family?"

"A half-million dollars, I'd go through that in less than five years. I didn't care about the affair."

"Shut up! You did care about the results of the affair if she divorced you. For someone who thinks they are brilliant, when you sent the videos you also sent motive." Travis opened a file on the computer and the video showed Tammy and Calvin talking about divorcing their spouses and getting married.

"That bitch thinks she was going to get rid of me like I'm trash and garbage, for him. She thinks that my lifestyle would ever be the same. Six-hundred thousand dollars, my friends earn that in a year. If she thought she could get rid of me without real cost, she was wrong."

Travis quickly sat back down.

"So, you killed him?"

"What, no. Come on, sending videos and murder aren't the same." Bill said with complete deniability on his face.

Travis opened another file. It showed the back of the auto body shop looking onto the dealership parking lot.

"Had you taken a real interest in how the dealership works, you would know about these cameras. You'll see that on the night of the murder when you said you were out of town, and your buddy confirmed, that doesn't seem to be true does it?"

As the video played it showed Bill removing golf clubs from one car and placing them into the back of a black, convertible mustang.

"The camera angle doesn't reach to the other side, but I can tell you that motive and opportunity along with the District Attorney's story telling in a court of law...not good. I can also tell you that a confession can help sometimes." Travis set back and stared at Bill.

"Fuck, shit, damn."

"Why did you do it?" Travis asked

"You already know why, but I didn't shoot him. I know who did, and I will testify but I didn't shoot Calvin." Bill blurted out and realized the mistake he had made.

"I need my lawyer and to see my wife."

Travis heard the two knocks on the mirror, indicating good job from Captain Montgomery.

"I'll get you access to your attorney, but I'm pretty sure your wife doesn't want to see you, but I'll ask." Travis walked out of the room and back into where Captain Montgomery had watched both.

"That was good Travis and you too VA, have him processed and get him his phone call." Captain walked out.

"This love triangle plus one is why I don't date." Travis said out loud.

Vania stared at Bill through the glass as officers pulled him from the room.

"Agreed, with friends like these people who needs enemies."

The Commissioner's assistant closed the door behind him when he walked into Captain Montgomery's office. His expensive shoes and suit were more than what most officers could afford, but being the right-hand man of the highest-ranking law official in the city had its privileges.

He pulled the blinds closed before he said a word.

"The last time I looked it was my name on the door Mario. Don't touch anything in here without asking me first. Why are you here?" he asked the assistant as he took the liberty to sit down.

"David, it's been a long time. I always knew that you'd make something out of this department. The word is getting around, and your name has been circulating about moving up." Mario sat forward and picked up a picture of the Captain's family.

"Oh my god, is that Jr.? He is a splitting image of you! How's Marcie doing, I heard she's finished her second master's degree. Seems like the job has been kind to you and the family. Evelyn and I almost divorced when the kids flew the nest, but she started taking on clients."

Captain Montgomery had listened enough to a man who had betrayed him once; taking credit for busting a narcotics ring at the height of the crack epidemic. It elevated him in the eyes of brass, and their two lives had taken different paths.

"Mario, I'm not your therapist, best friend or partner anymore. I've never wished anything on you that you don't deserve, but unless you are here on official business, you need to get the hell out of my office." Captain Montgomery didn't mince words. He and Mario had been partners with the same ambition. Over the course of three years, they had forged a bond of trust, but ambition could prevent vision. It was the final time that Captain Montgomery trusted anyone other than himself on the force.

"Your department is outperforming everyone else in the city, and like I said there is a promotion for Deputy Chief when everyone moves up in about a year, and I see no reason we can't support a thirty-five-year seasoned veteran like you. Concentrating on current cases, like you've been doing is the key. Thirty-year old cases with the statute of limitations expired can look like a waste of time." Mario sat back in his chair and watched the Captain come to understand the reason for his visit.

"Is this a threat Mario? You've known me for three decades, have I ever done well with threats?"

"David, that's not my purpose. If you take anything from this discussion, I need you to realize that there are many eyes on you and your detectives." Mario paused as if he was contemplating something.

Captain Montgomery understood everything he had just been told. His Detectives had disturbed the hornet's nest within three days of being asked to investigate the Kuper shooting.

"I won't apologize for taking my shot David, you were better than I was and more ambitious, but you never knew how to play the game. You have another shot and I'm here giving you...no, sharing with you. You can do as you have always done and put principal over practice, or you can let all the good work you have done for this city finally pay off." Mario shook his head. He knew David could be stubborn, but hoped his old partner was better at reasoning as he grew older.

"If that's it, you can excuse me. I have real police work to get done." Captain Montgomery stood from his desk and walked to his office door.

Mario hesitated, seemingly waiting for an indication that the Captain would accept his advice. He extended his hand without the Captain shaking it.

"Very well." Mario walked out.

Malcolm was excited to be diving into an unsolved crime that no one else had made progress with in over thirty years. He confirmed that the crime scene photos were doctored, the autopsy report indicated that the entry wounds came from one gun, when he could see that the suspect was shot with two separate guns. Kuper's Gun was a 9mm, but some entry wounds showed at least two were shot from a .38 caliber handgun. The inconsistencies kept mounting, and Malcolm was excited to be diving in.

Malcolm wanted to get his hands on the actual witness statements; he knew that would require a trip to the city's archives.

The old building was connected to the newly constructed Downtown Plaza. He remembered the last day he spent in the musty basement nearly ten years ago before being transported into a modern forensic lab.

He walked down the stairs after remembering how the elevator often broke down. Malcolm passed his old lab, looking inside of the room brought back memories. It was the last time he had been in love.

"Whoa, if it ain't Mr. Worldwide Crime Solver. Malcolm what's good my man?" An older officer with graying hair looked through the gated window.

"Boss Man, what's happening. I see Doris is making sure you stay healthy; you got a six pack of baby chickens in there?' Malcolm laughed and pointed at his belly.

They gave each other a fist bump between the gated barrier.

"I need to take a look at a case from a few years back." Malcolm gave him his badge and signed the log to gain entrance to the restricted area.

"Doris, made this homemade peach cobbler and I have two pieces my friend." Boss said as he pressed the electric release to allow Malcolm entrance.

"You mean you have one piece for you and one piece for me." Malcolm asked where the old file cases were situated to cut down on the time looking.

"Shit, this is from over thirty years ago. I hope it hasn't been purged, ya know I don't think brass really cares about this stuff." Boss said as he looked at each row of files, categorized in a manner that made Malcolm grateful his old friend was lending him a hand.

"These three rows should have what you want. Put everything back where you found it." He walked away singing a made-up song about the peach cobbler.

Malcolm had spent countless hours in this department. He dove into his work after breaking off his engagement with his fiancé at the time. She was a heroin addict and after two years of breaking a promise to get help, he had to walk away.

The labels on the boxes had faded so much that he had to pull out his readers until he located the correct one.

Malcolm carried it to the table and opened it. The contents were scarce with redacted information on the statements taken blacked out. He found several photos like the ones he already had, along with a series of negatives. He noticed variations in the photos from the box, from those already in his possession.

Reading over the statements provided, too many inconsistencies were apparent. He took copies of the photos with his cell phone but knew that what was under the redacted information could be the key to understanding why Captain Montgomery kept running into dead ends.

"He pulled two statements from the box and slipped them into his sports coat. He placed everything back in the box and placed it on the shelf.

"I'm going to be smelling like hot dogs when I leave." Malcolm approached the desk again.

"You're lucky I like you." The guard pointed to the baked delight wrapped in saran wrap.

Malcolm smiled and they shook hands before a quick embrace.

"Tell Doris anytime she wants to share her recipe with me." Malcolm picked up the pie and made his way out of the building and back to his lab.

He blew up the pictures he had taken from the archives on his cell phone and compared them to each other.

He noticed that the body of the suspect was not in the same position in each photo. What he originally believed were marks left by the gurney in the grass, appeared to be actual indicators of the suspect's body being dragged roughly five feet. Malcolm did quick mathematics and verified his assumption.

Lastly, the suspects gun had also been moved.

He called Everett and Cole and they arrived shortly after.

He laid his preliminary findings out for them and explained them slowly.

"We need to update Captain immediately." Everett told Malcolm to collect everything before making their way to Captain Montgomery's office.

Captain Montgomery was speaking with Vania and Travis as they approached.

"The B-team just solved the Powell case." He said out loud for the entire office to hear.

"Captain can we talk with you?" Everett asked.

Captain Montgomery saw the concern on Everett's face and directed them into his office.

"V.A. and Travis, I want you on the triple homicide case now that you have your cherry popped."

The two young detectives decided to jump into the new case while leaving their senior partners with the captain.

Cole closed the Captain's office door as Everett detailed information about their brief conversation with Terry at the nursing home.

The Captain listened on. Malcolm brought his revelations next.

"I believe the photos were doctored, the body was staged..." Malcolm paused and laid two additional photos onto the Captains desk.

"The whole crime scene was staged, and with the autopsy report being a cross between a bad script and lack of originality; I am certain there is at minimum, a cover up, at worst, a conspiracy wherein the former partner of Officer Kuper and now Commissioner of Police was a participant."

Captain Montgomery took another look at the photos. He inhaled a deep breath and pushed his chair back from his desk. Staring up at the ceiling, he began to wonder what the result of the investigation would be, especially if no one could be arrested. How many lives would be changed if he allowed his detectives to pursue any more leads. How would it affect his ability to achieve his lifelong goal of being Chief of Police where he could make a real difference?

"Captain." Everett's voice broke through the silence.

"Yeah Clark." He walked to his office window and stared out.

"For now, hold off on any further investigation. Leave the files on my desk and don't speak of this again." He turned to face the three men he had placed trust in.

"Captain?" Malcolm asked as he placed the remaining files in his hands on the desk.

Everett sat on the edge of his seat, unsure what to say.

"For now, I said. Dismissed."

The men filed out of the door and closed it behind them.

They had found out more about an old investigation in two days of work than others had.

"I guess the meeting with the Commissioner's assistant came with a heavier weight than he wants us to carry." Malcolm walked away from the detectives. His curiosity sparked, he needed to throw himself back into his current cases to take his mind off what he had found.

Everett pulled Cole into the stairwell to make sure their conversation was private.

"Capt. is feeling pressure, that quick. We are going to follow orders and stay clean, but if he gives the word, I want to bury the pencil pusher first."

Cole shook his head in agreement.

"I never liked that piece of shit or his boss..." Cole paused as he followed Everett down the stairs to the parking garage.

"...but yeah, we will follow his orders. Can you believe the b-team, one case and now the Capt. makes them the lead on a triple homicide?"

"Let's meet them on site and take them to lunch before they get their tattoos."

Cole began laughing loudly.

"What?" Everett asked with a grin.

"Travis is not going to like it."

Everett started laughing with him.

"Most definitely not."

STAY TUNED...

OHIO 10

BOOK II

AVAILABLE ON AMAZON

SEPTEMBER 2020

ABOUT THE AUTHOR

A.V. Smith is an athlete turned writer. With a passion for storytelling, he paints with words that captivate readers. Smith writes on an emotional level to empower readers to engage in deeper conversations about their past, their relationships, and their connection with the Universe. With his first book, *Madison: God's Fingerprint 1.618*, he won the 2019 Author Academy Award for Best Romance. Smith has also finalized the next two installments in the Madison series: *Madison: In the Presence of God* and *Madison: Vengeance Is Mine*. In *OHIO 10* and *OHIO 10 Book II*, Smith takes a break from romance and focuses his literary talent on crime and social issues that divide us.

Through life and love, Andre' has learned our steps are temporary, yet the journey intensely meaningful. This understanding led him to donate a kidney to his younger brother. As the father of three children, his desire is to see his children overcome the fear of success by being the best version of themselves. He strives to lead by example, at times falling short, but understanding human beings are still a work in progress. When he is not engaged in his passion, you can find him with a fishing pole in his hand, coaching youth level football, or attending a local artist event.

Other Books by A.V. Smith

While in College, Madison befriends a second-generation Colombian who gets bullied until she steps in. Madison receives more than a simple warm welcome when her friend takes her to visit Colombia for his family's gratitude. Unbeknownst to Madison, a familial bond is illuminated that changes her future. Love dares to awaken Madison's soul; however, with the darkness that surrounded her teenage years, she has constructed walls of protection.

As passionate, erotic themes and emotional conflict shift her vision of the world, she is forced to face the event that paralyzed her father and sent her parents to prison. The murder of a family of three combined with a harassing phone call at work puts Madison on a collision course with the man who had her friend's father assassinated, and who tainted the narcotics found in her father's possession the night her life was forever changed. Madison is a woman with a tumultuous past struggling to escape her demons all the while blindsided by love at a poetry event. Longing to feel normal, Madison attempts to balance her desire for justice with her need for swift, deadly punishment. With the help of her grandmother and sister-friends, she discovers who she really is as well as the courage to let love in.

Made in the USA
Monee, IL
12 August 2020

38187786R00197